AF574056

MARCO BERTIN

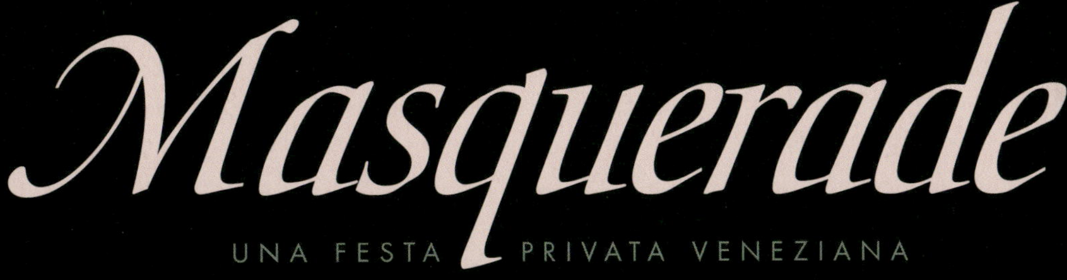

UNA FESTA PRIVATA VENEZIANA

Poetic texts by Antonio Giarola

With Music from Vivaldi to Verdi

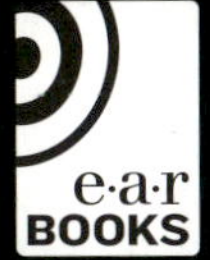

Foreword by Marco Bertin
Poetic Text by Antonio Giarola

ISBN 3-937406-33-6

Editorial Direction by Astrid Fischer/edel
Music compiled by Bernd Kussin/edel
Art Direction and Design by Marco Bertin
Translation by ar.pege translations sprl

Produced by optimal media production GmbH, Röbel/Germany
Printed and manufactured in Germany

earBOOKs is a division of edel CLASSICS GmbH

For more information about earBOOKs please visit **www.earbooks.net**

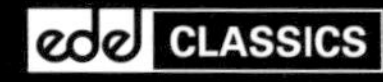

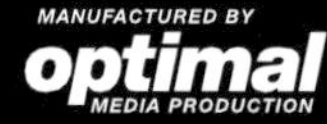

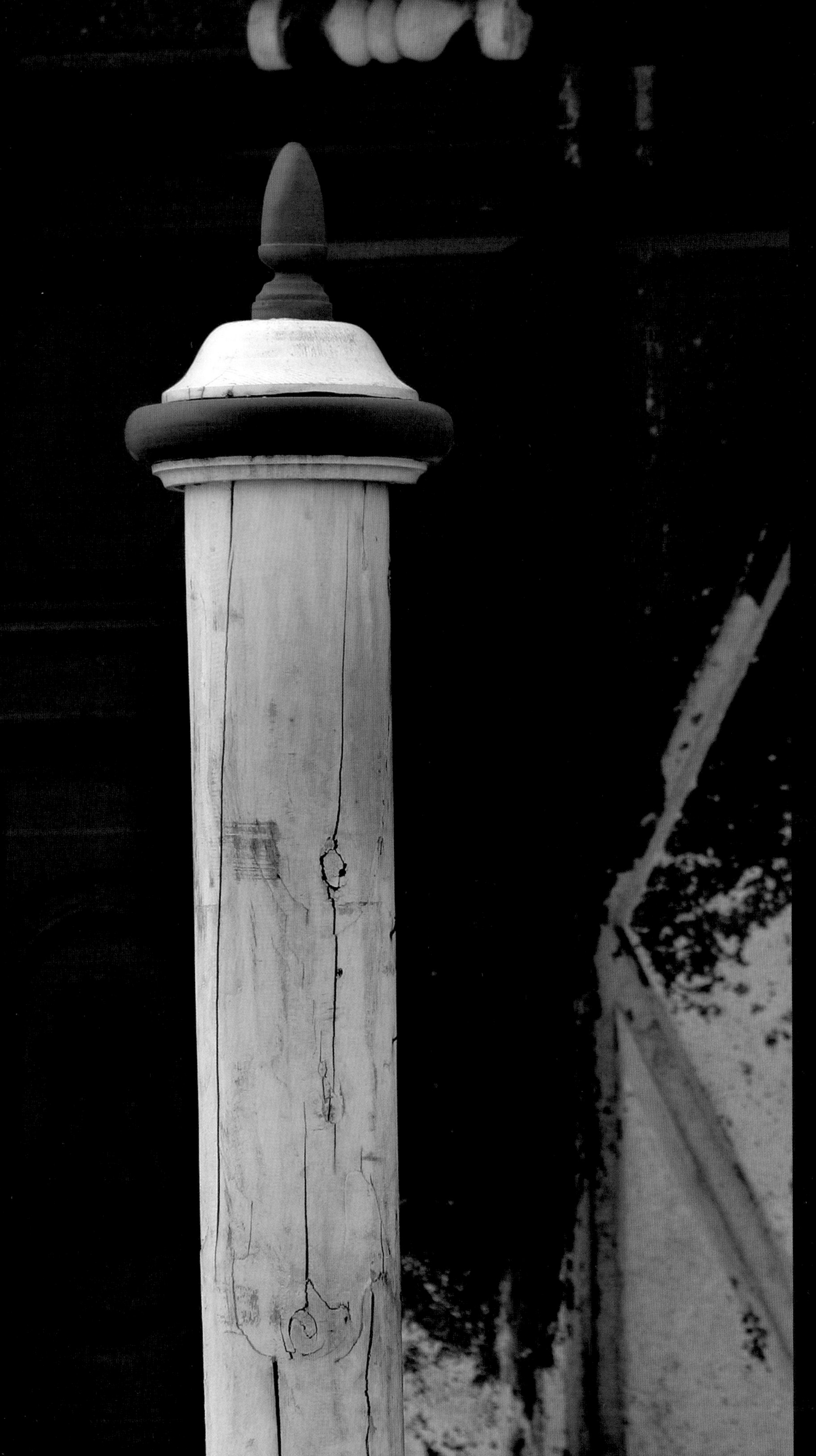

The human art of disguise
and the metamorphosis of personality
have always aroused my curiosity.

Carnival masks are a way of hiding
one's own identity and projecting another.
The projection imitates nature, whilst disguise,
the suspension of identity,
leads to the exploration of the unknown,
mediation of magical rituals, or forms
of transgression.
At times, men seek out their doubles,
who are opposite in terms of social standing,
for the simple, or perhaps,
complex pleasure of appearing other than
they are.

Marco Bertin

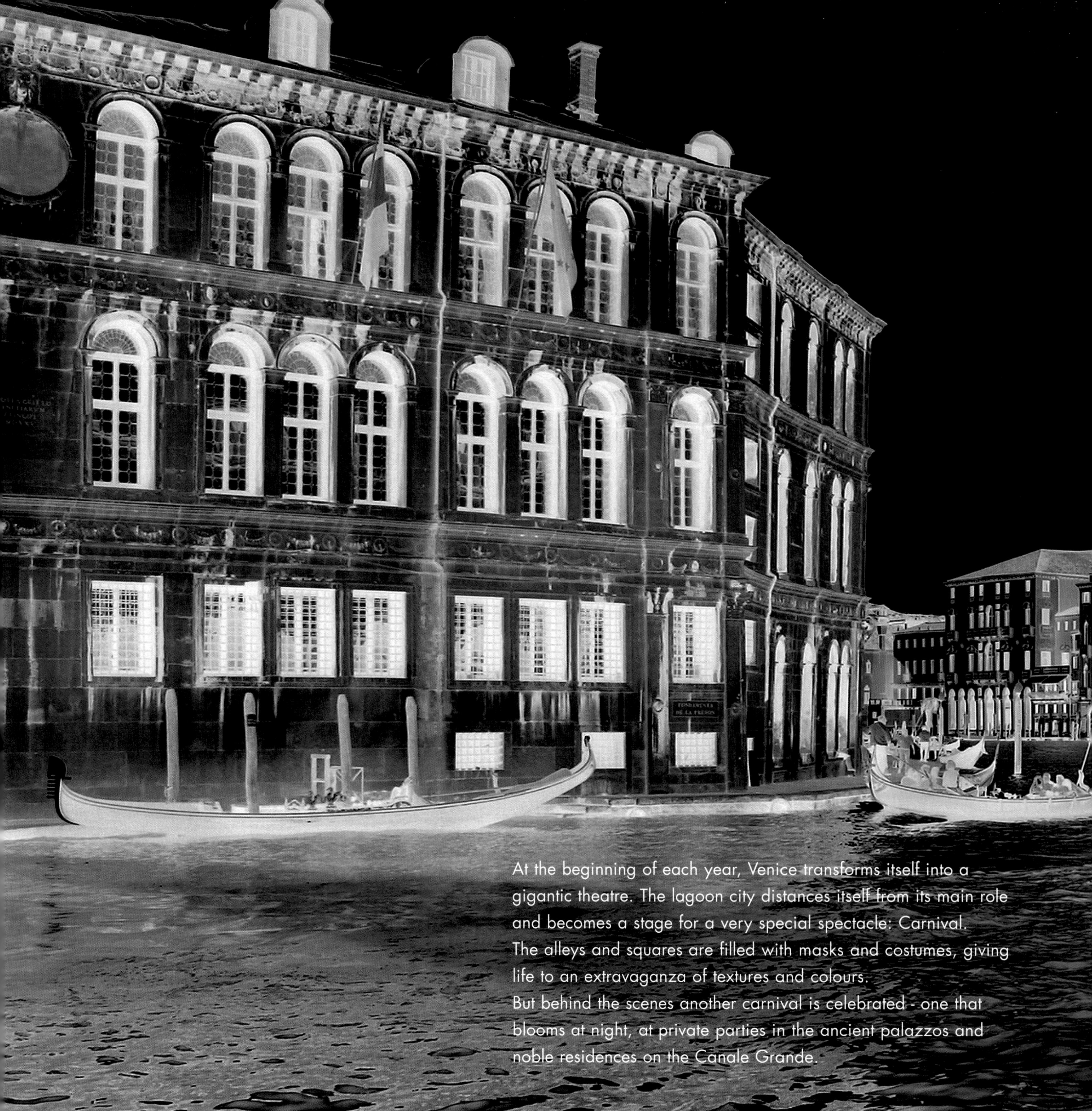

At the beginning of each year, Venice transforms itself into a gigantic theatre. The lagoon city distances itself from its main role and becomes a stage for a very special spectacle: Carnival.
The alleys and squares are filled with masks and costumes, giving life to an extravaganza of textures and colours.
But behind the scenes another carnival is celebrated - one that blooms at night, at private parties in the ancient palazzos and noble residences on the Canale Grande.

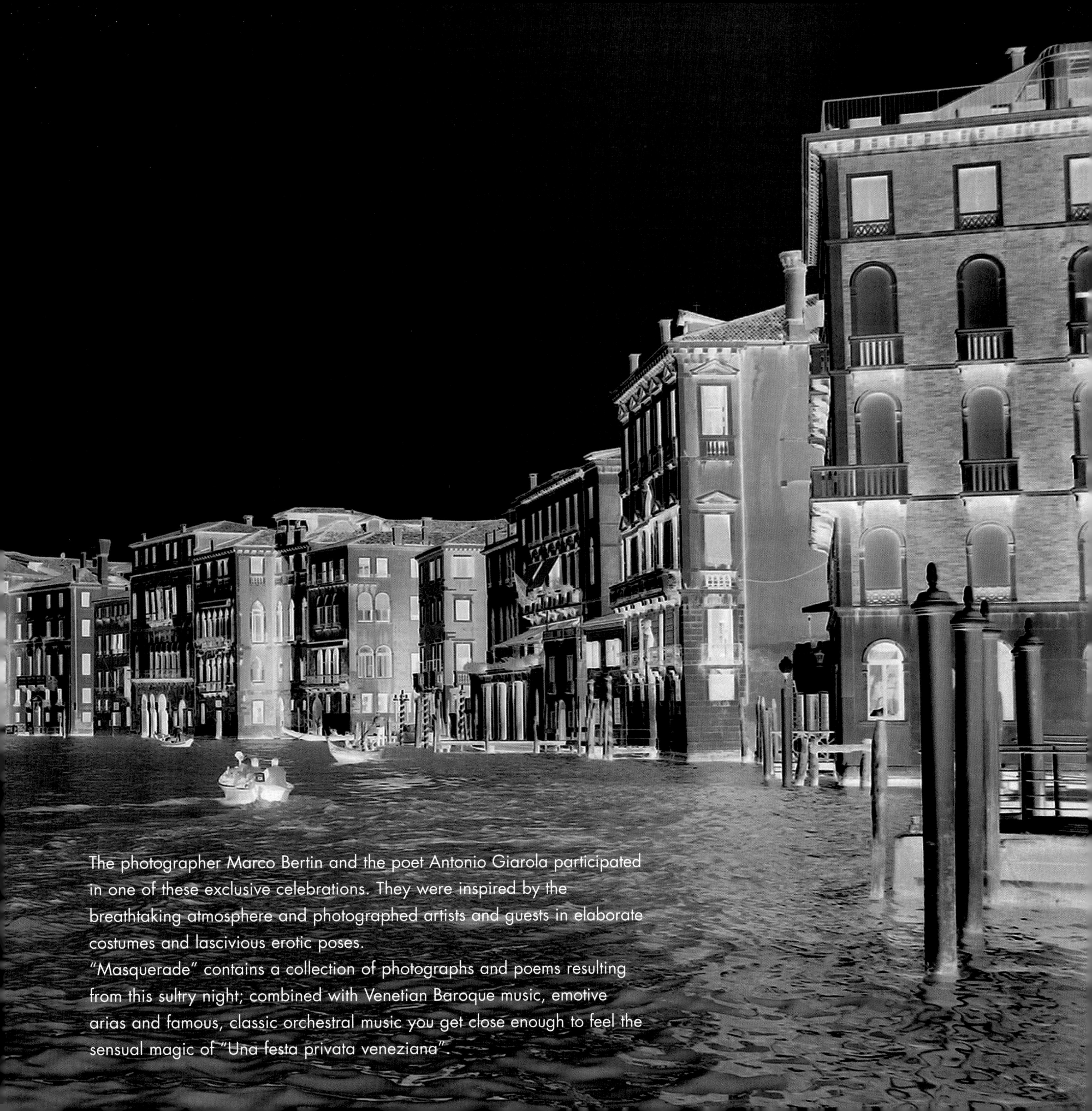

The photographer Marco Bertin and the poet Antonio Giarola participated in one of these exclusive celebrations. They were inspired by the breathtaking atmosphere and photographed artists and guests in elaborate costumes and lascivious erotic poses.
"Masquerade" contains a collection of photographs and poems resulting from this sultry night; combined with Venetian Baroque music, emotive arias and famous, classic orchestral music you get close enough to feel the sensual magic of "Una festa privata veneziana".

Behind a mask
there is always someone.

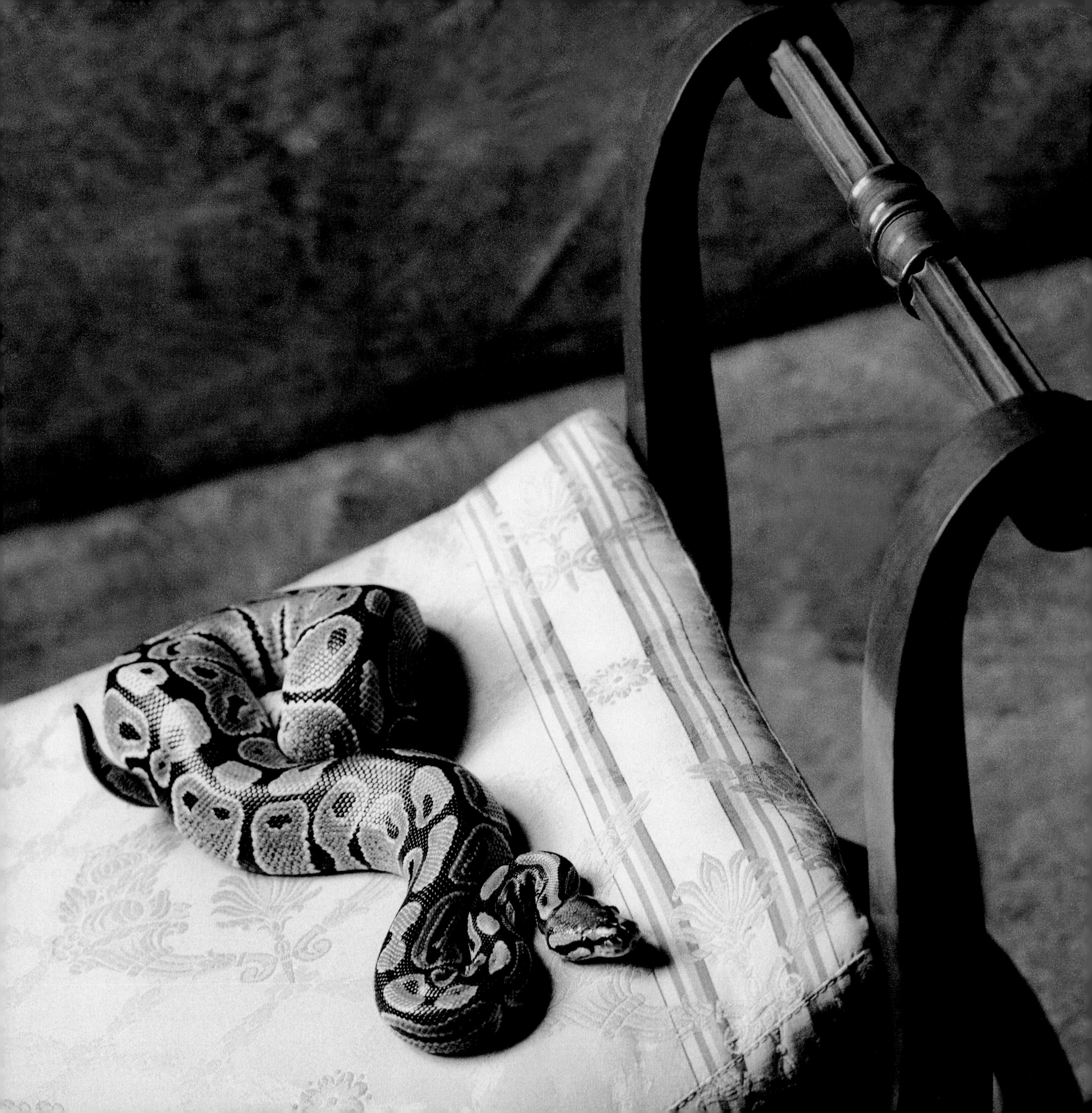

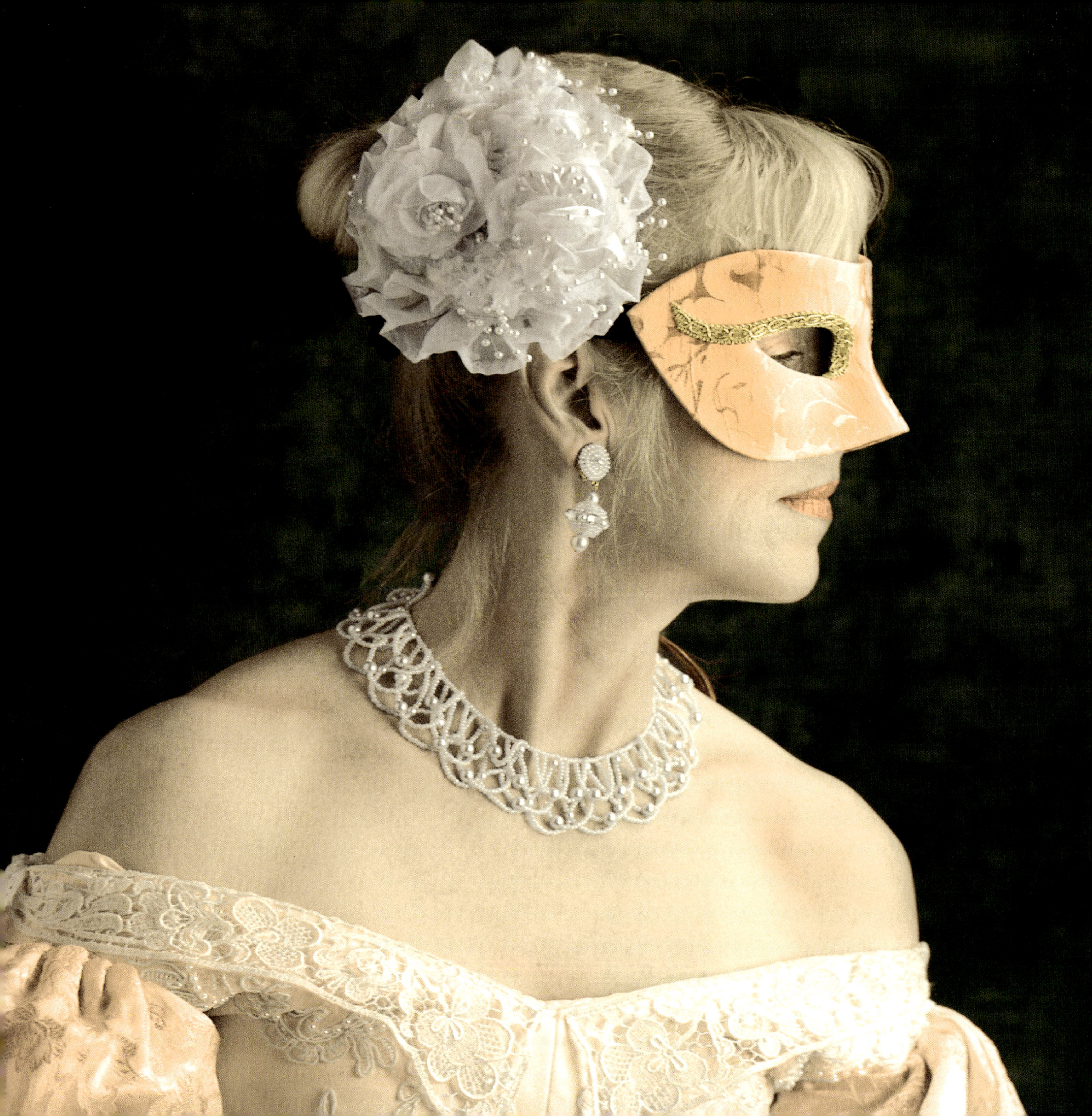

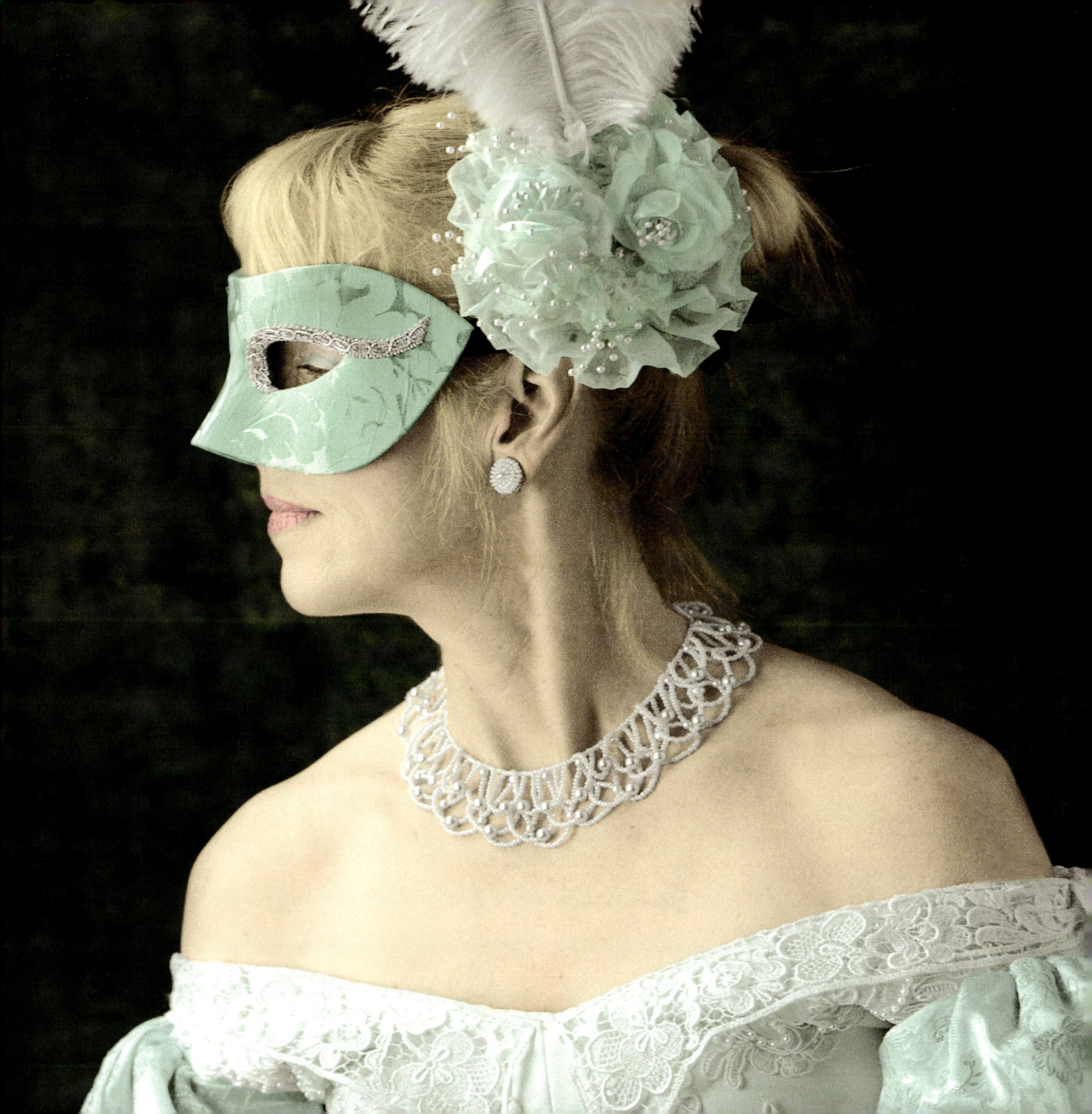

Rustling roams
Cloth gliding
On the polished pavé

Keen and persuasive
Audacious thought
Takes slow steps

An indiscreet eye
Insinuates and investigates
Transcending movement

Close and unquiet
Furtive quenching
In the whirling tide

Festive pressures
Precarious events
Make stumbling simple

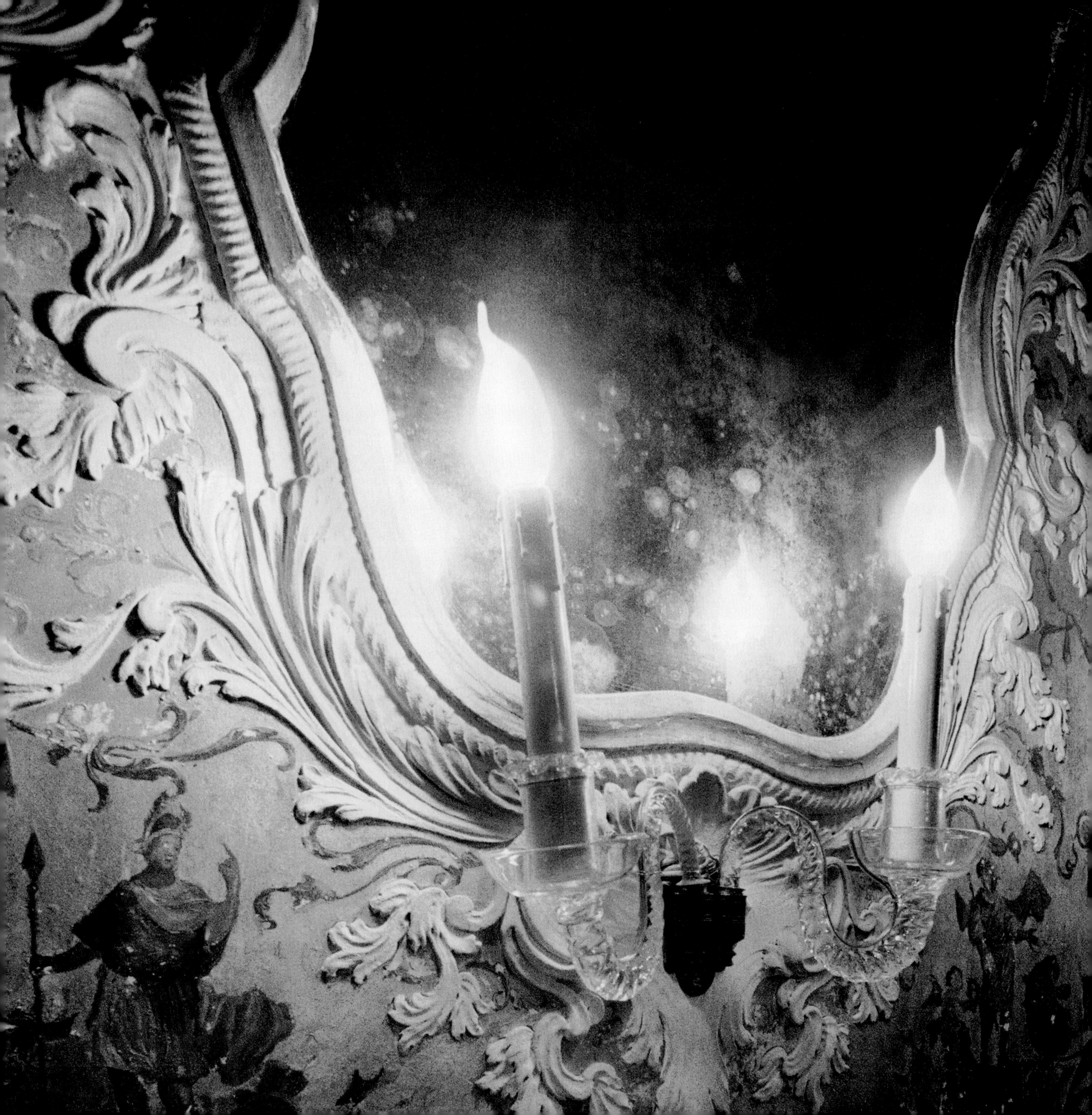

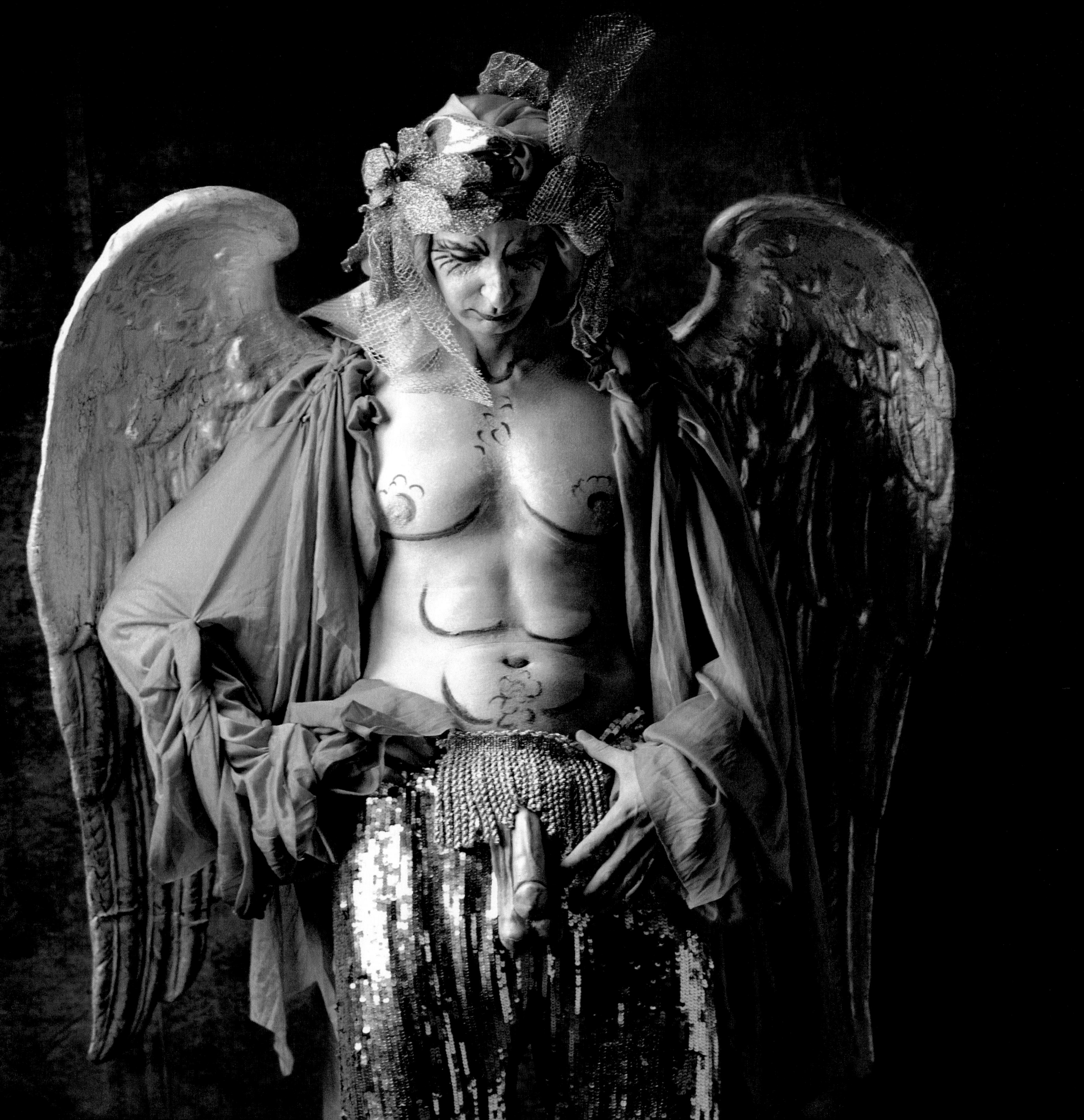

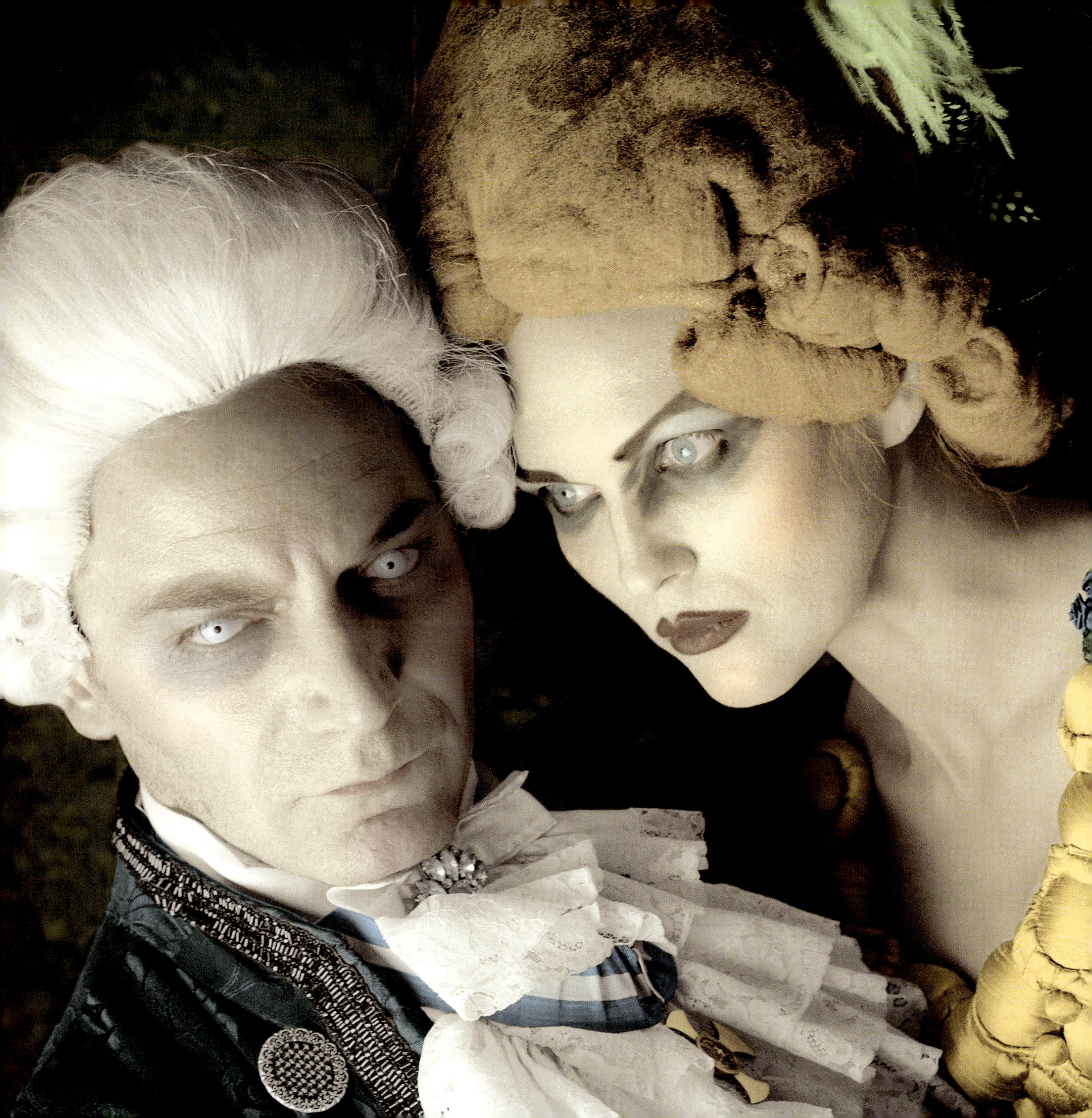

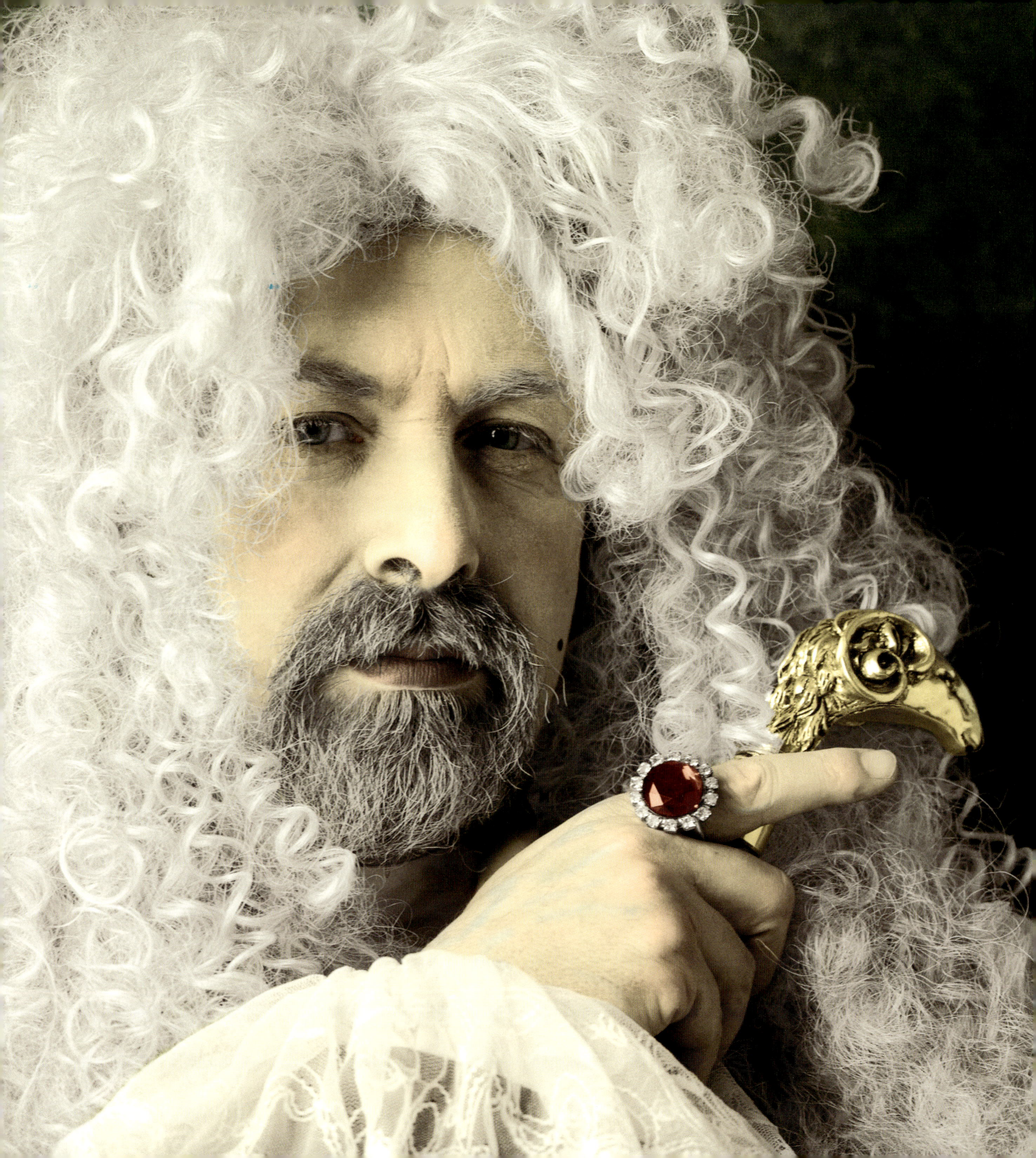

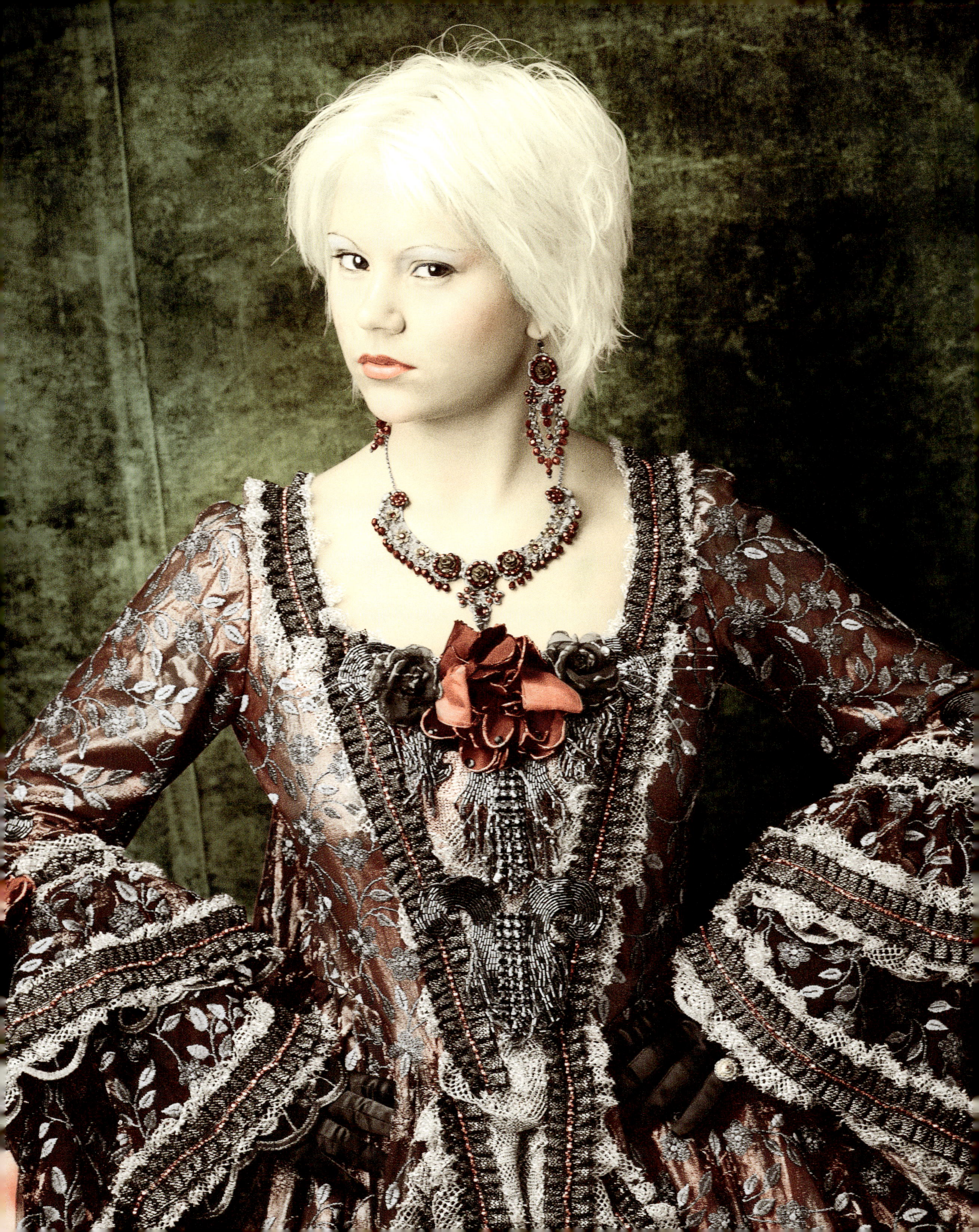

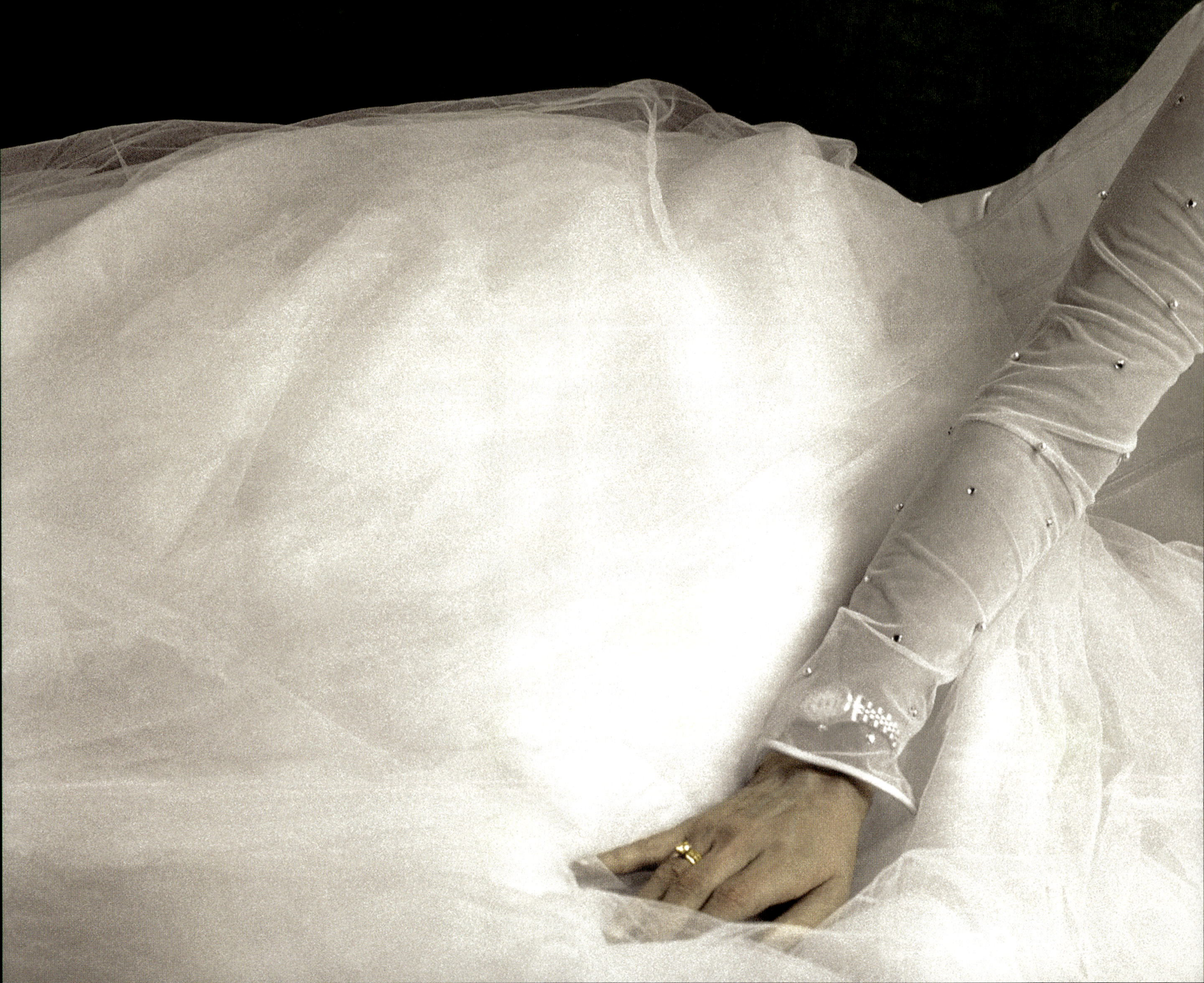

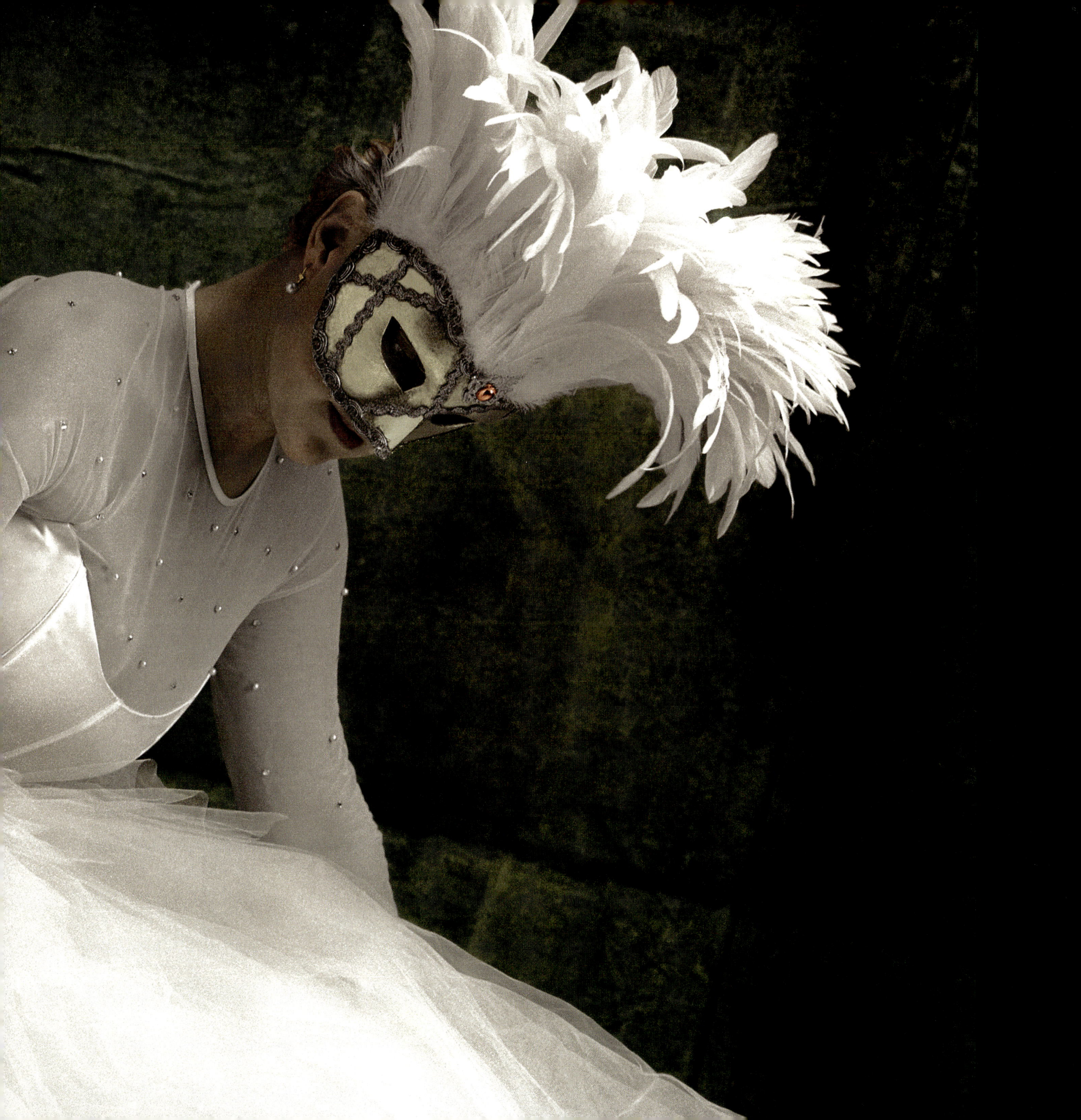

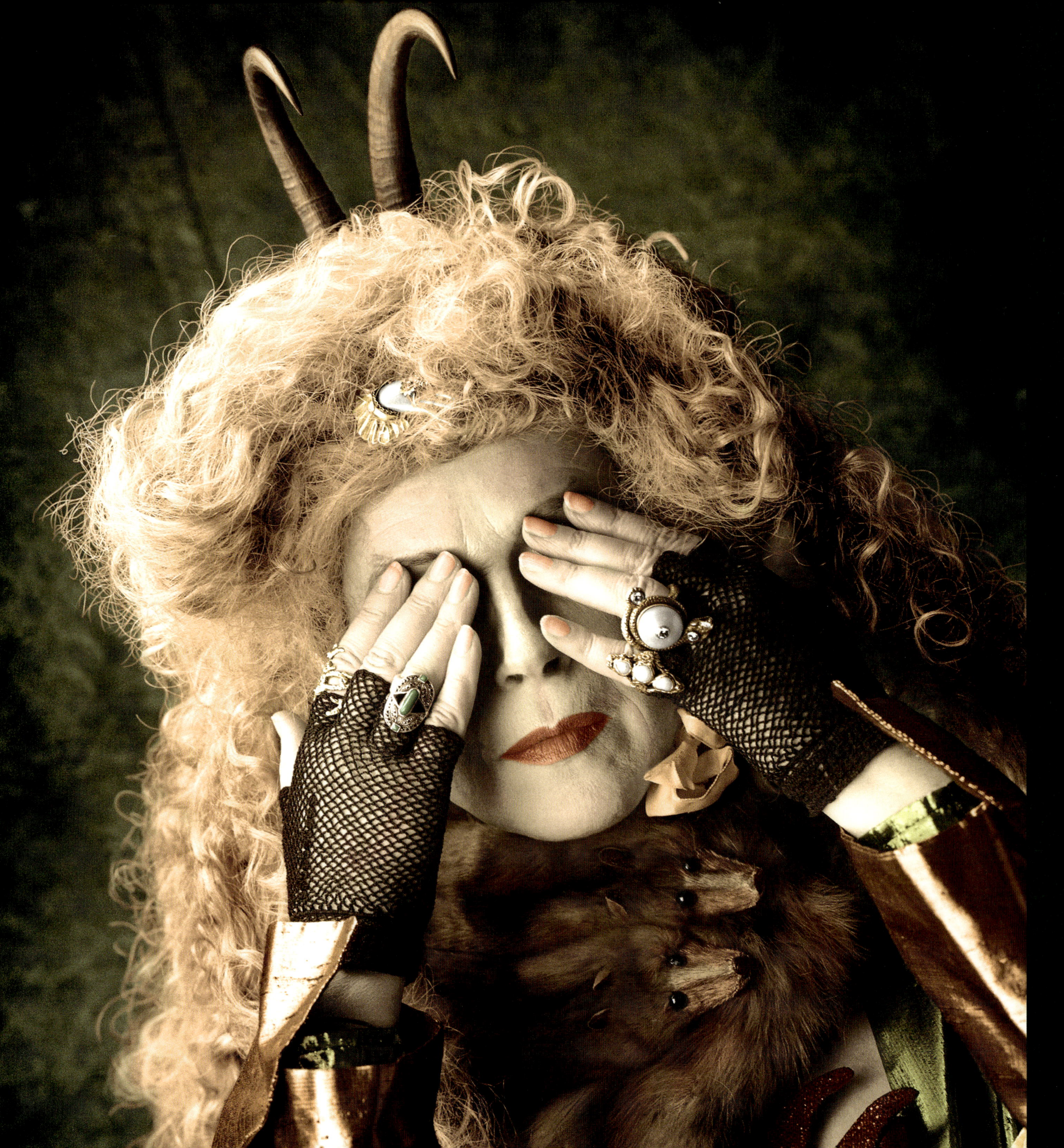

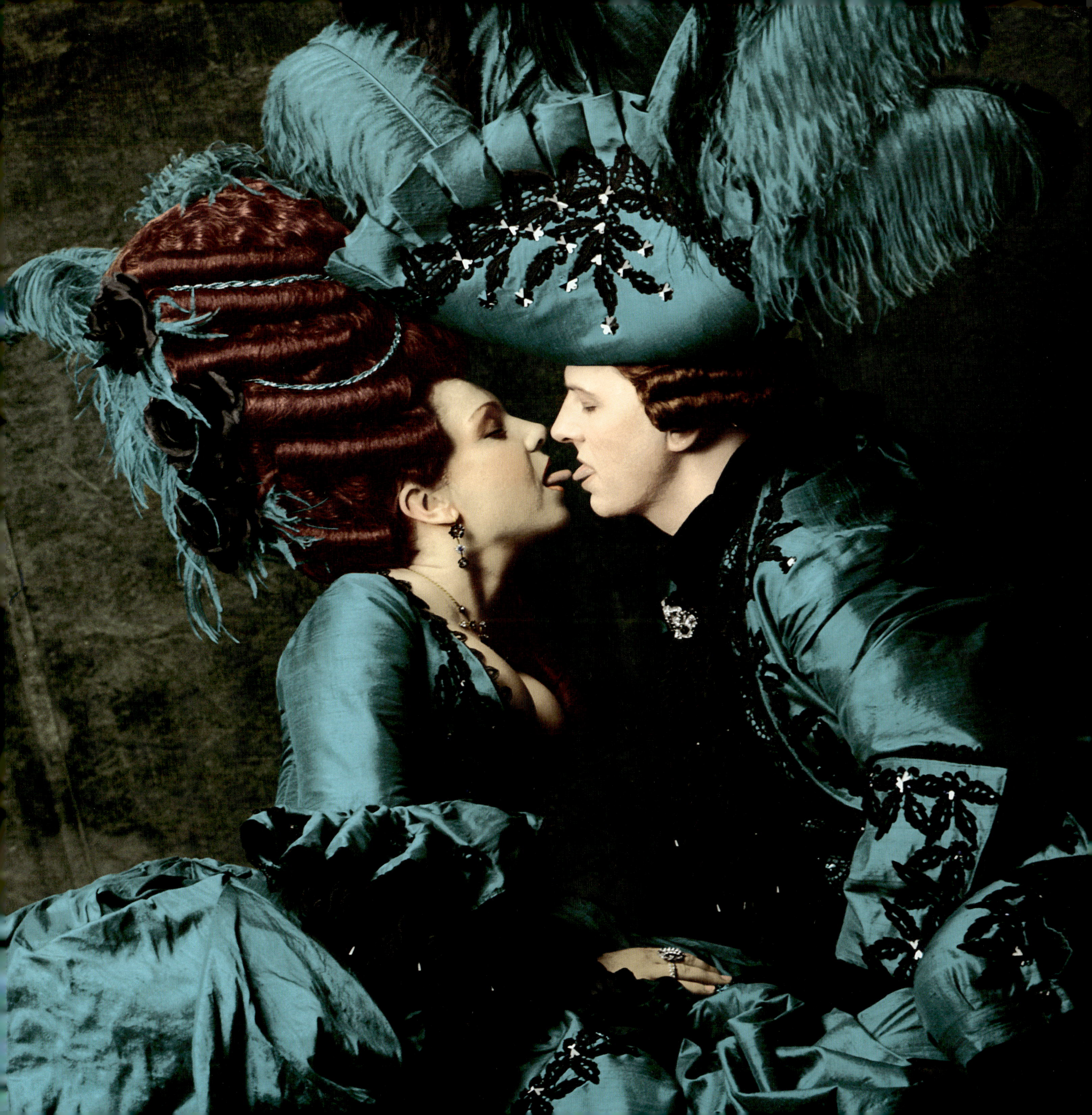

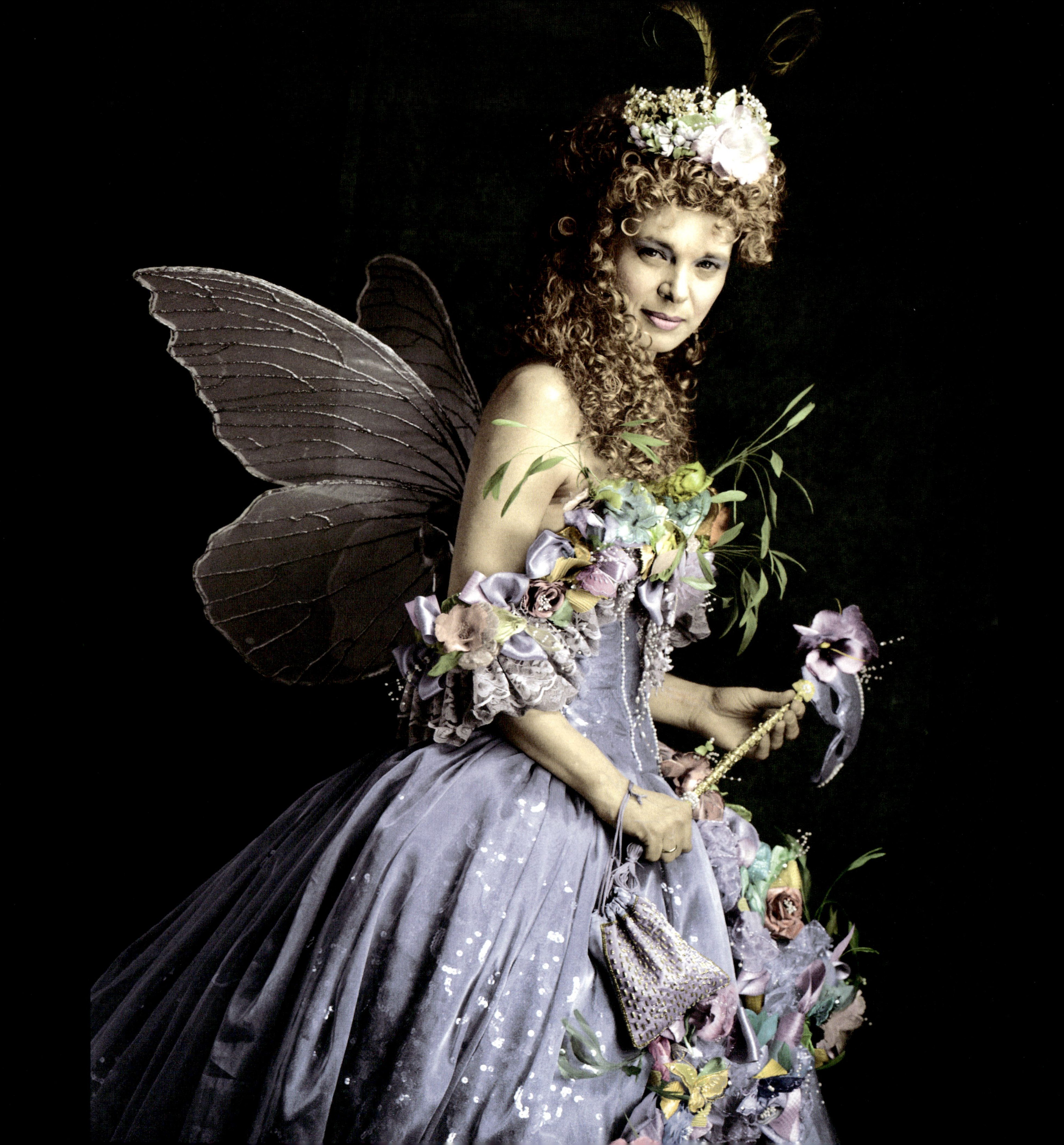

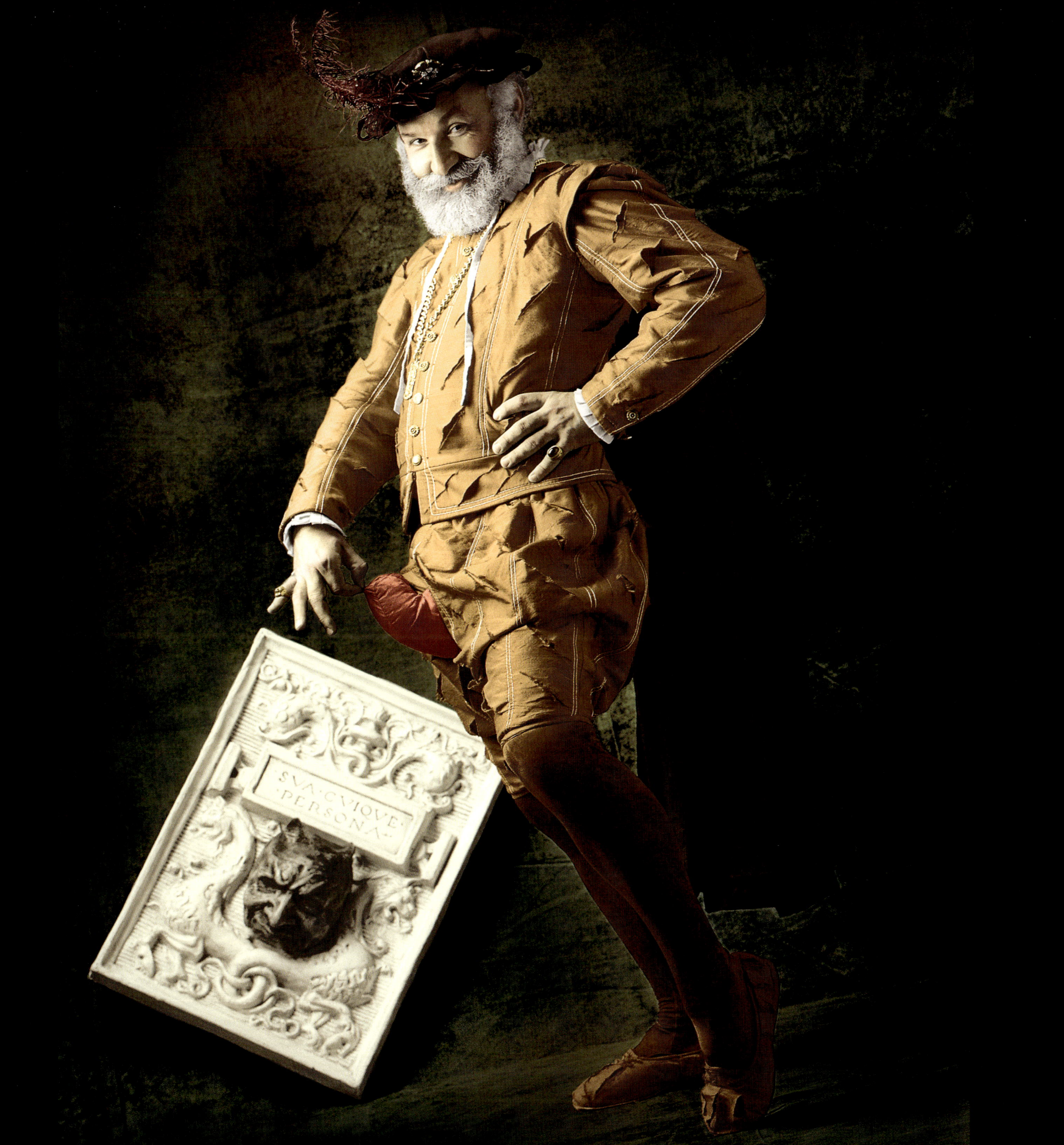
·SVA·CVIQVE·
·PERSONA·

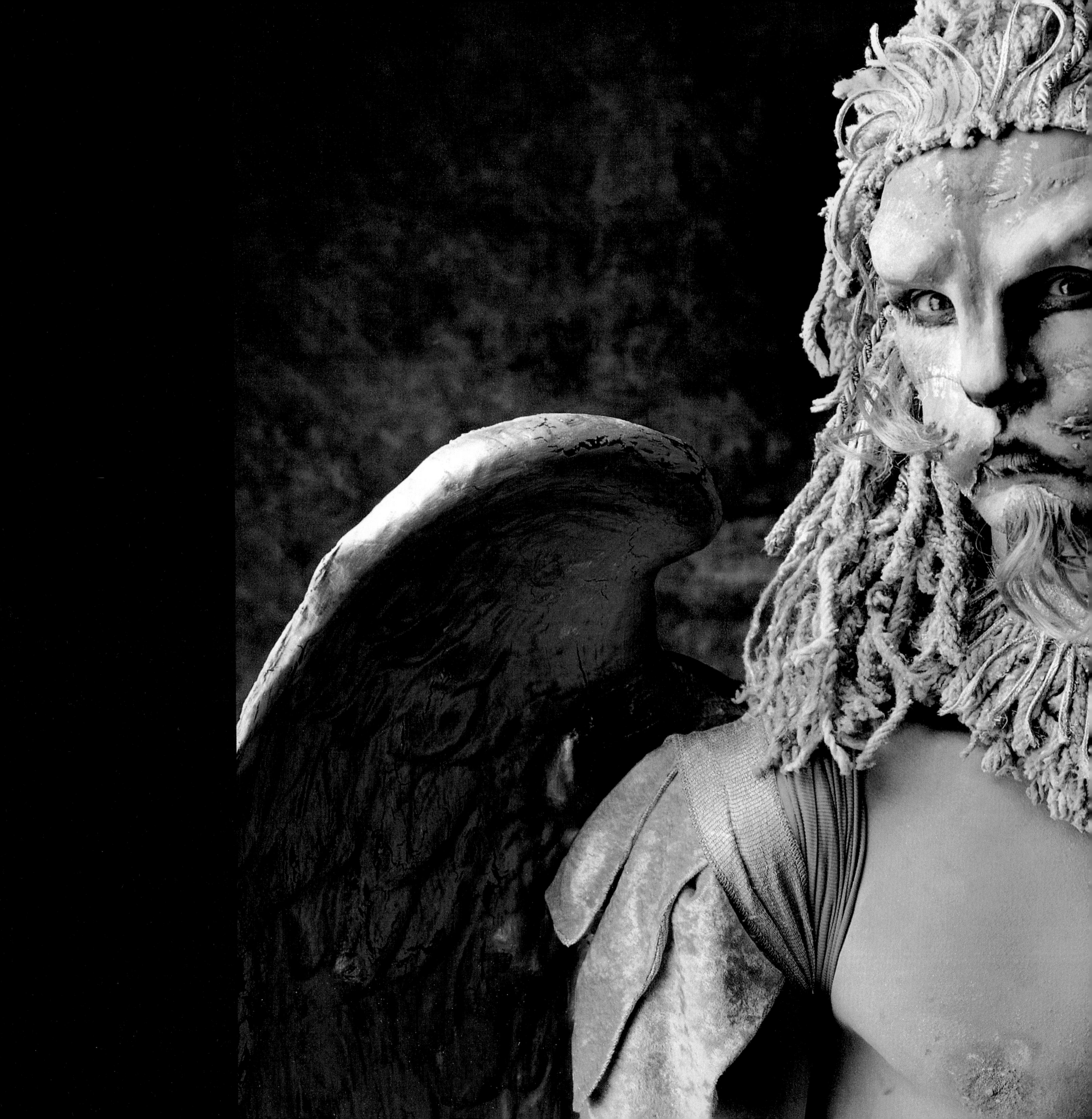

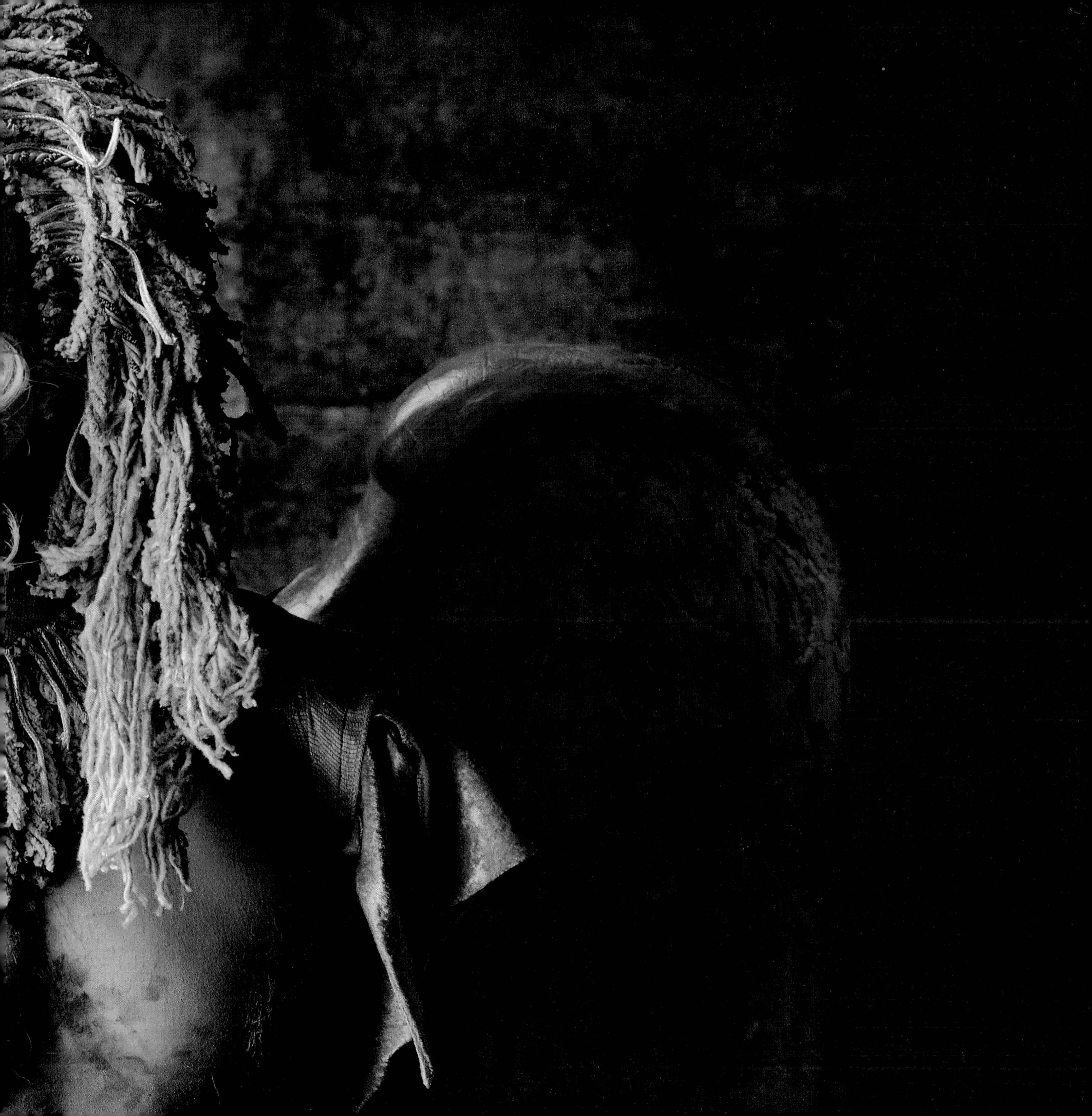

Luminous rambles
Nurtured longing
Latent and frothy

With dense sensuality
Persistently posing
Wickedly devouring

Piercing and deep
Dominating glances
Of changeable eyes

Suggestion emerging
Alluring and deceptive
With eddying dance

Fragile in play
Festive texture
Of profane symbols

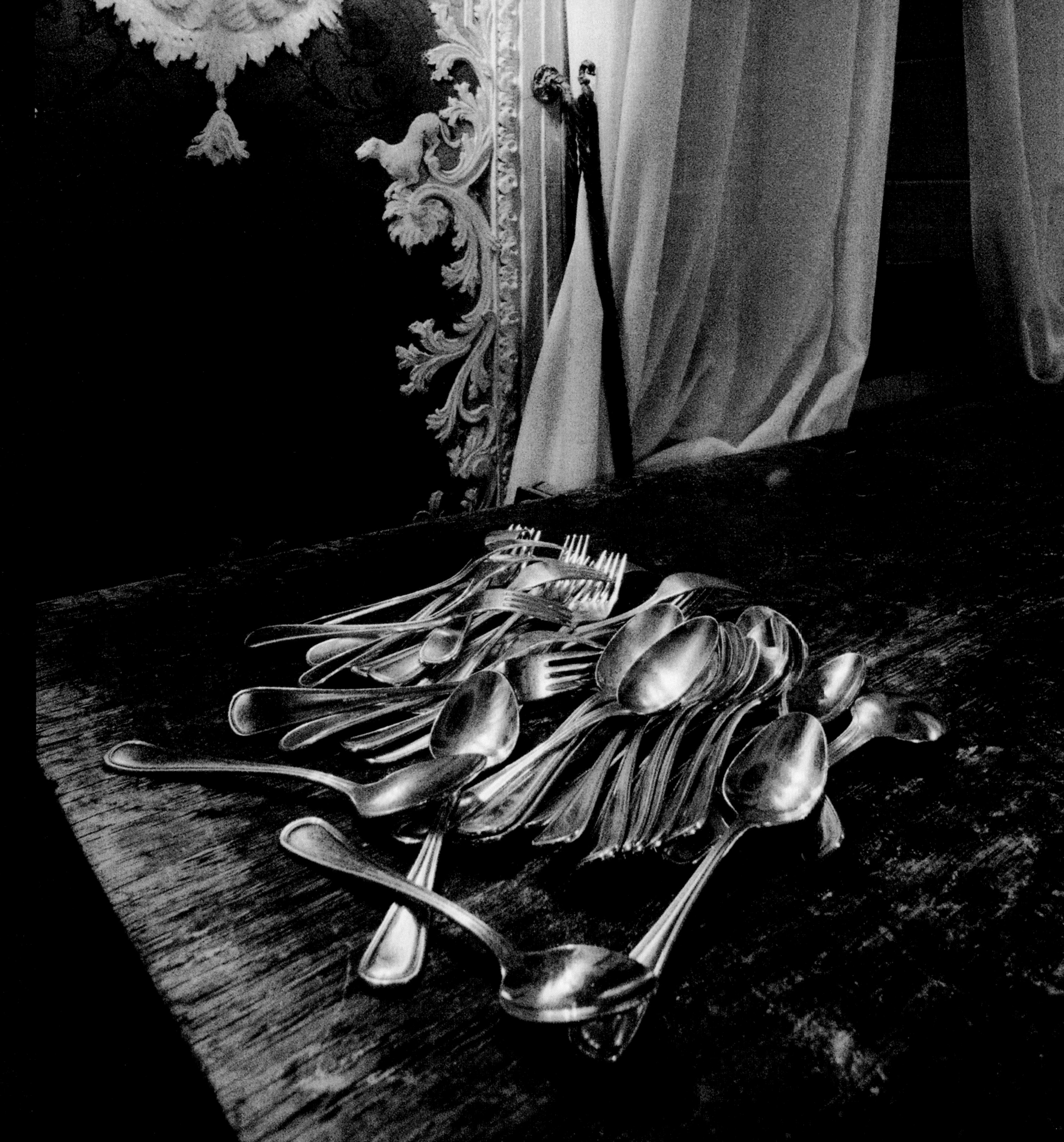

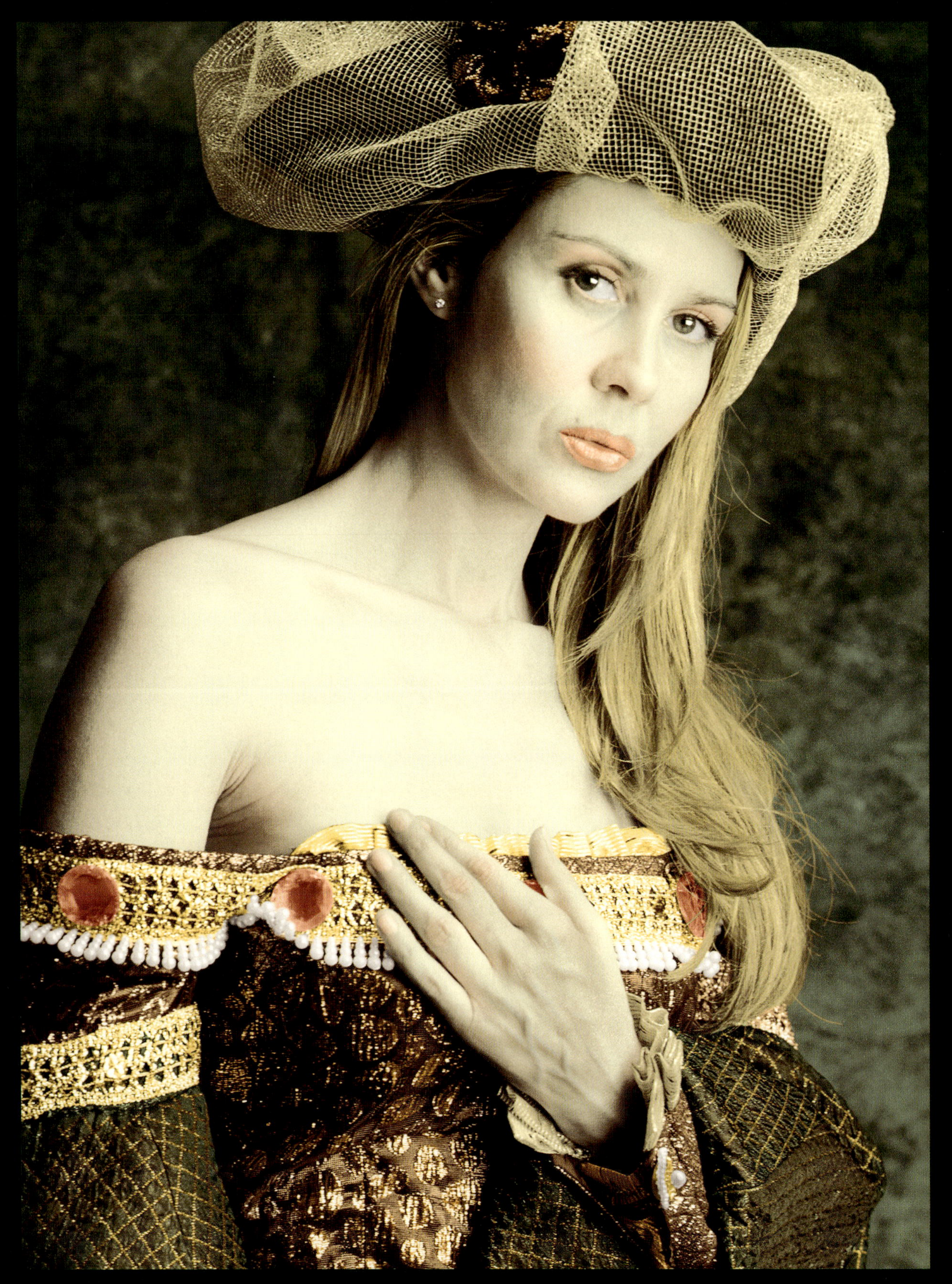

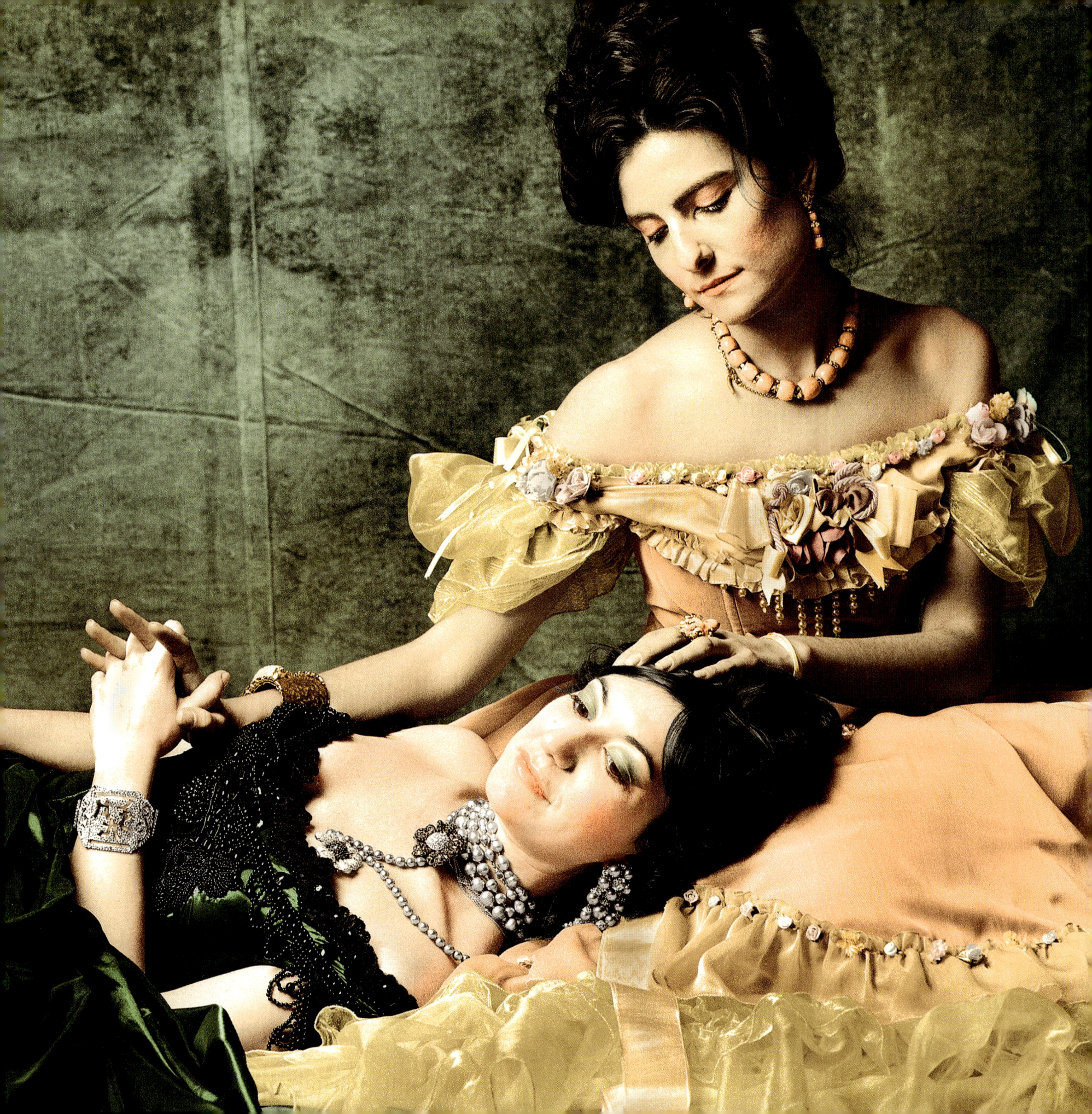

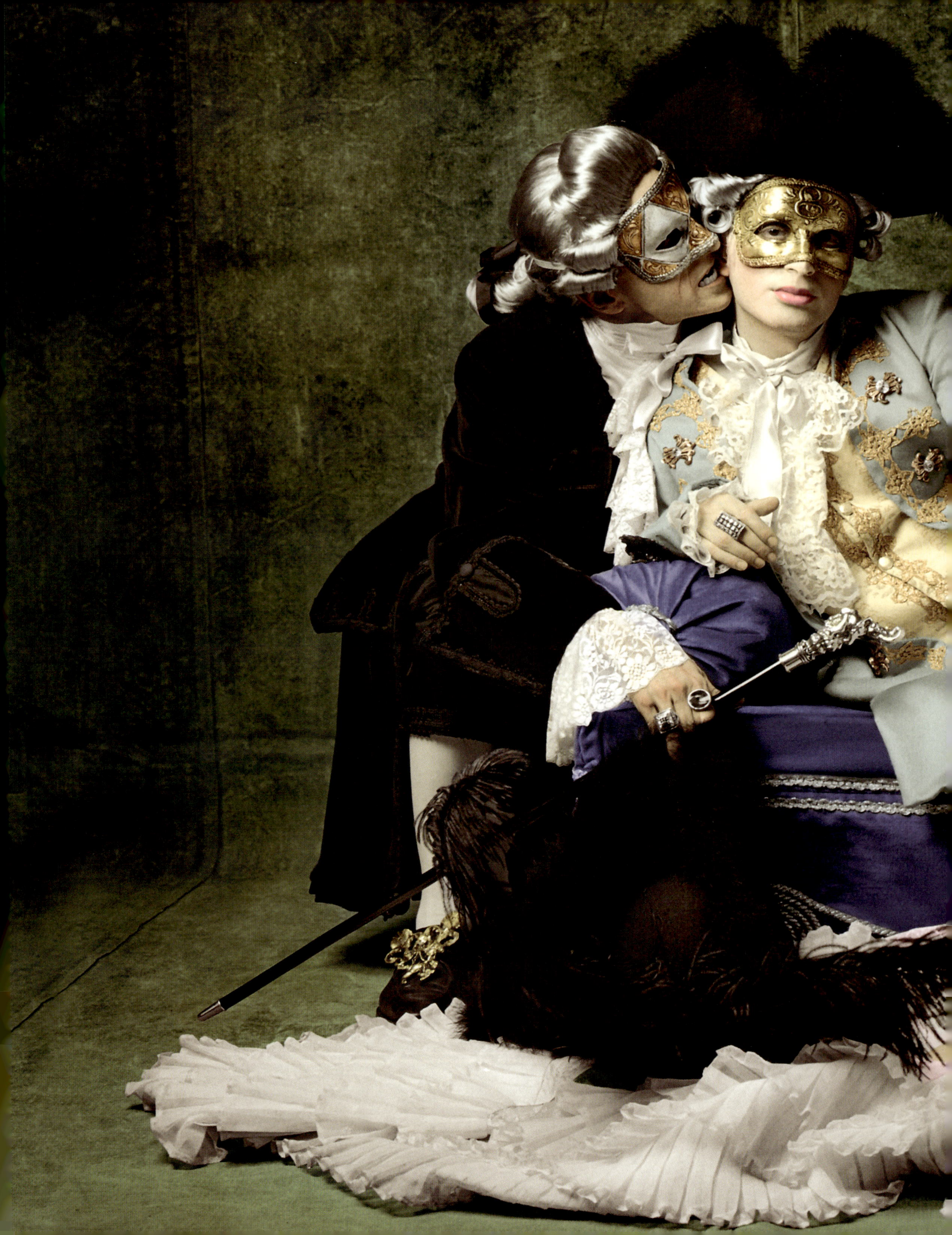

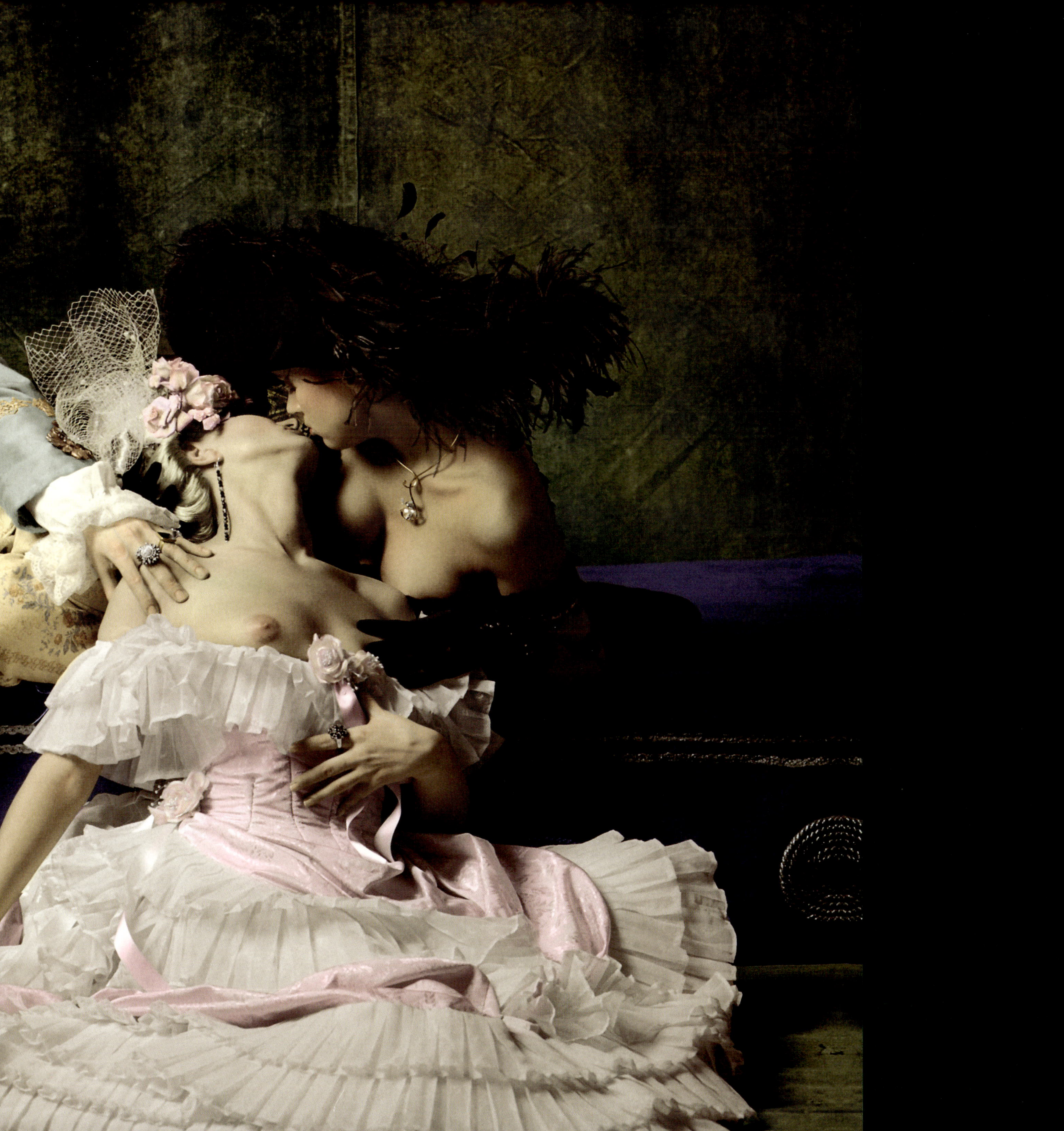

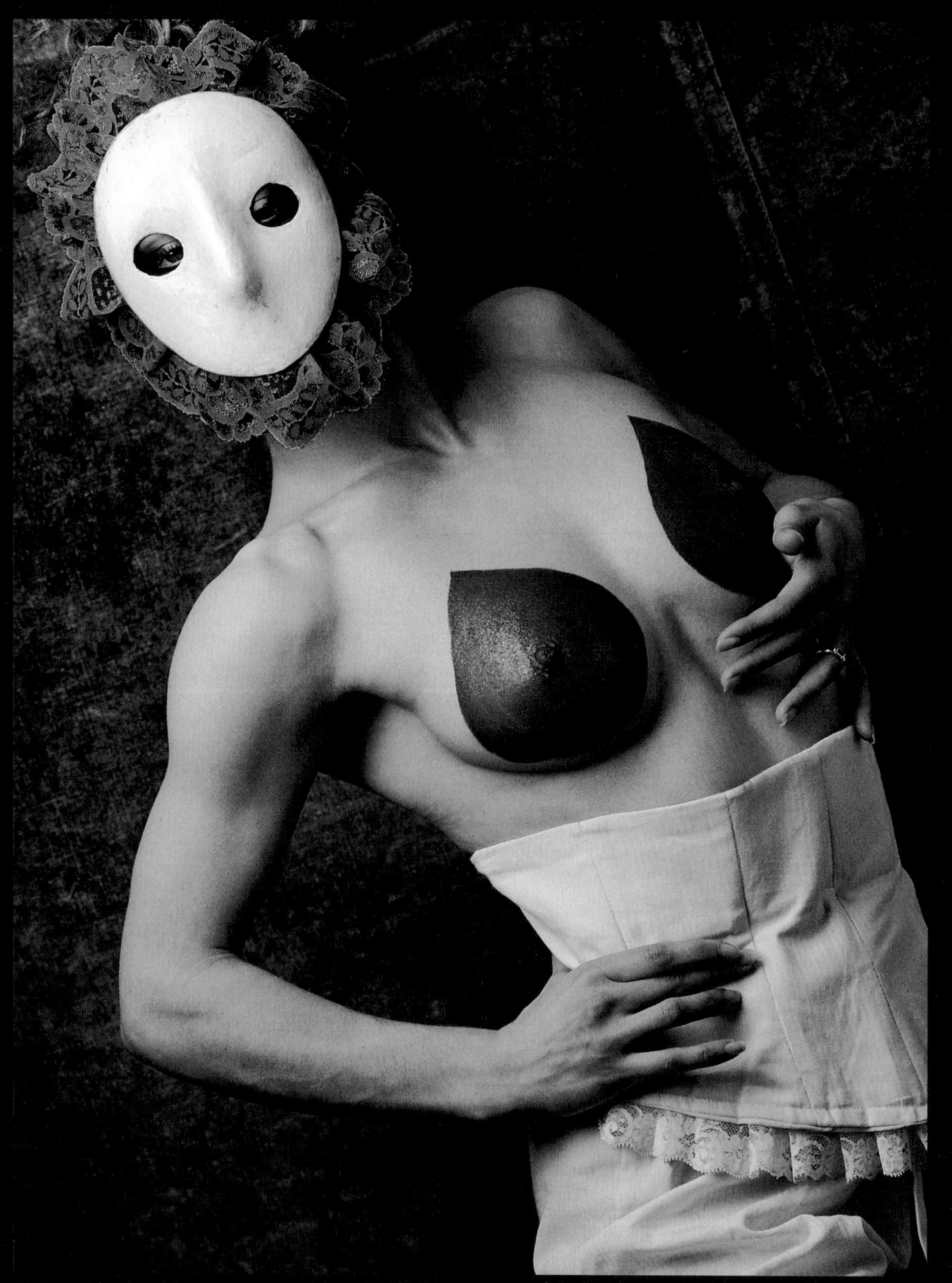

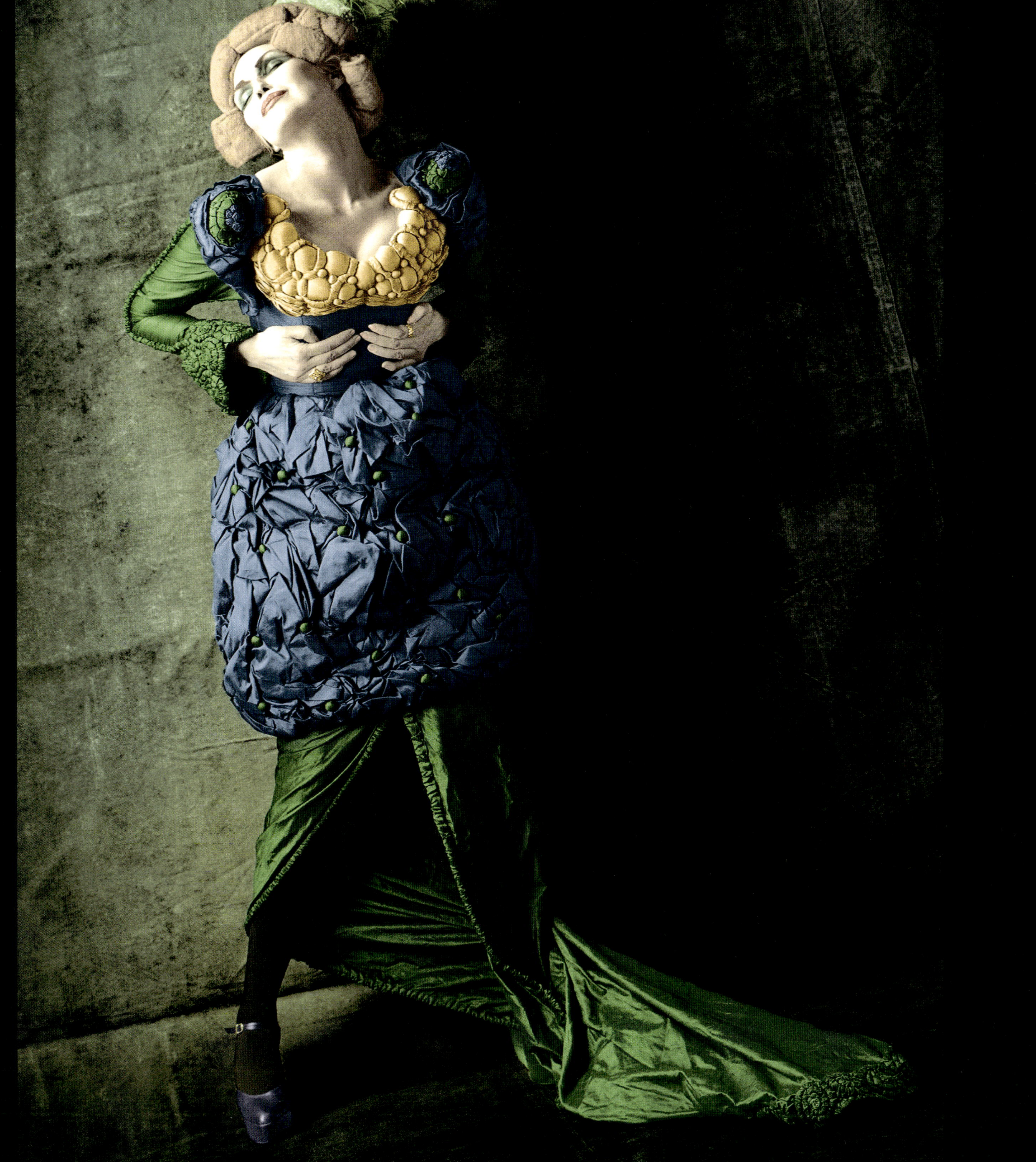

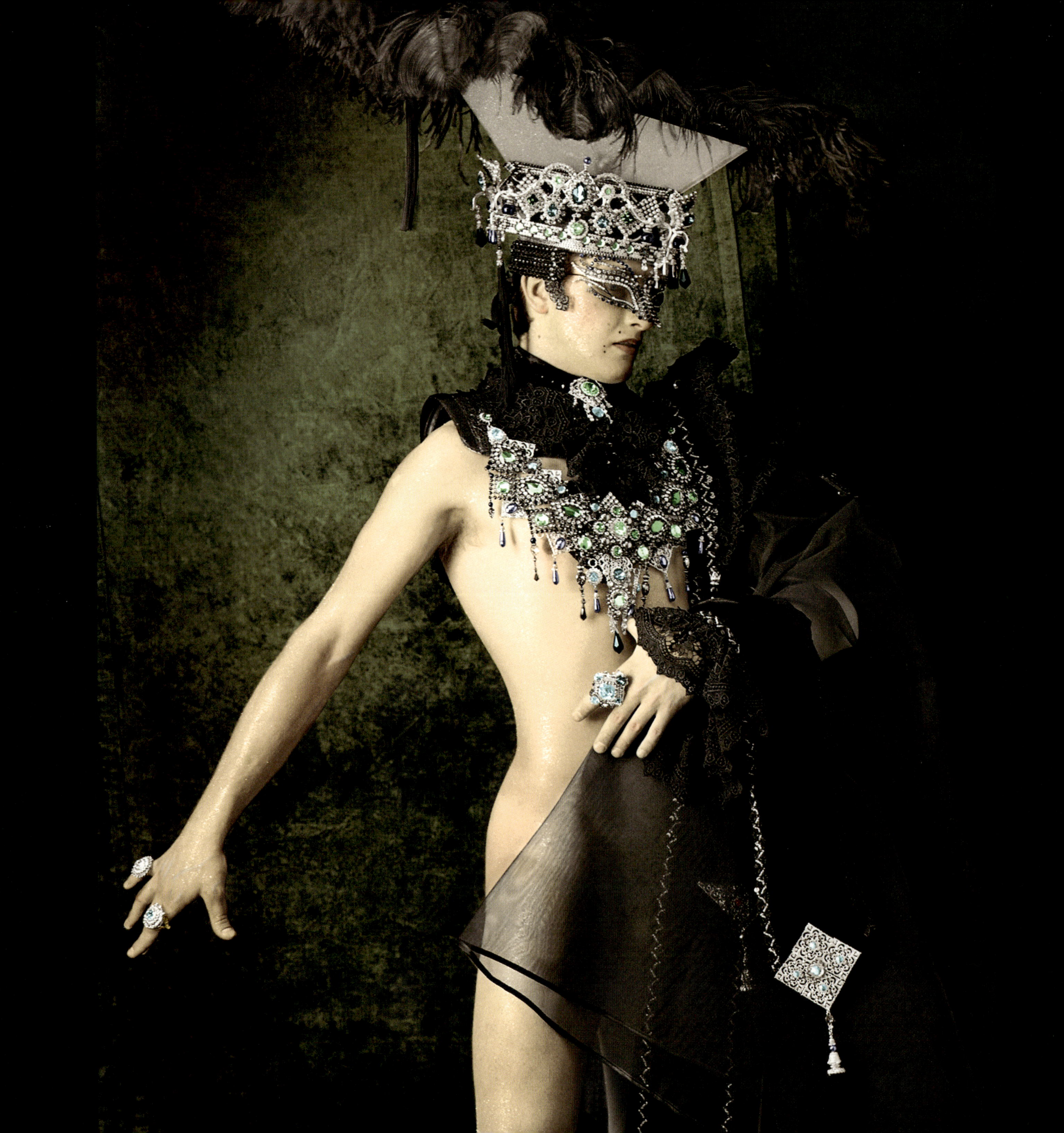

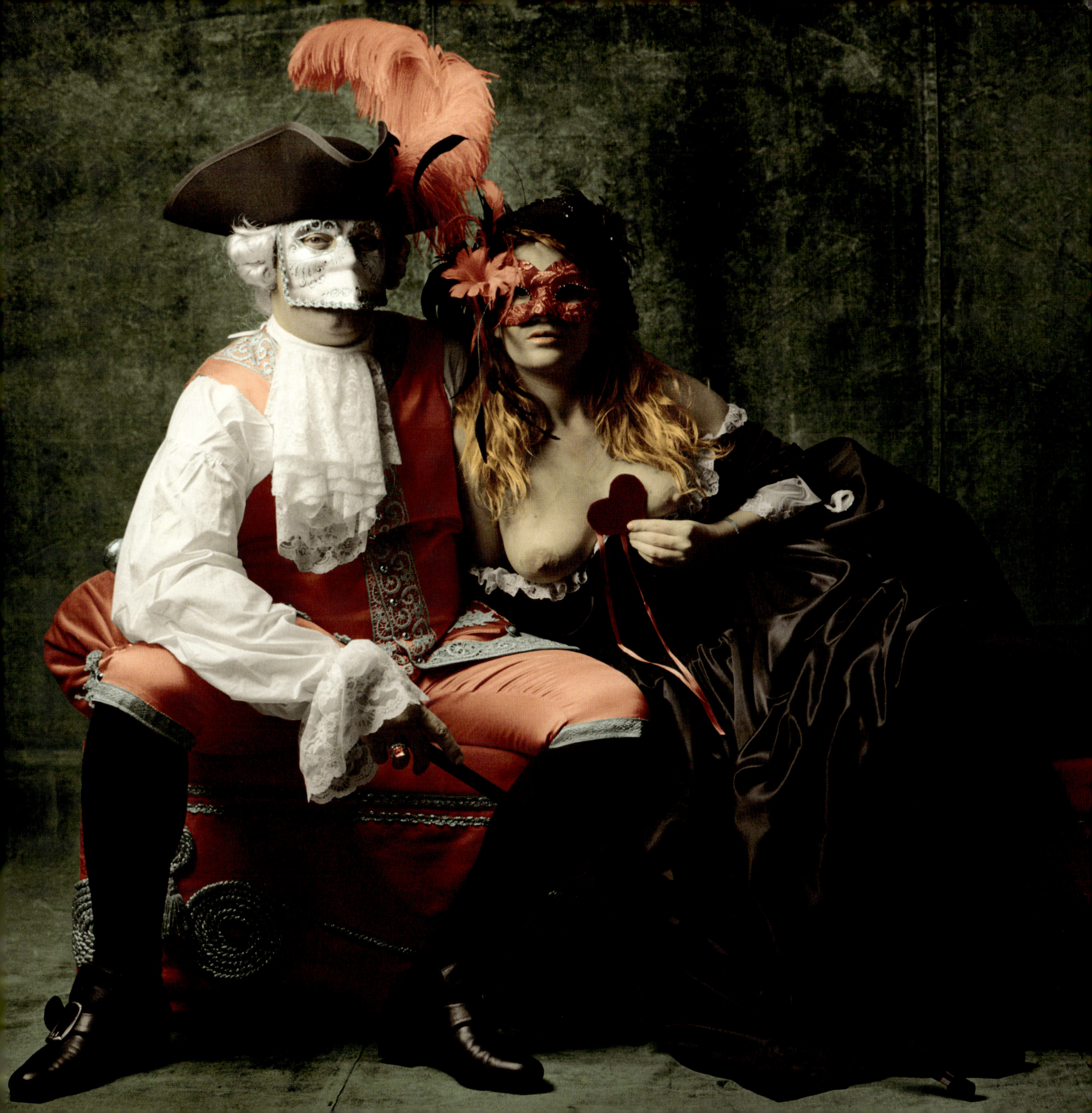

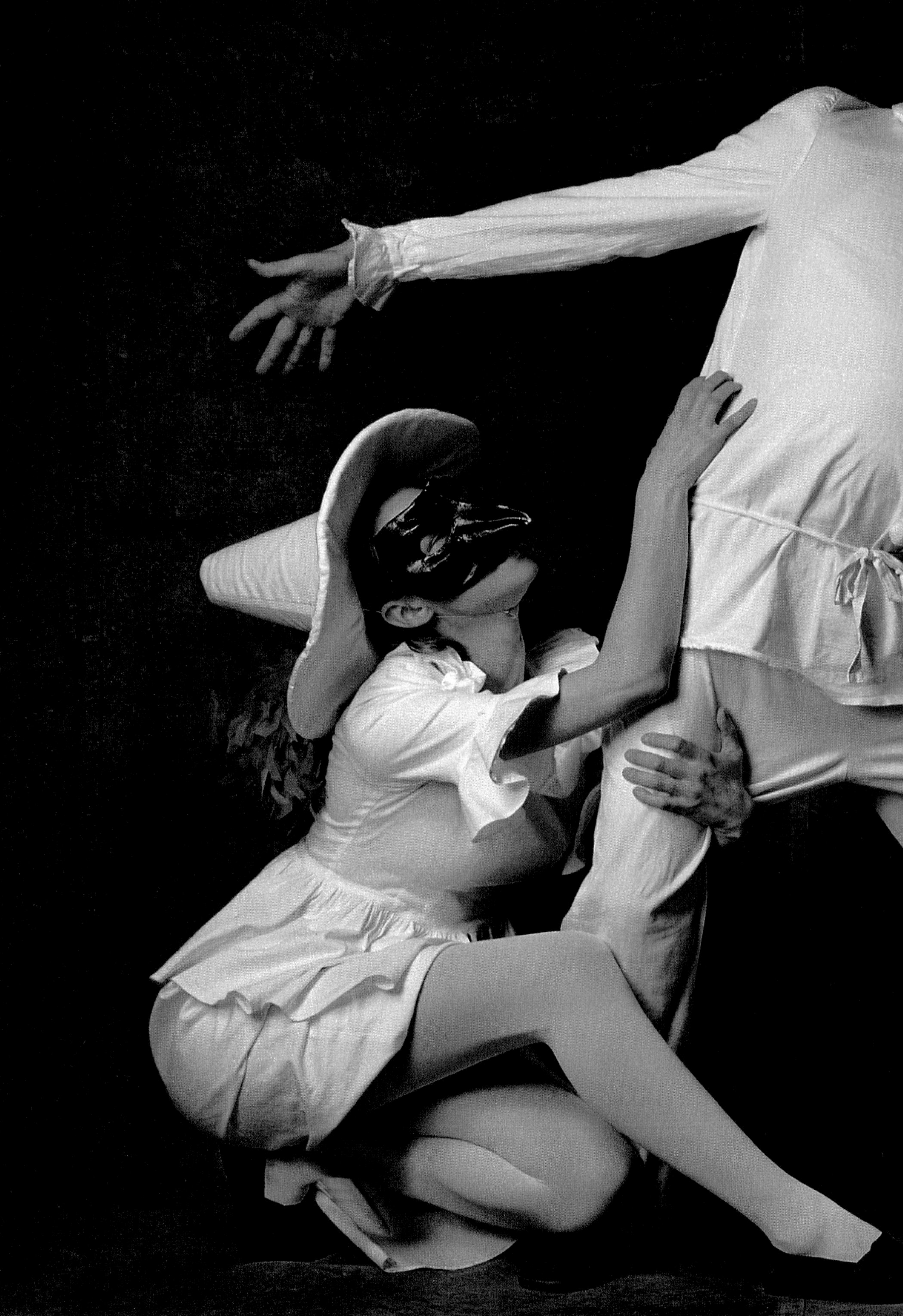

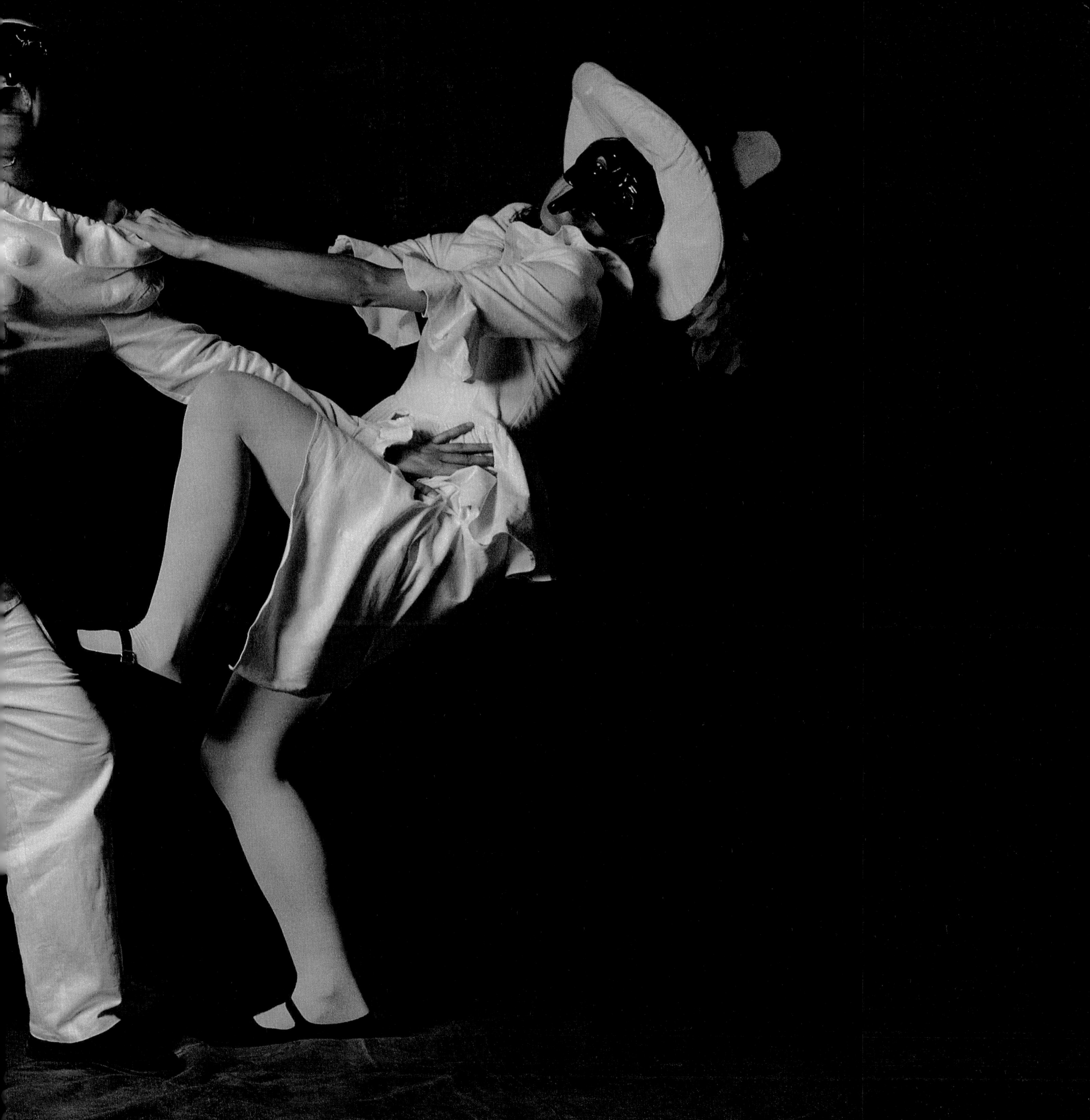

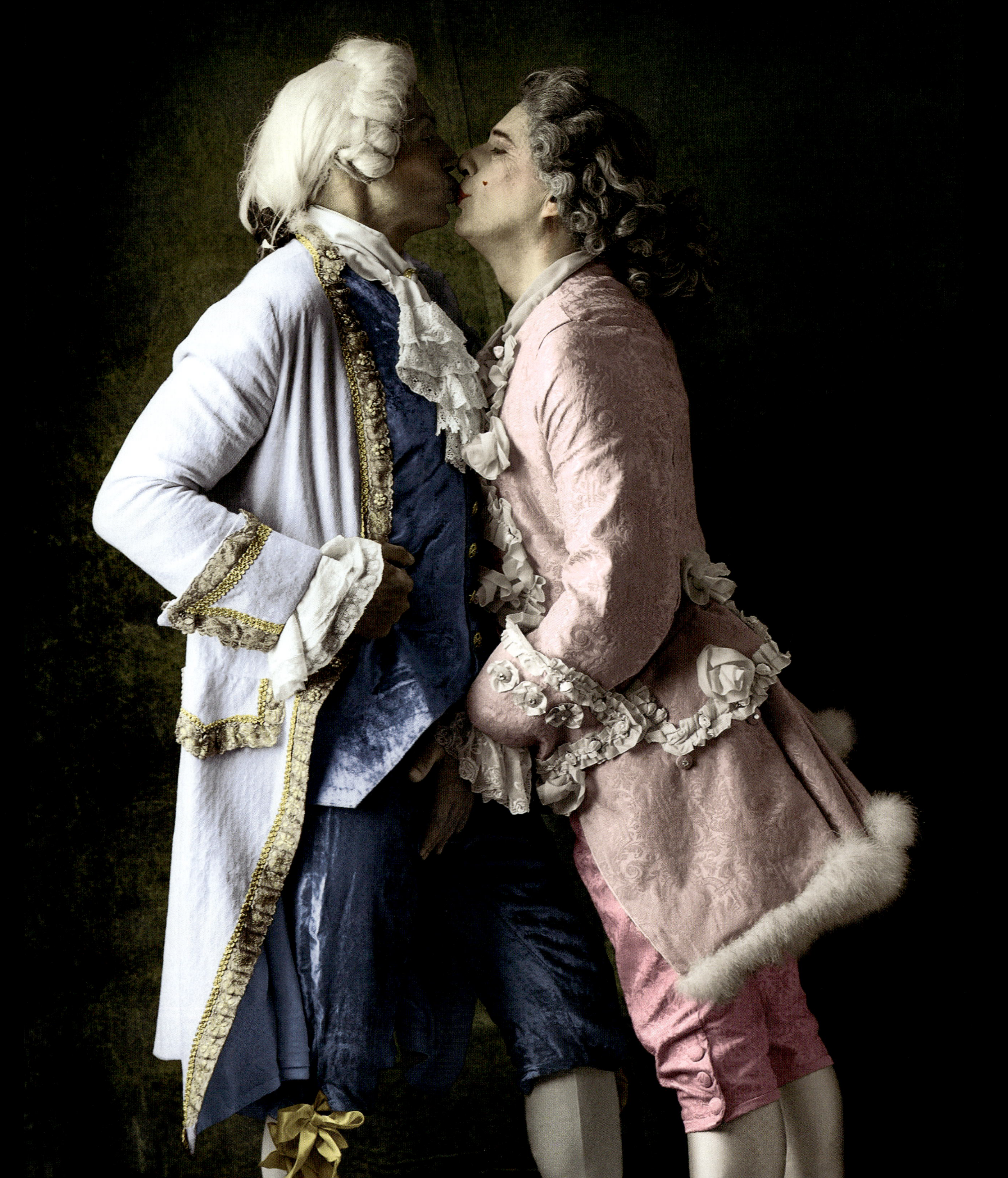

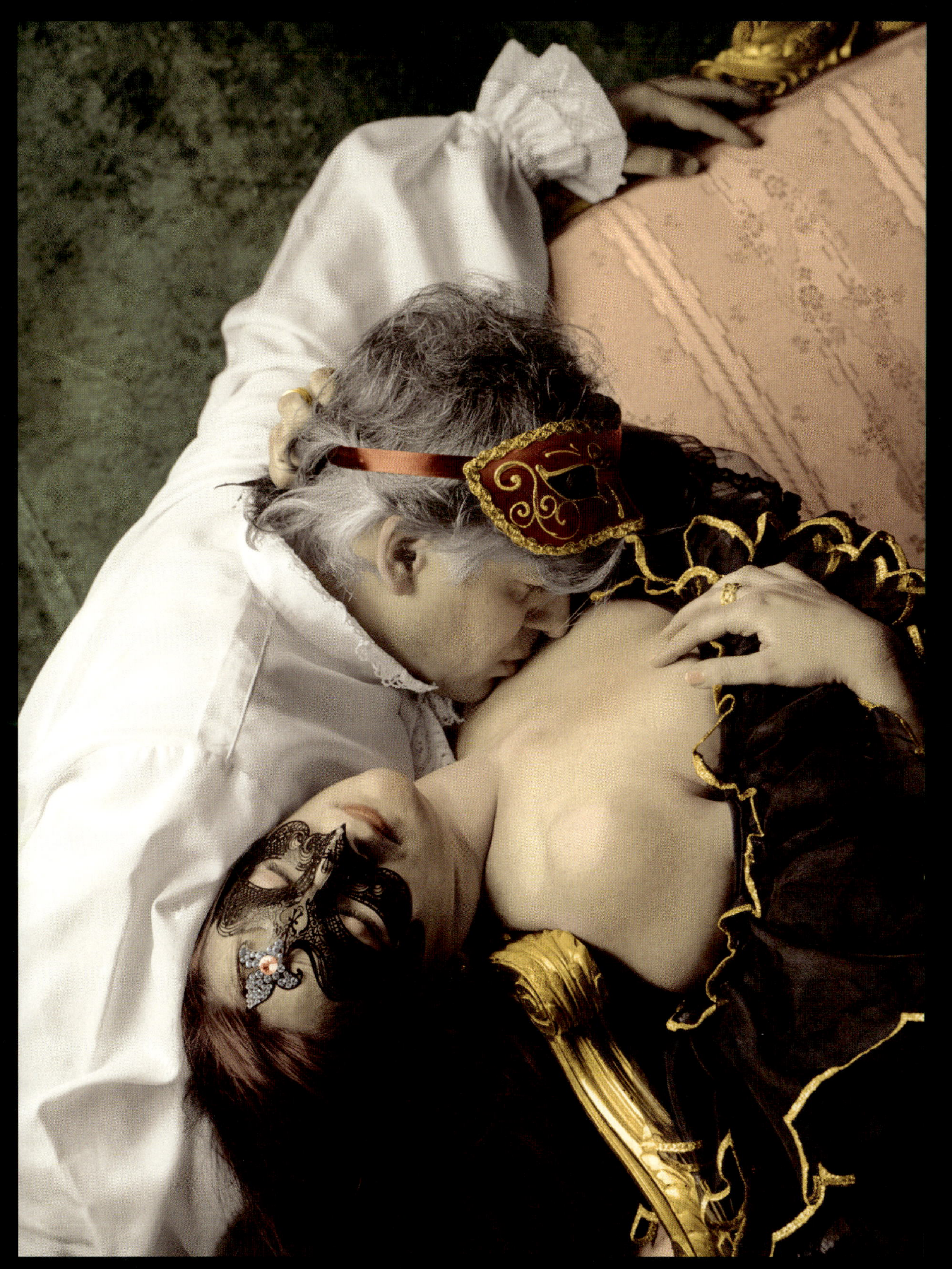

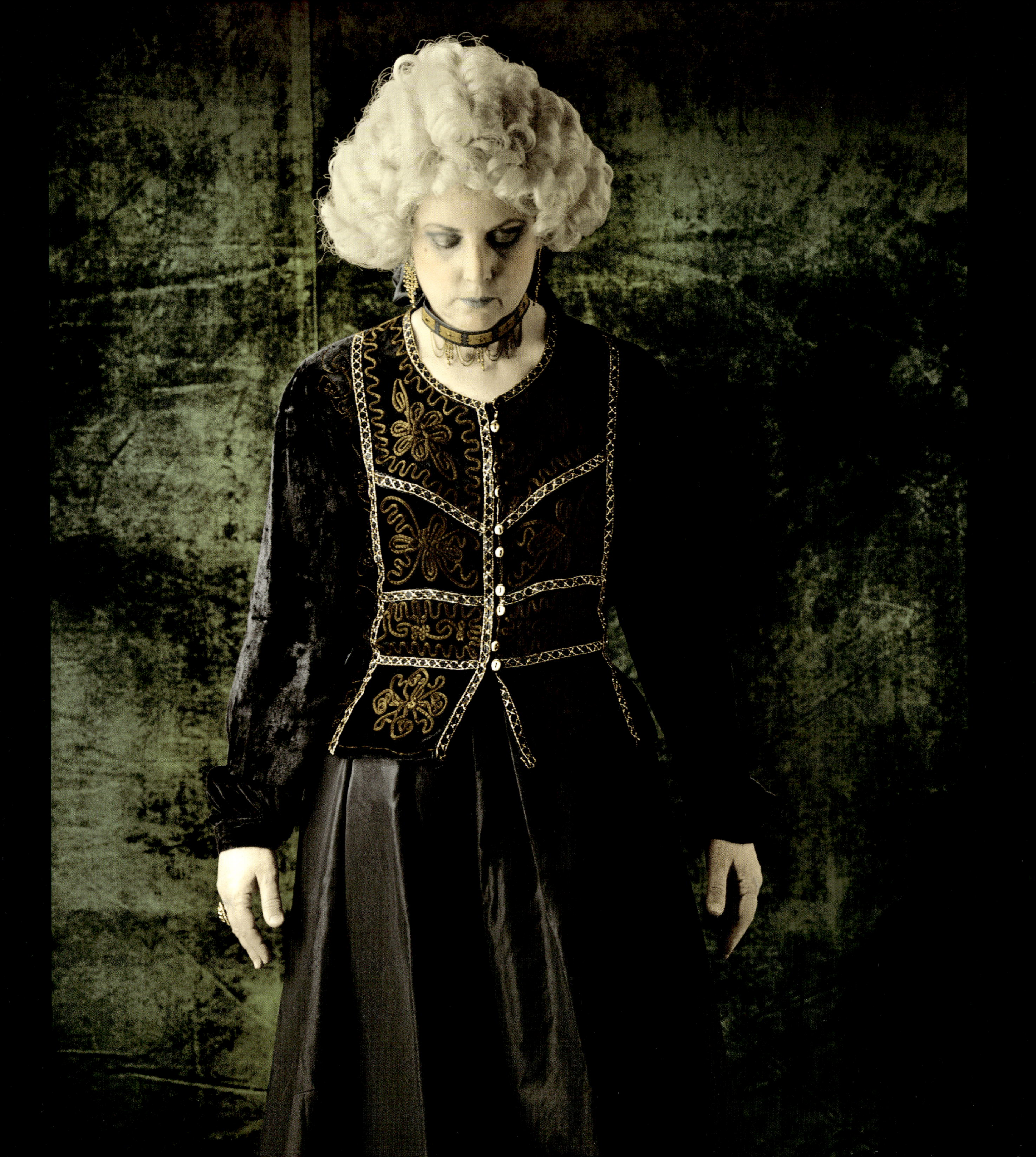

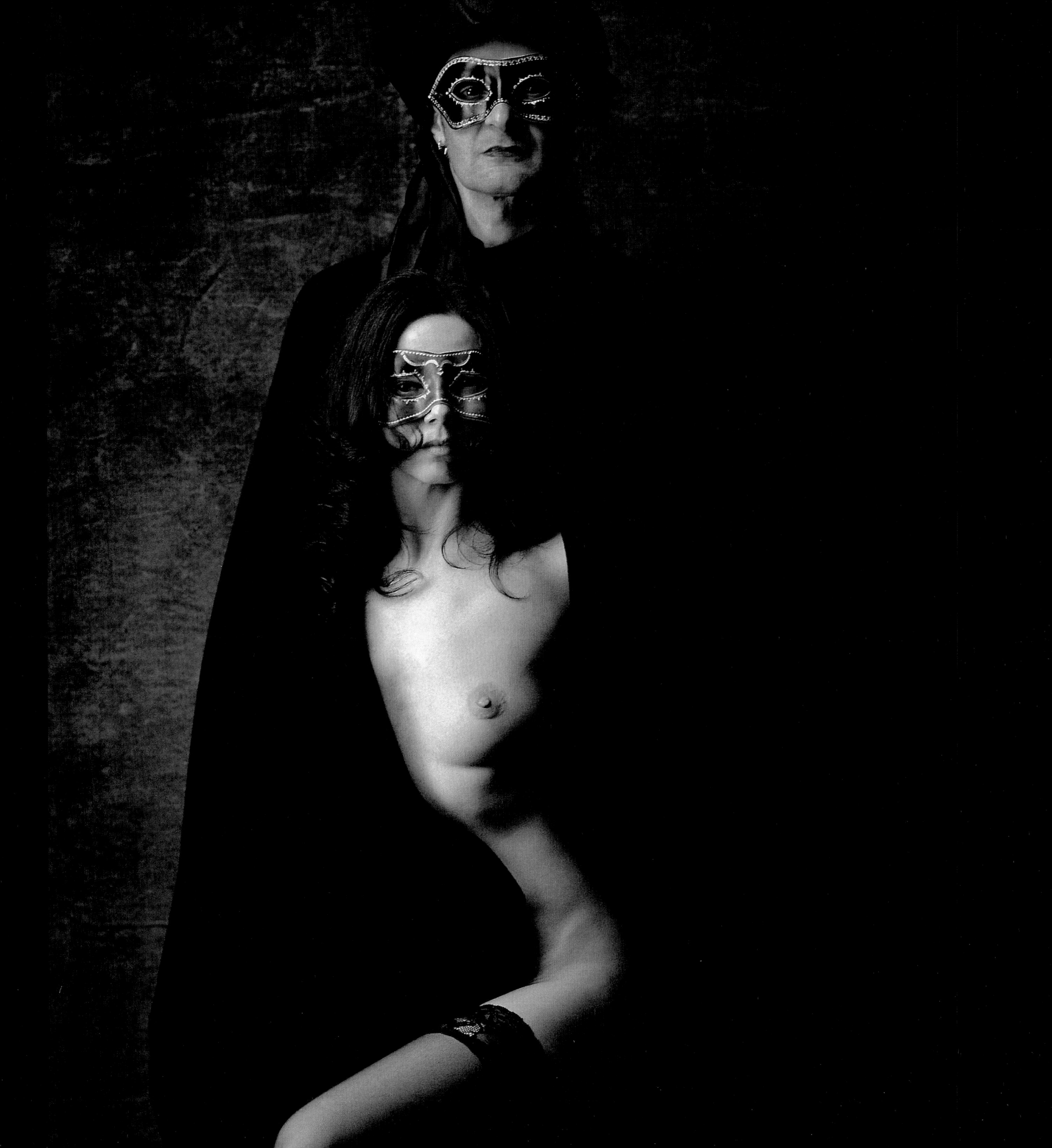

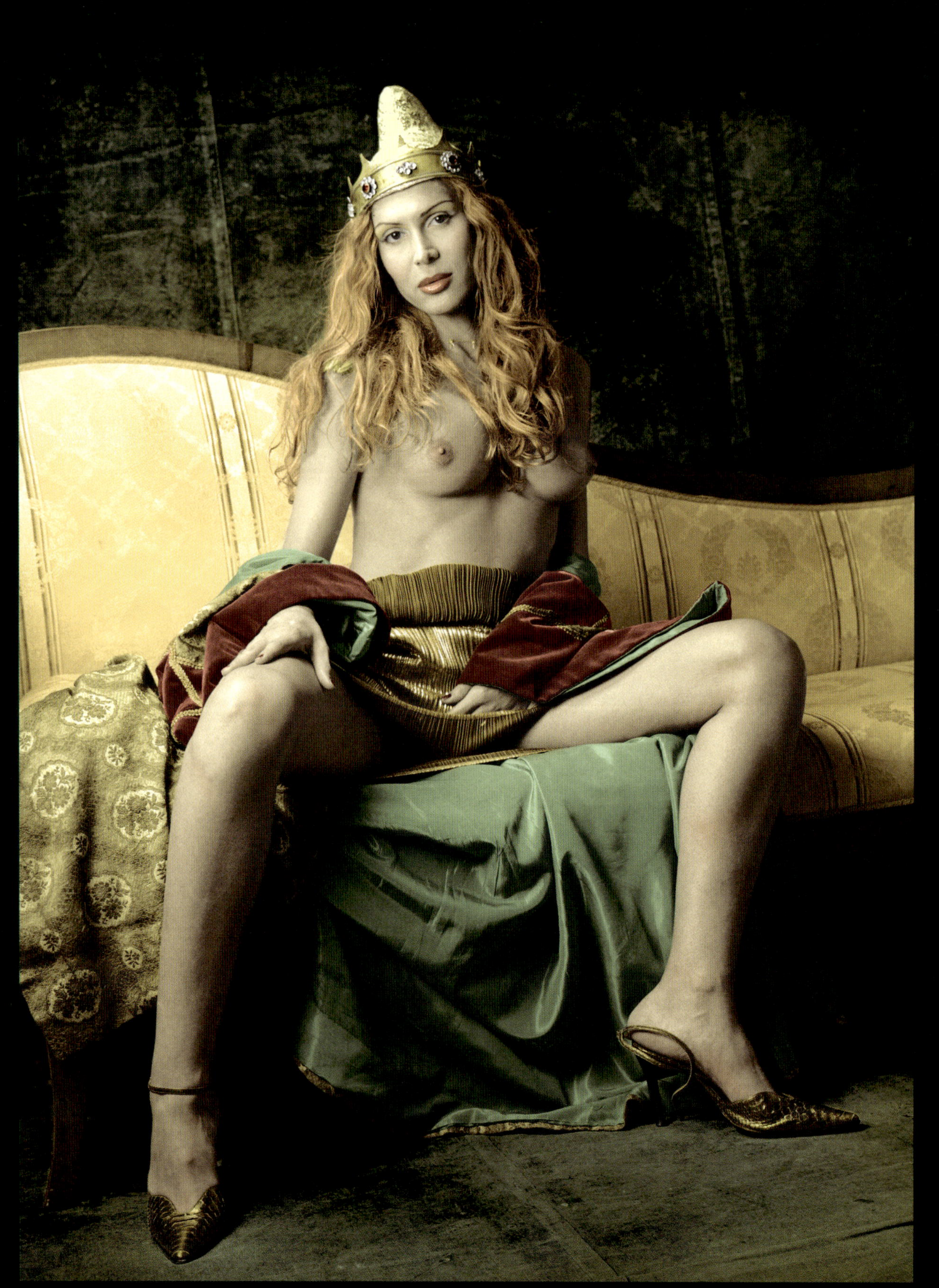

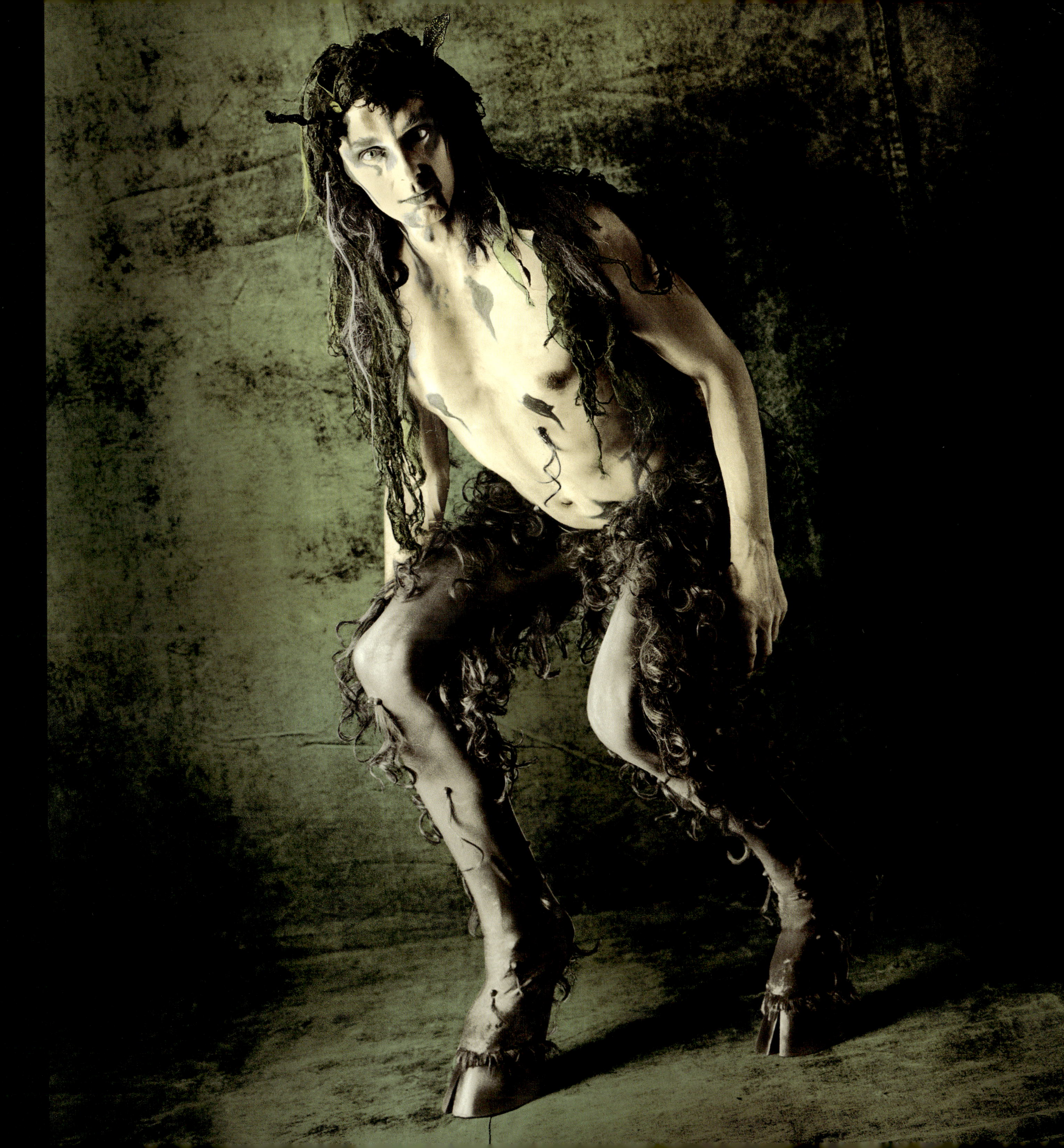

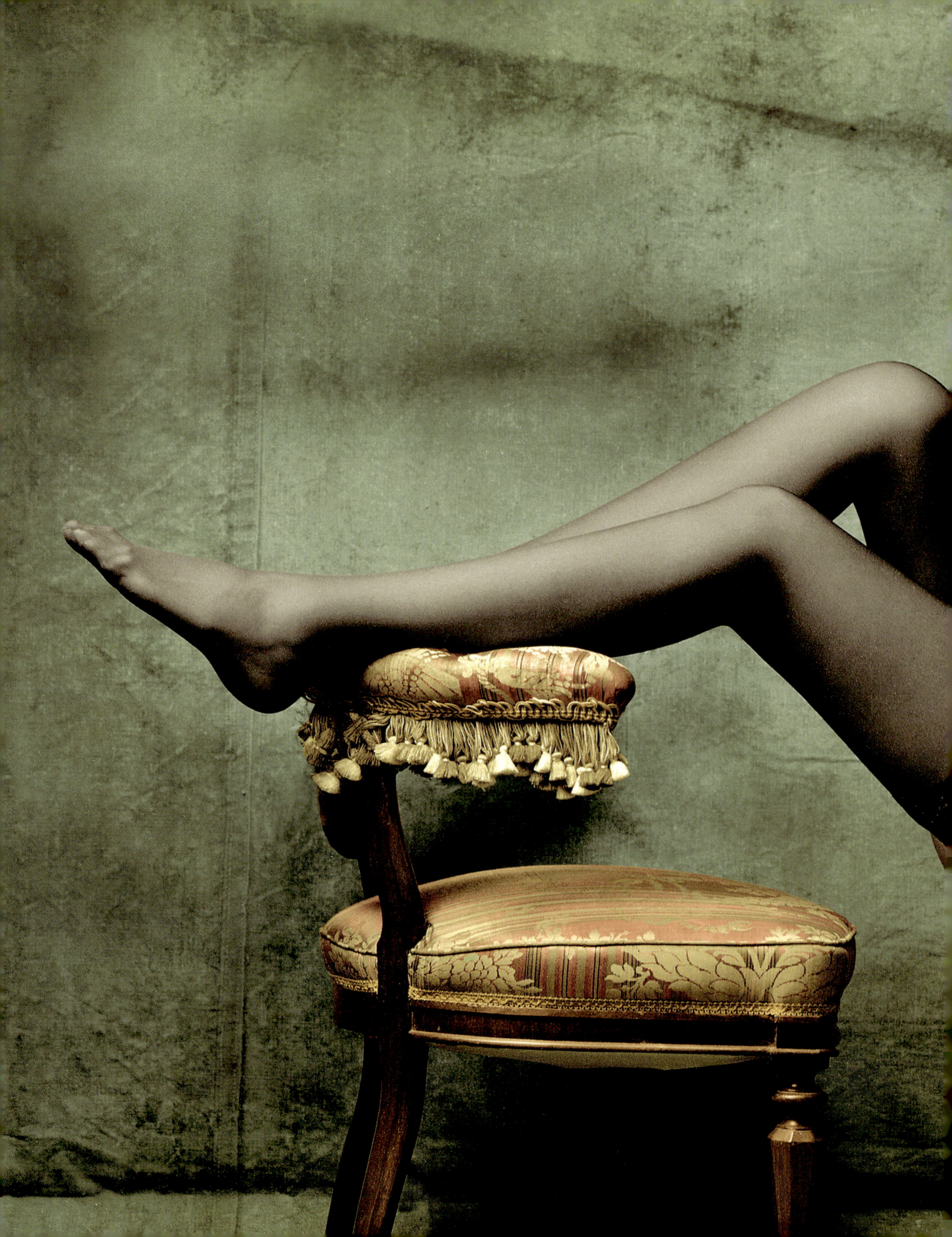

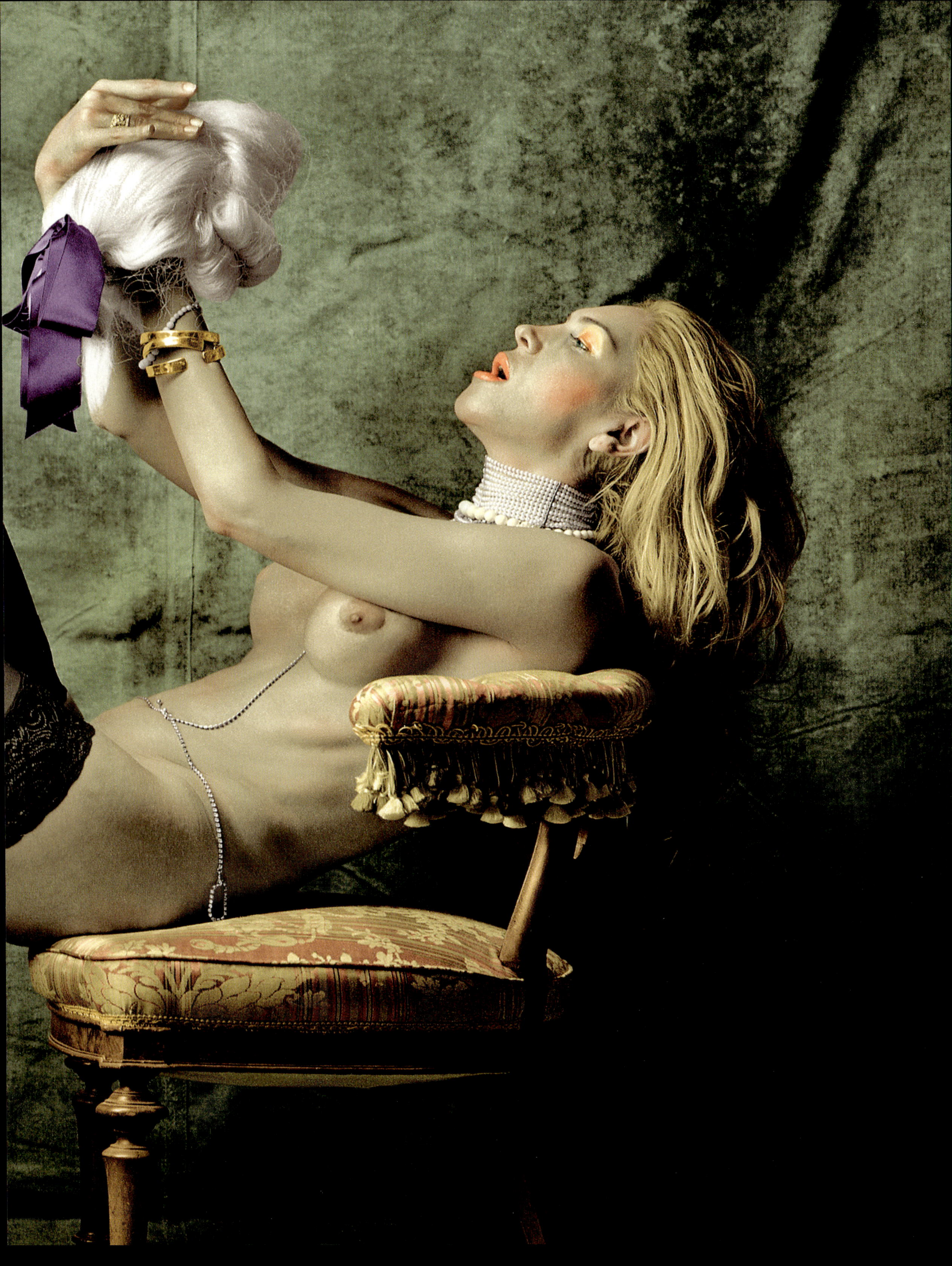

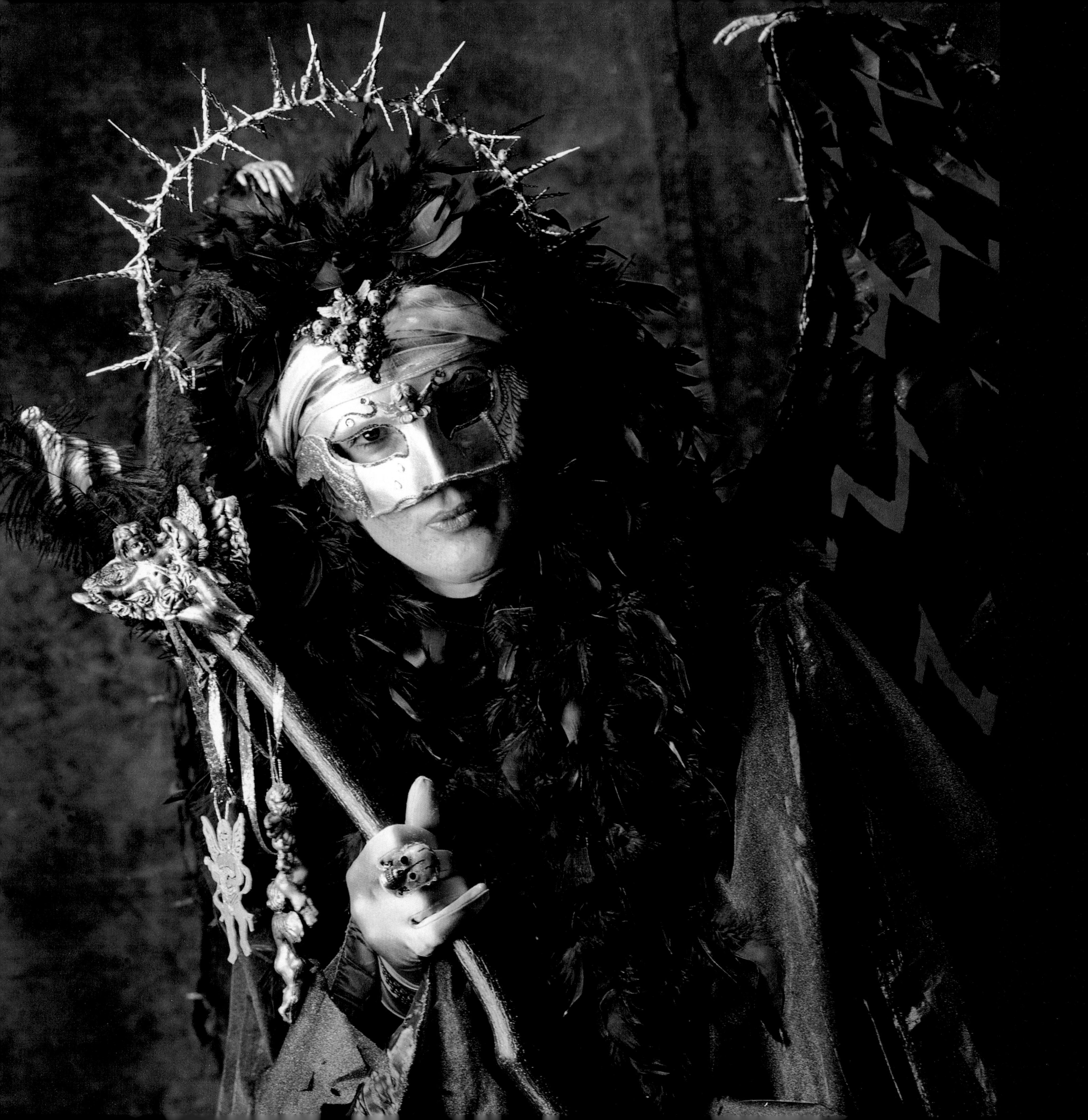

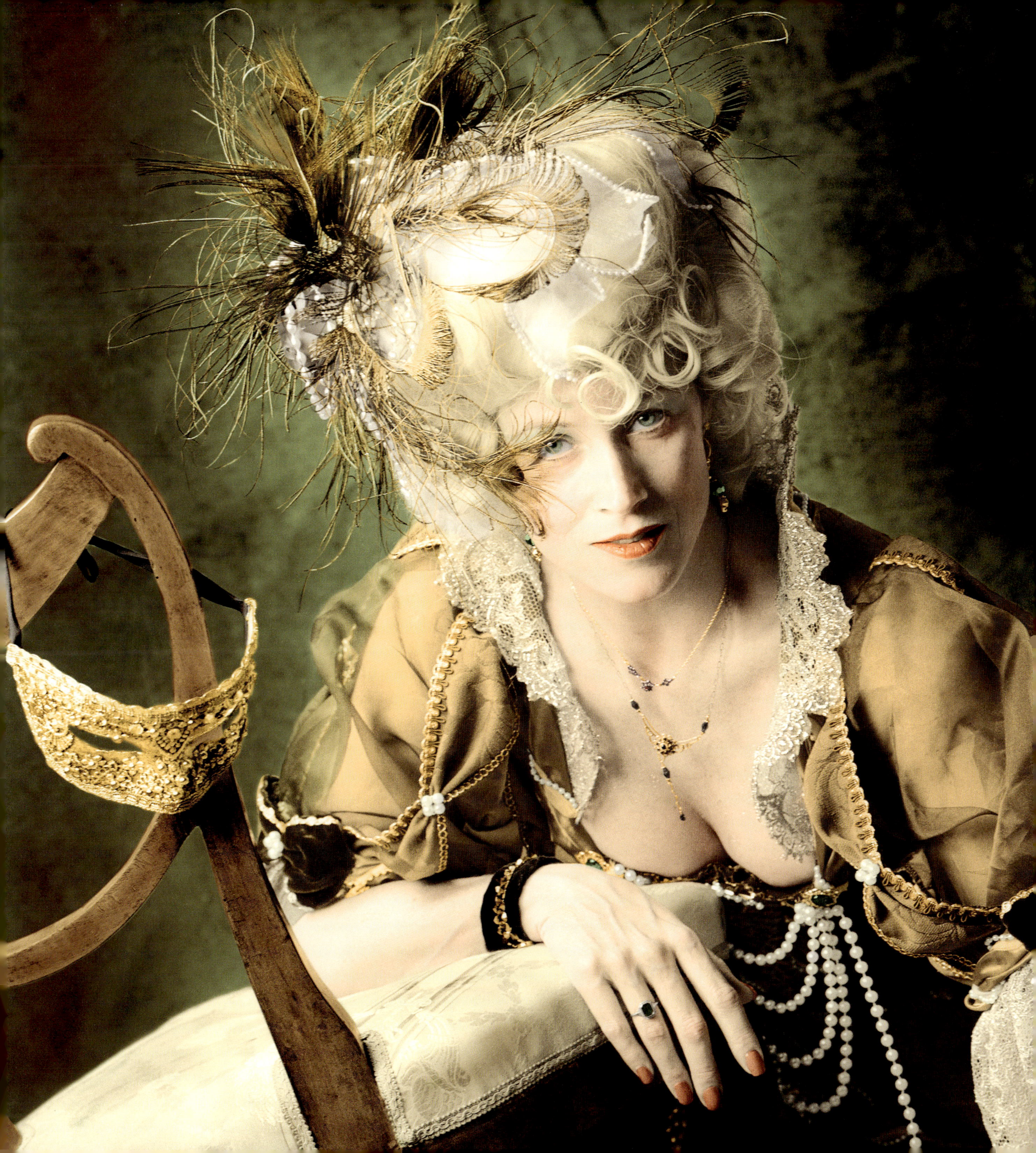

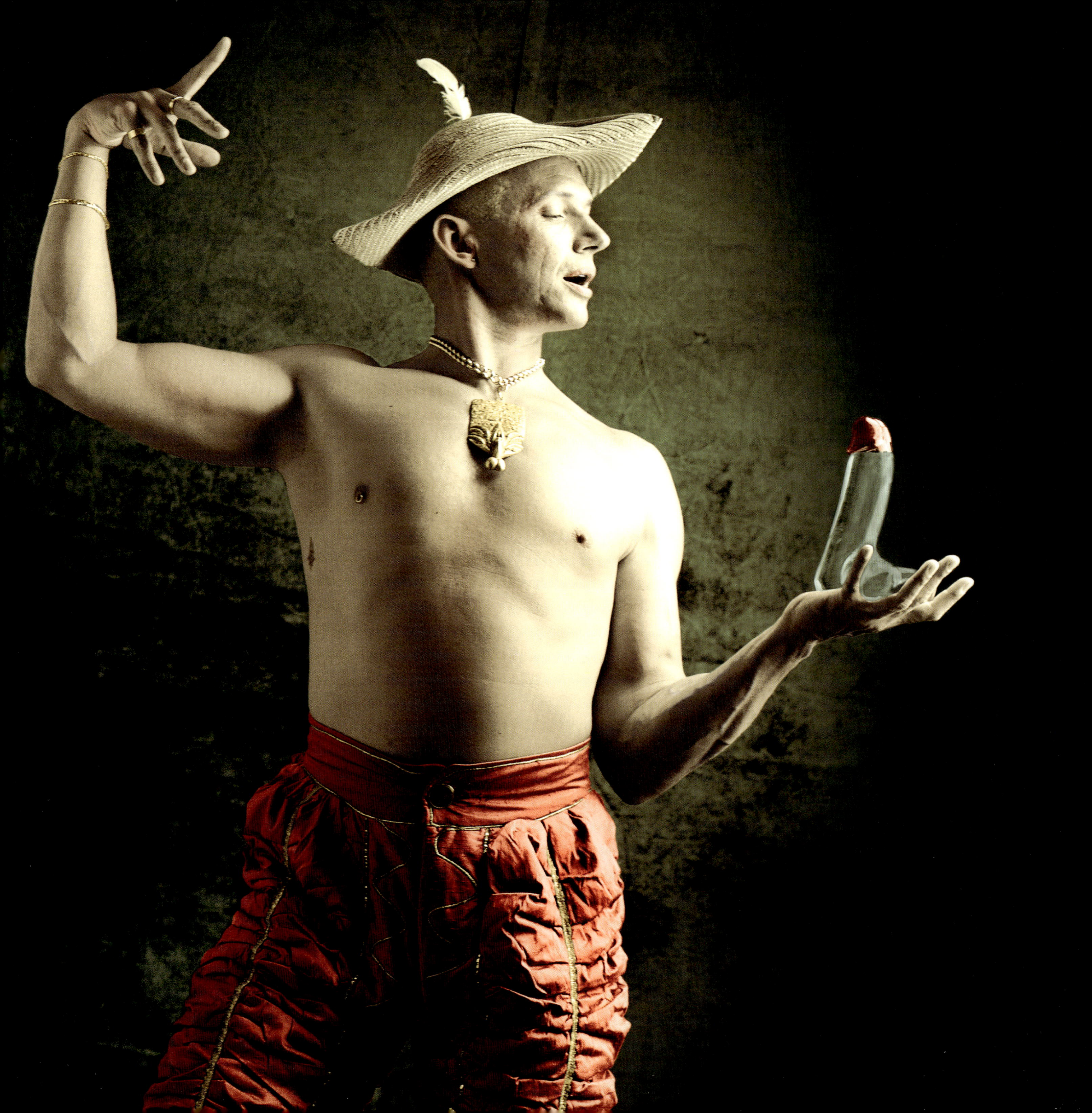

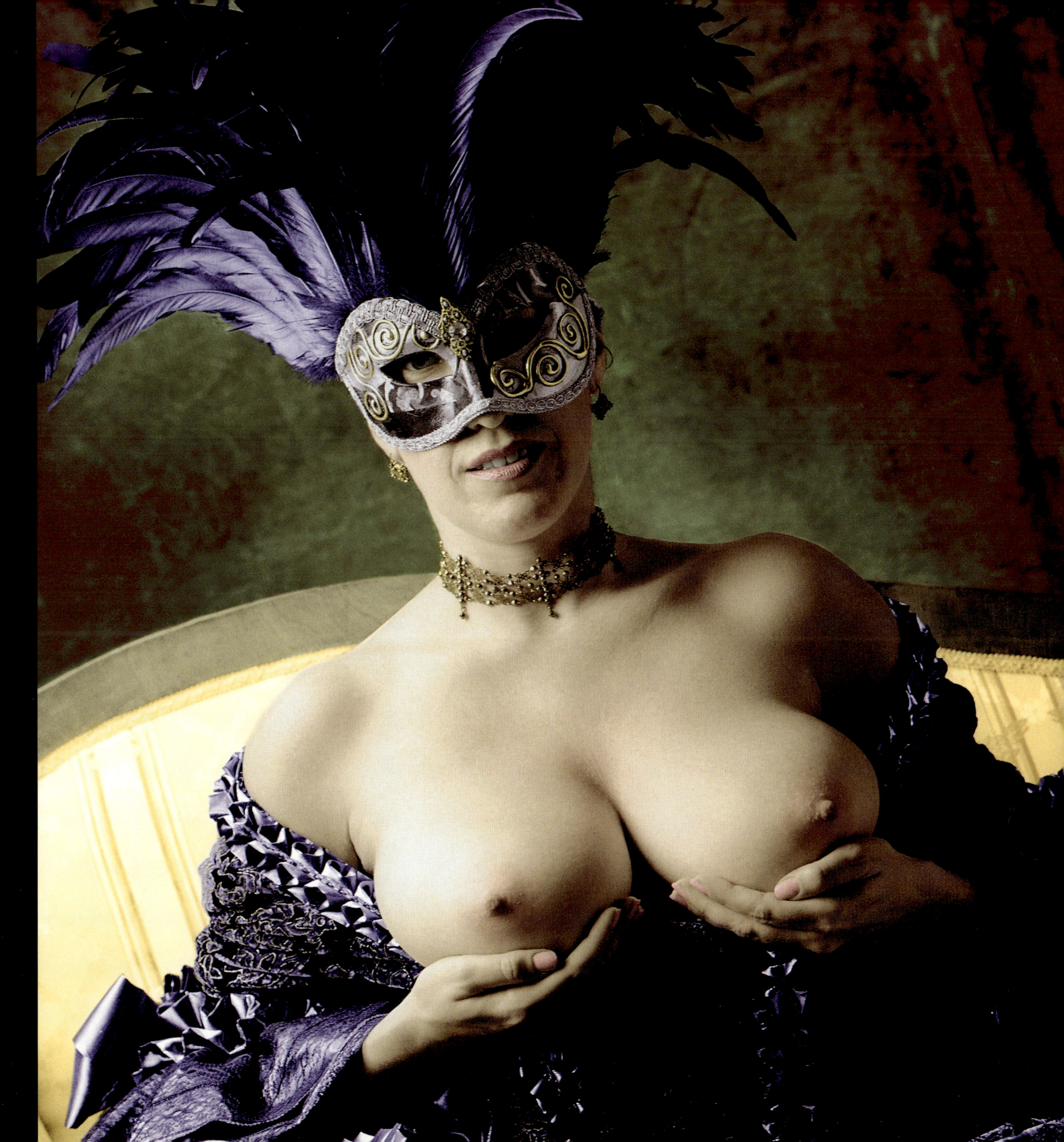

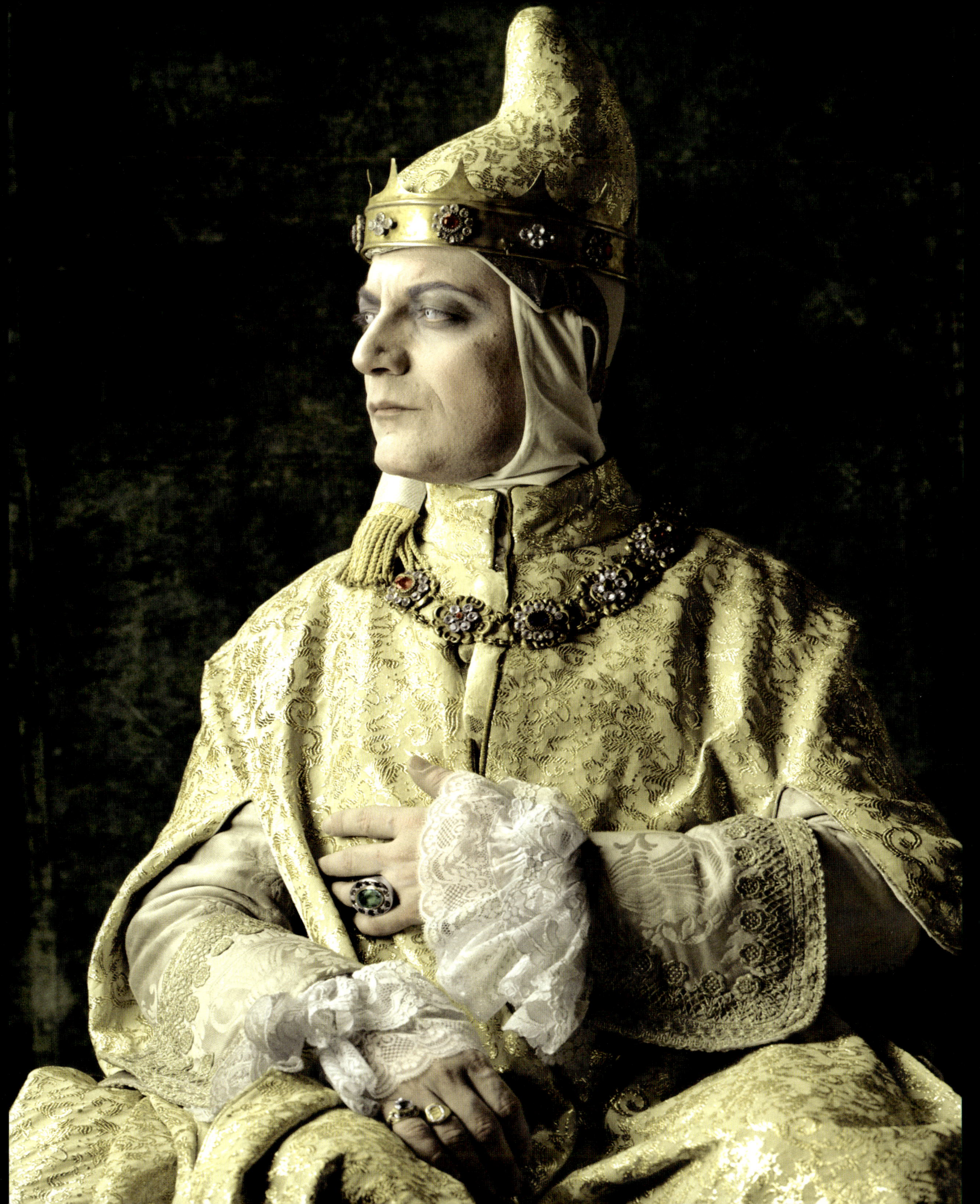

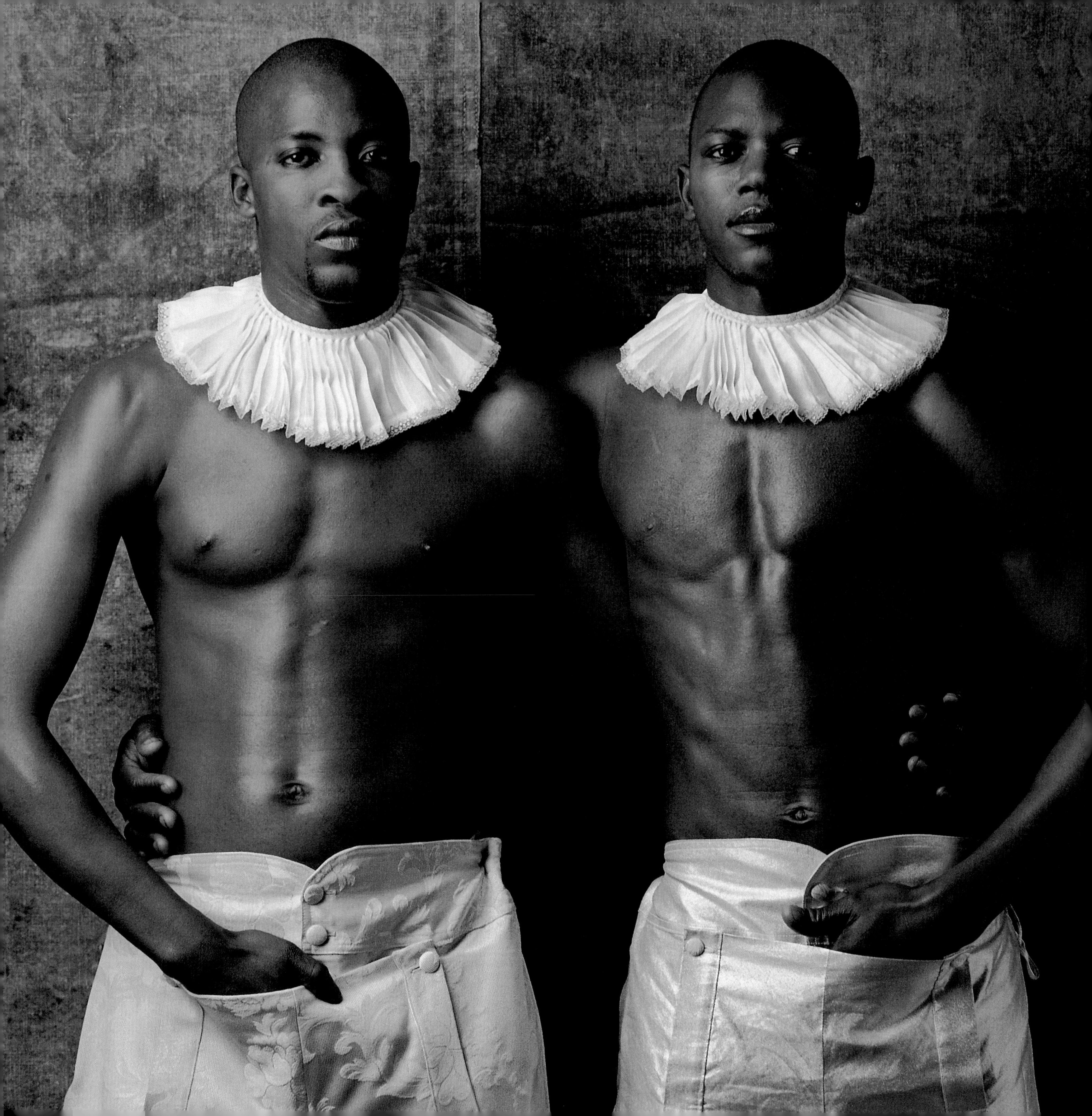

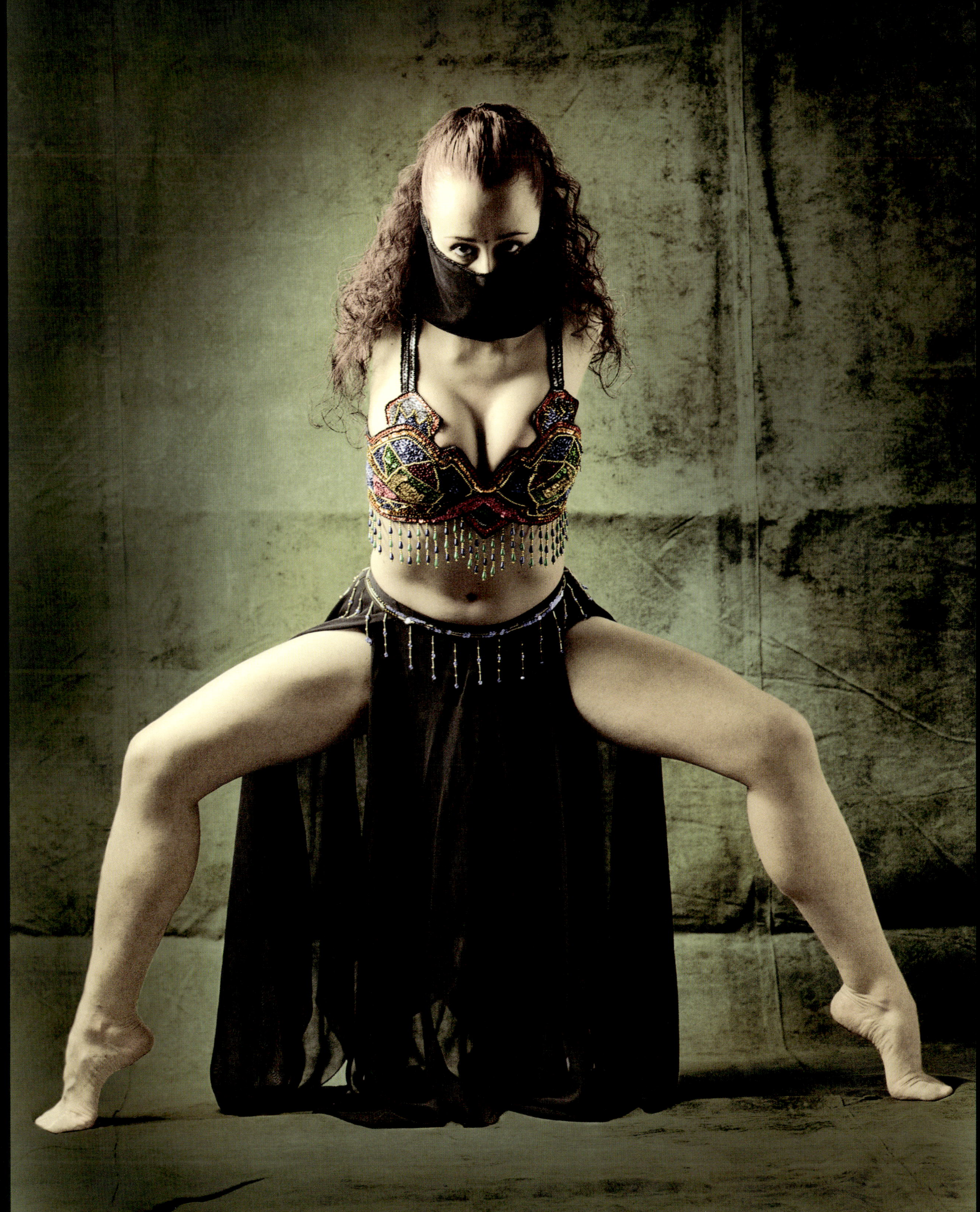

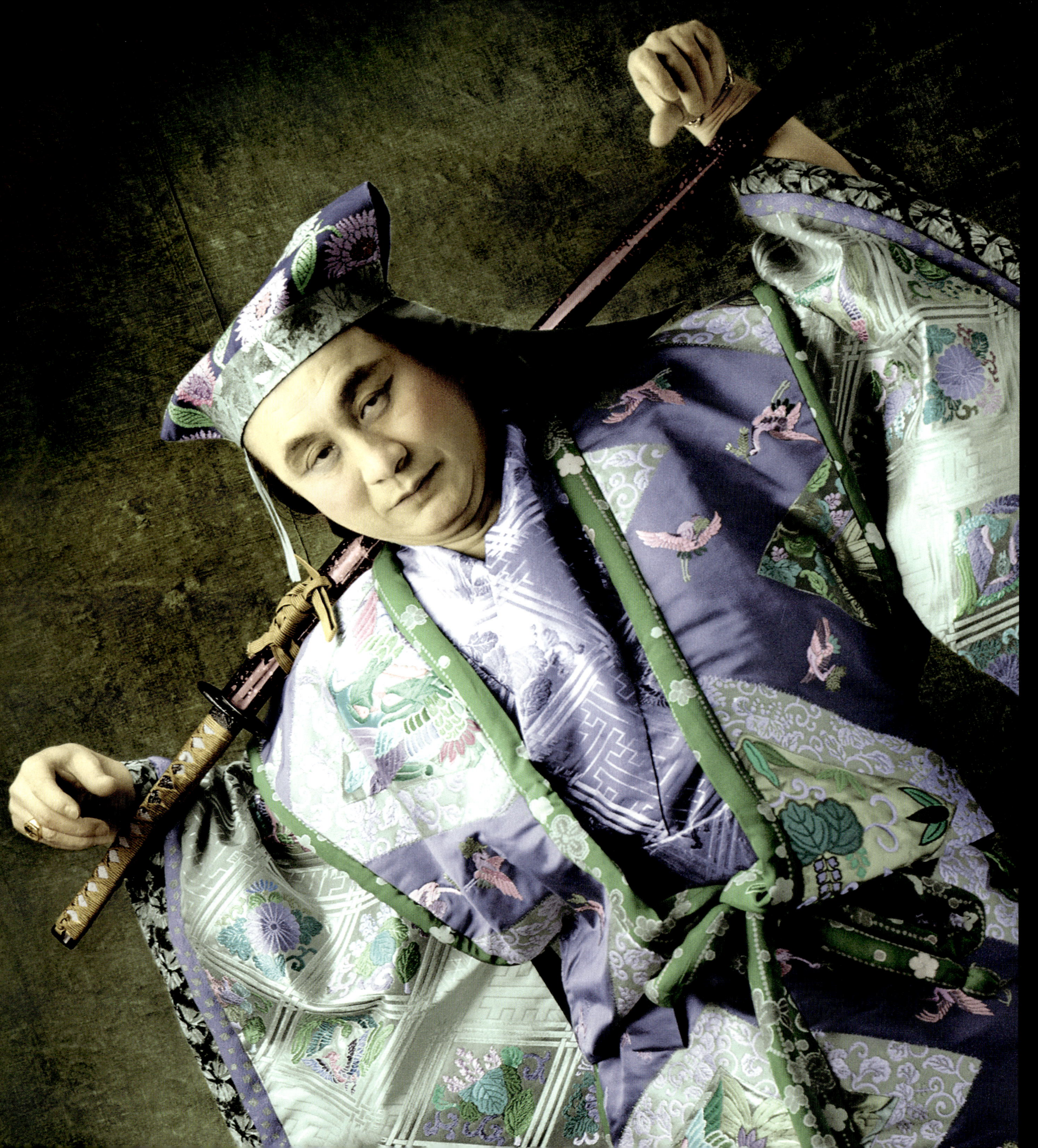

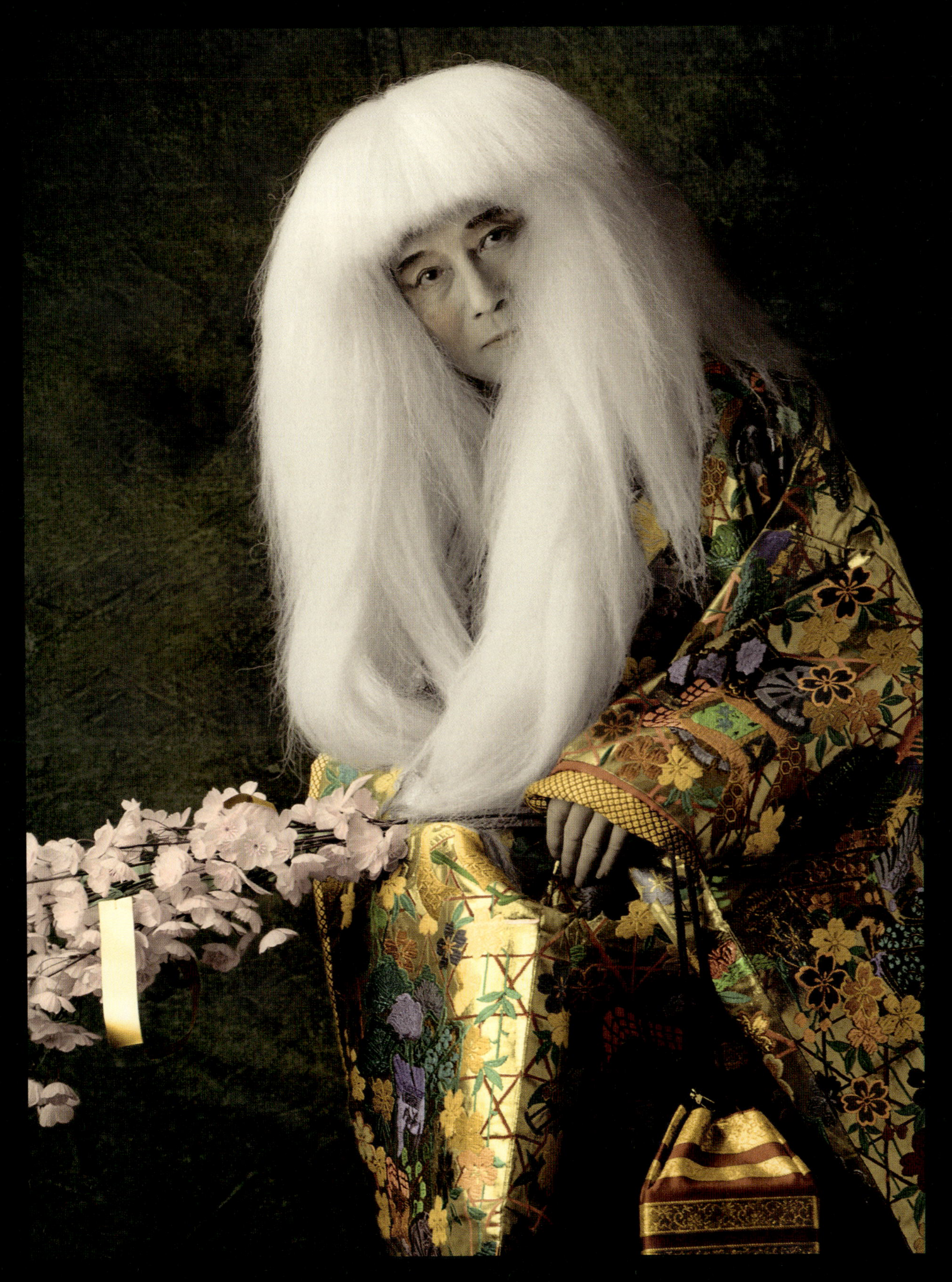

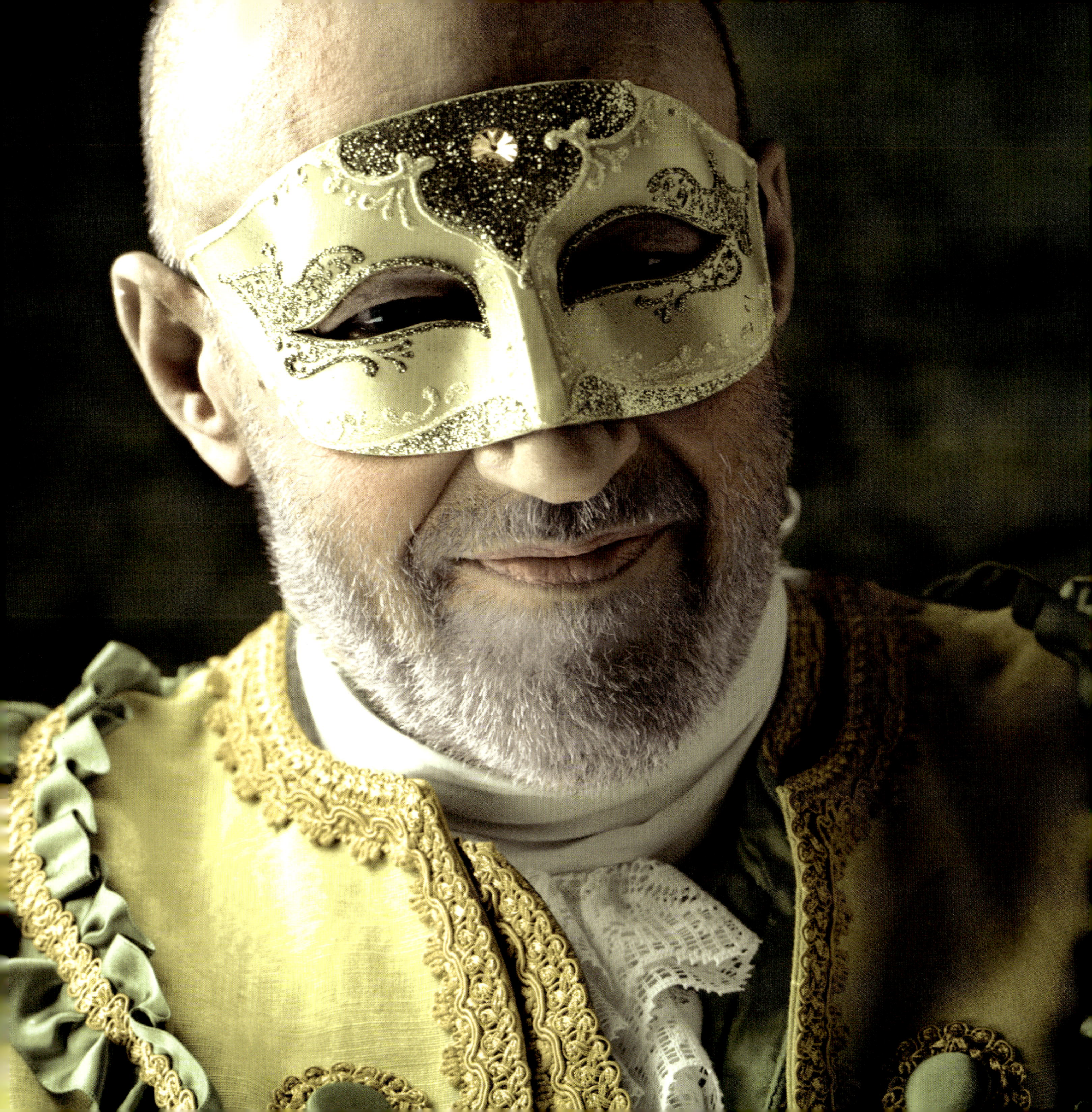

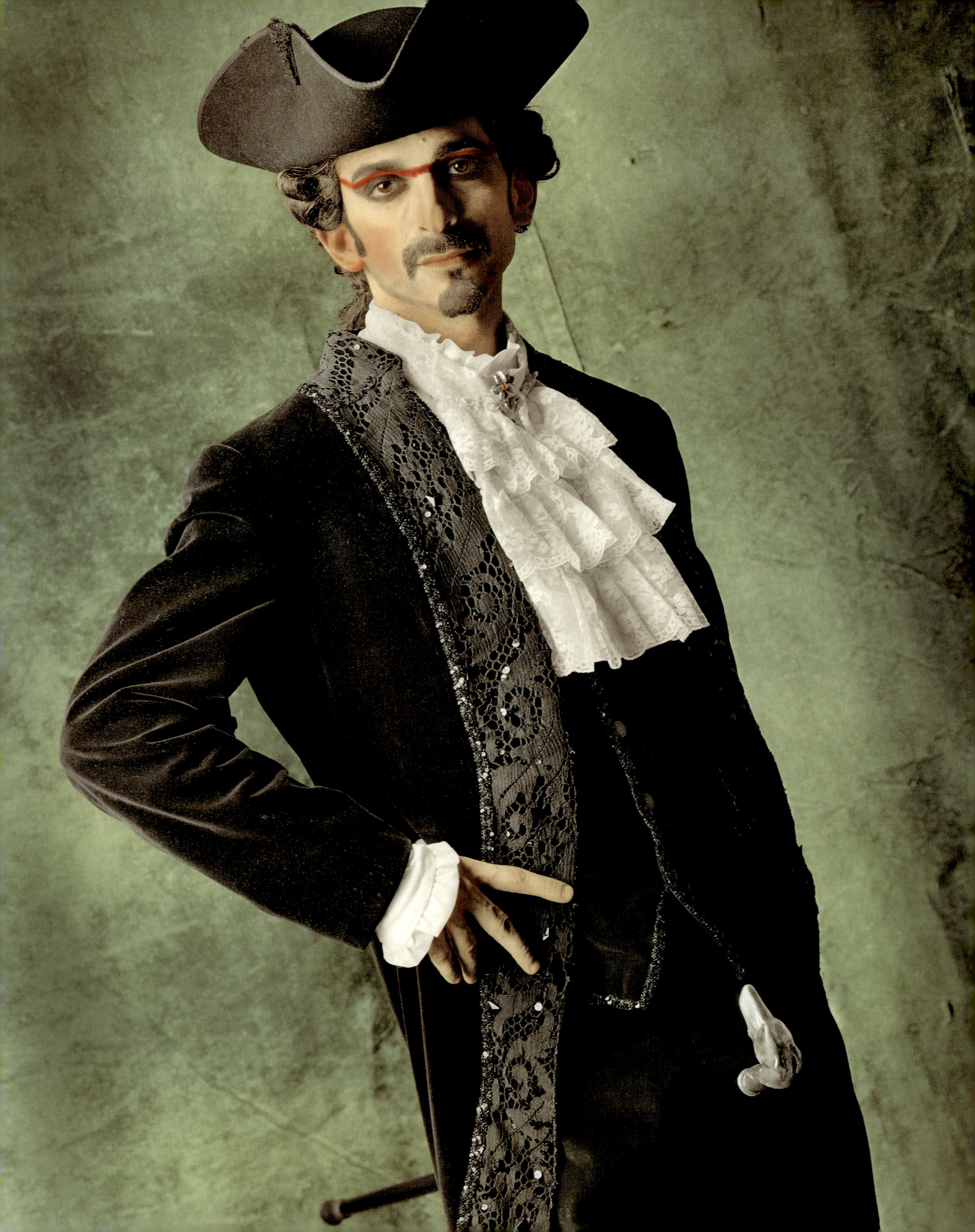

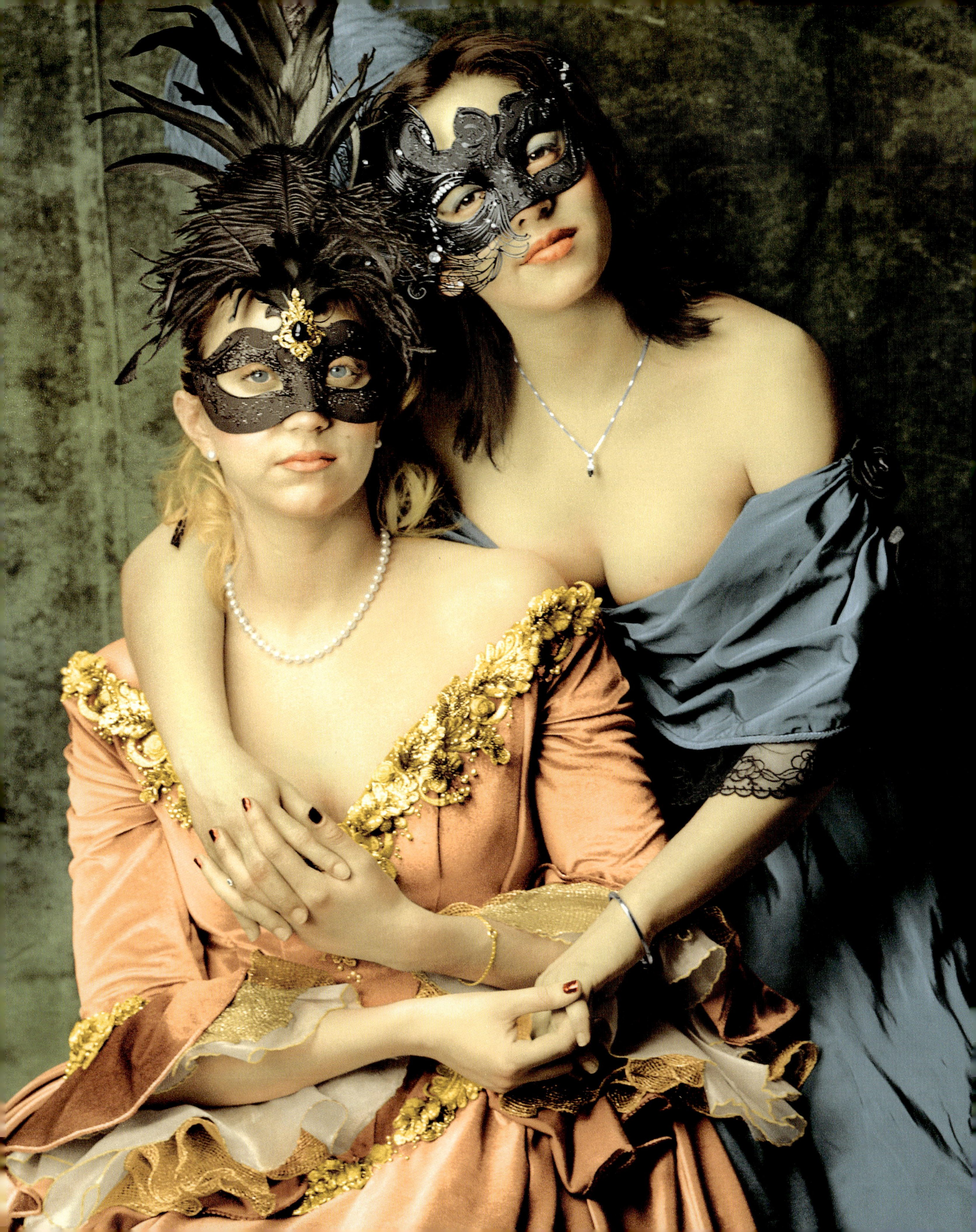

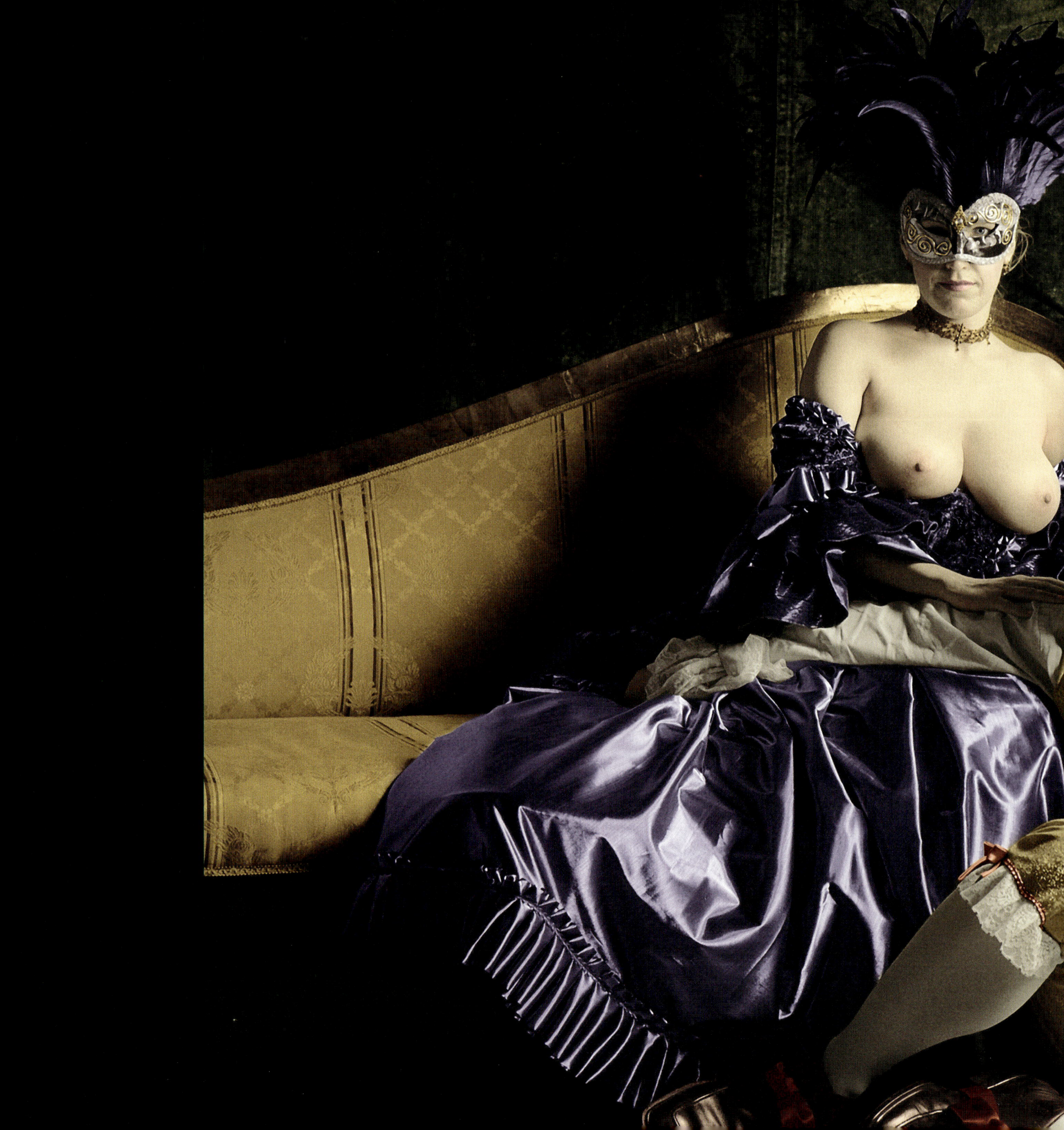

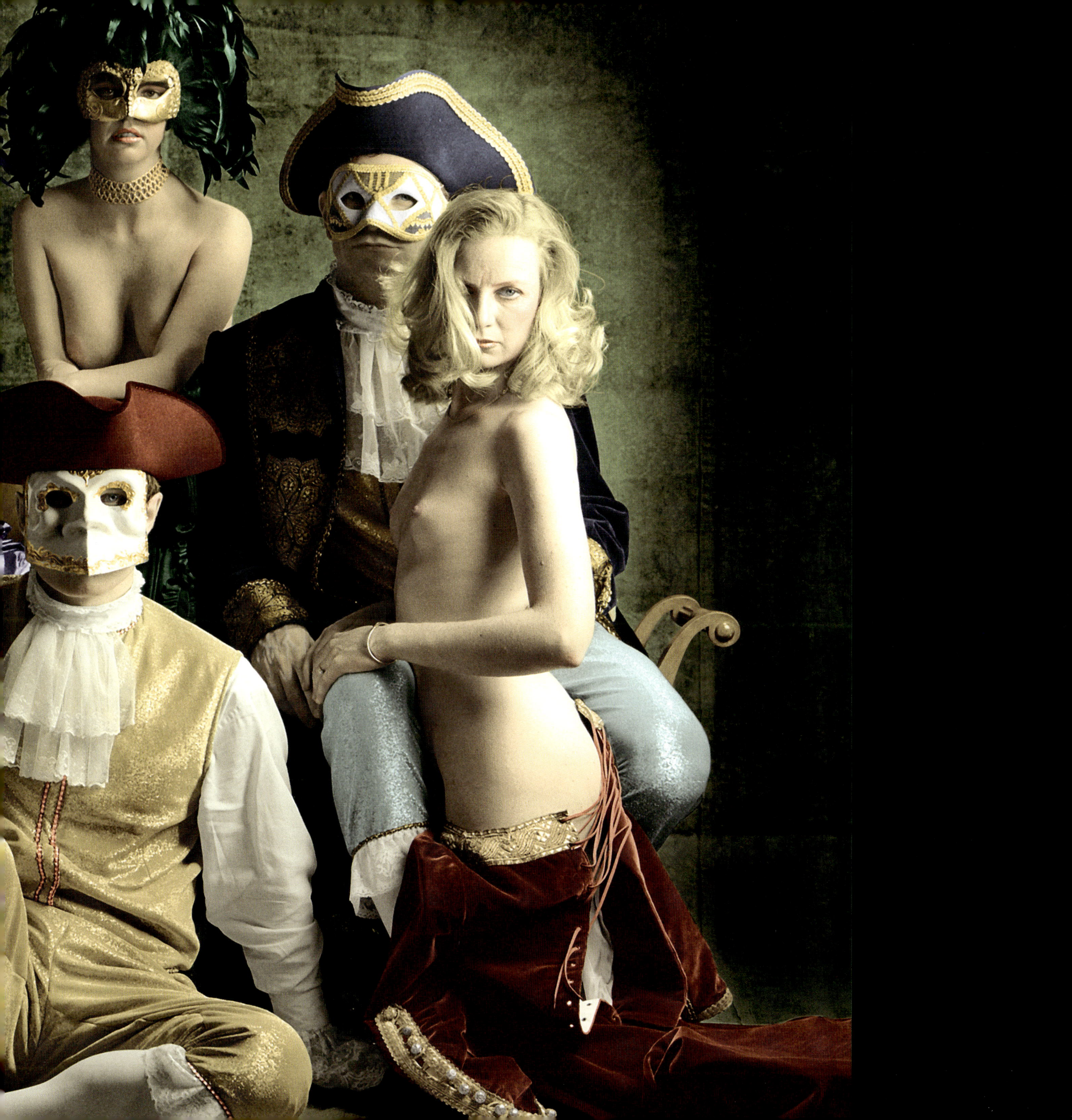

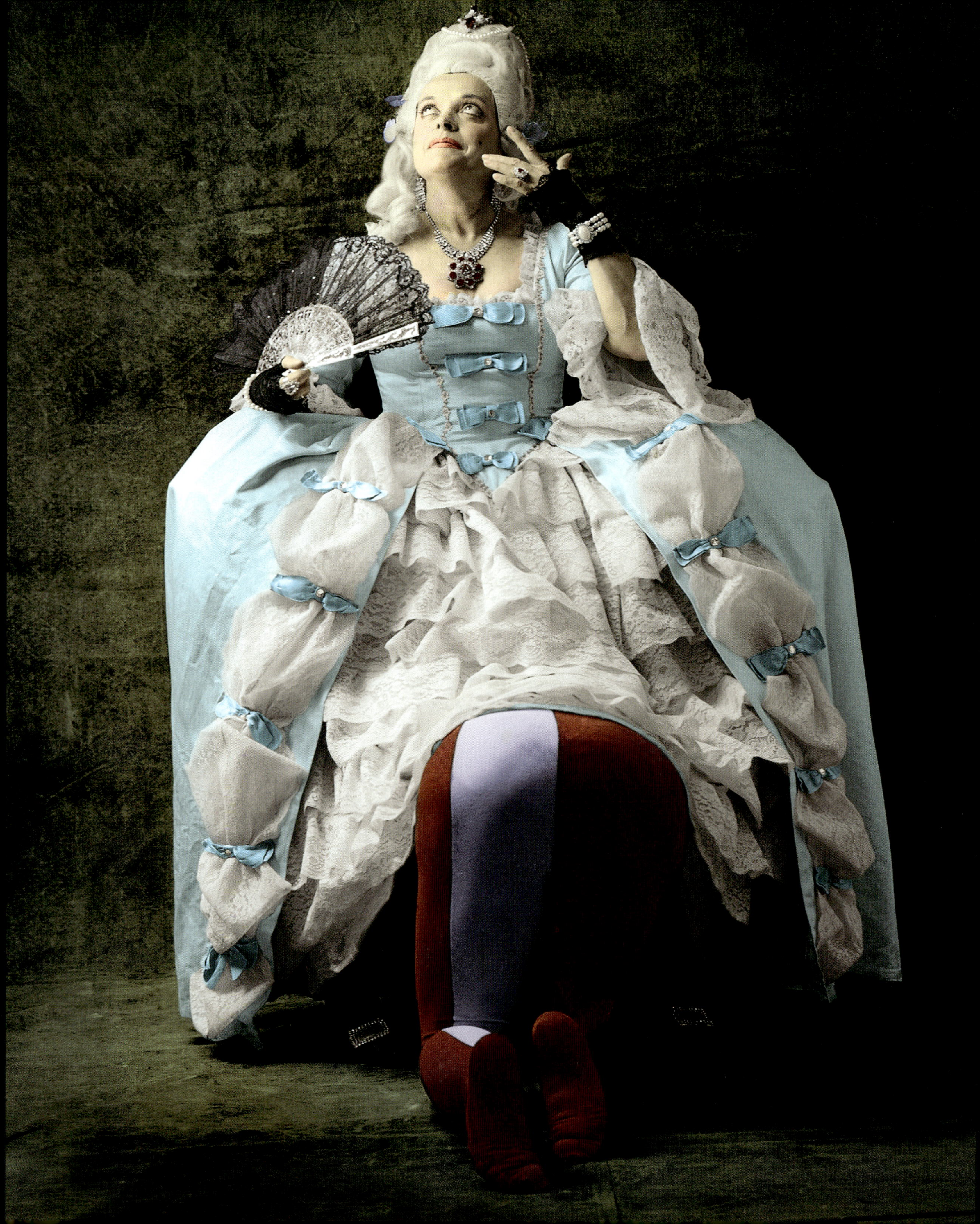

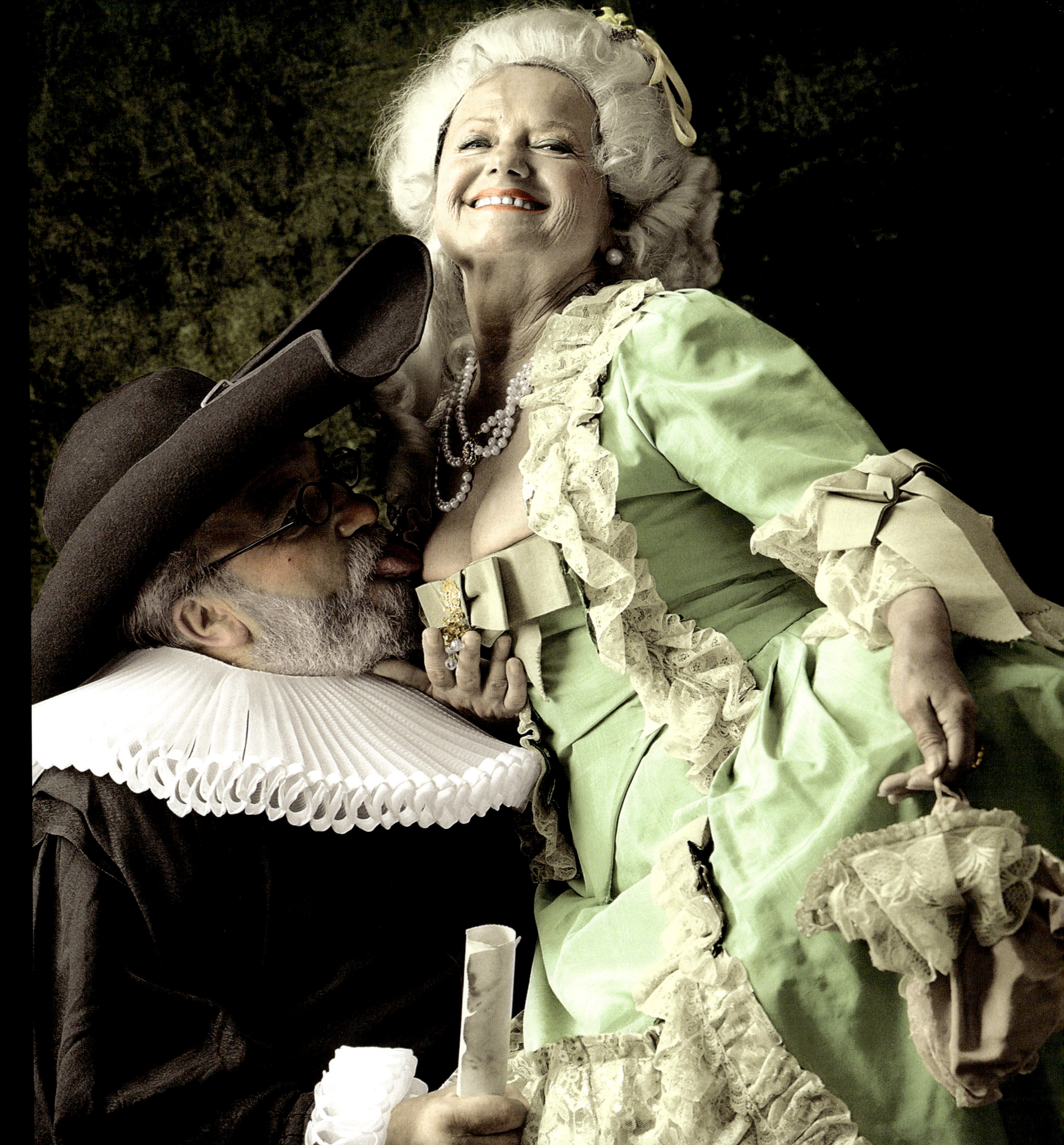

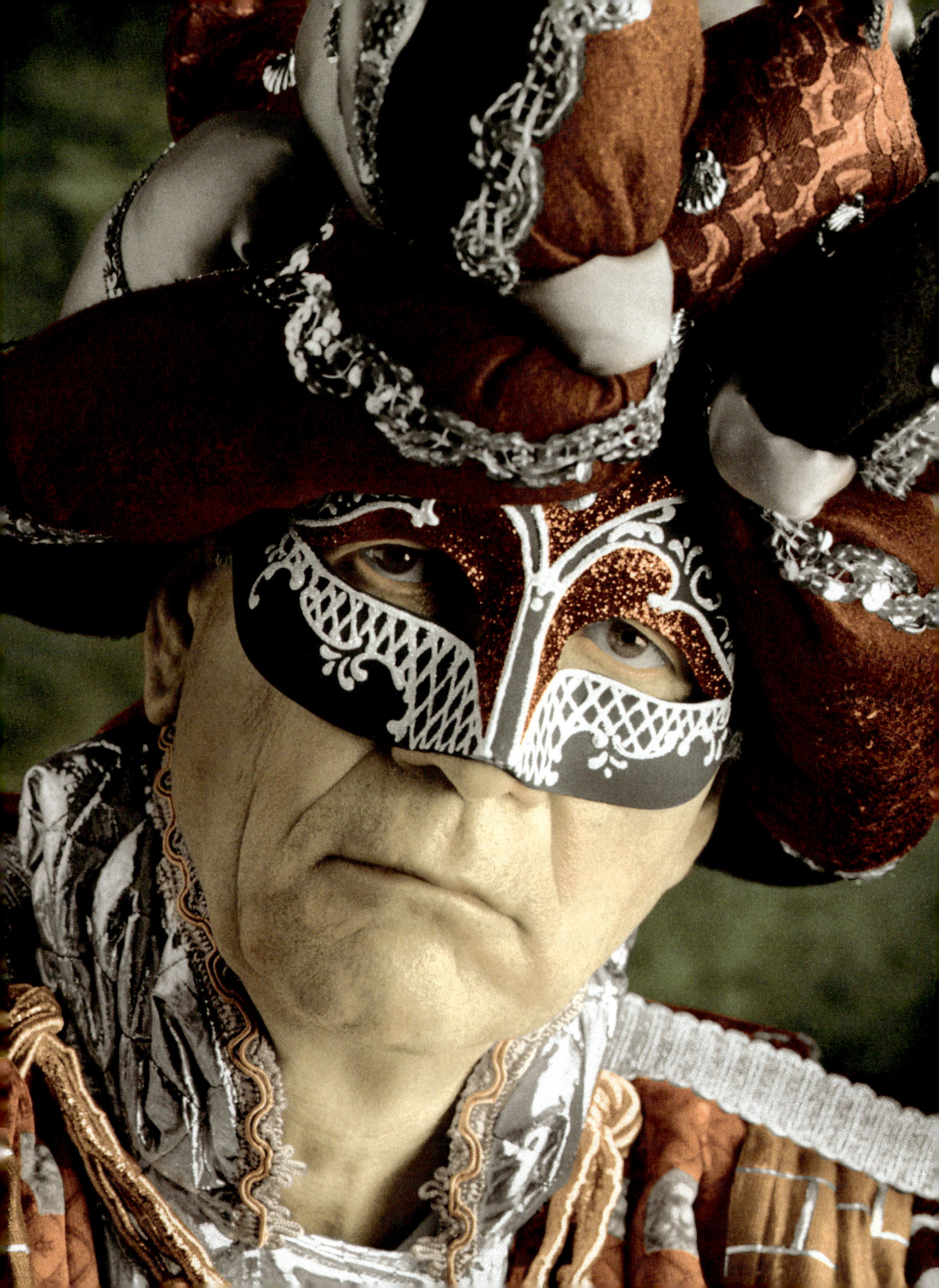

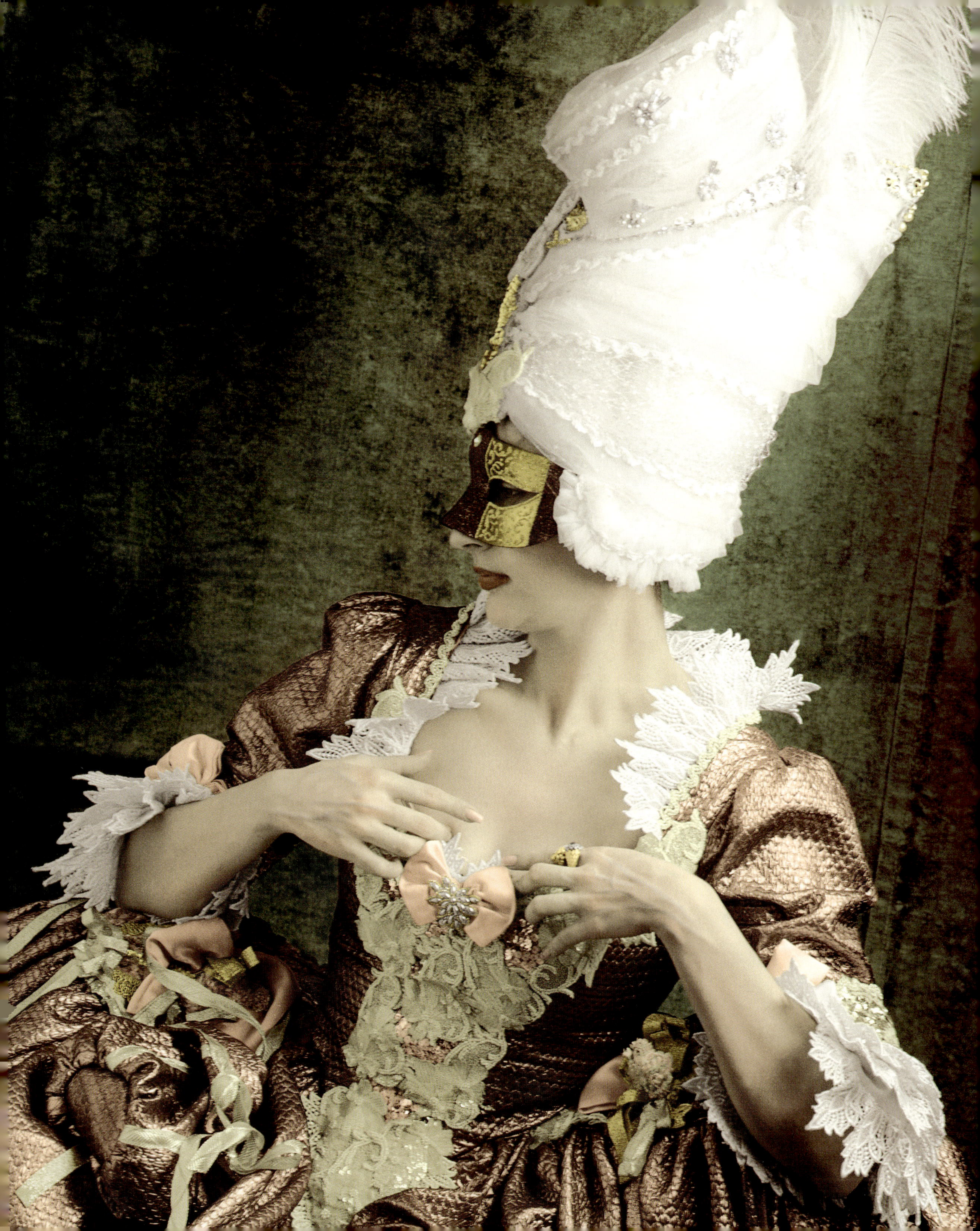

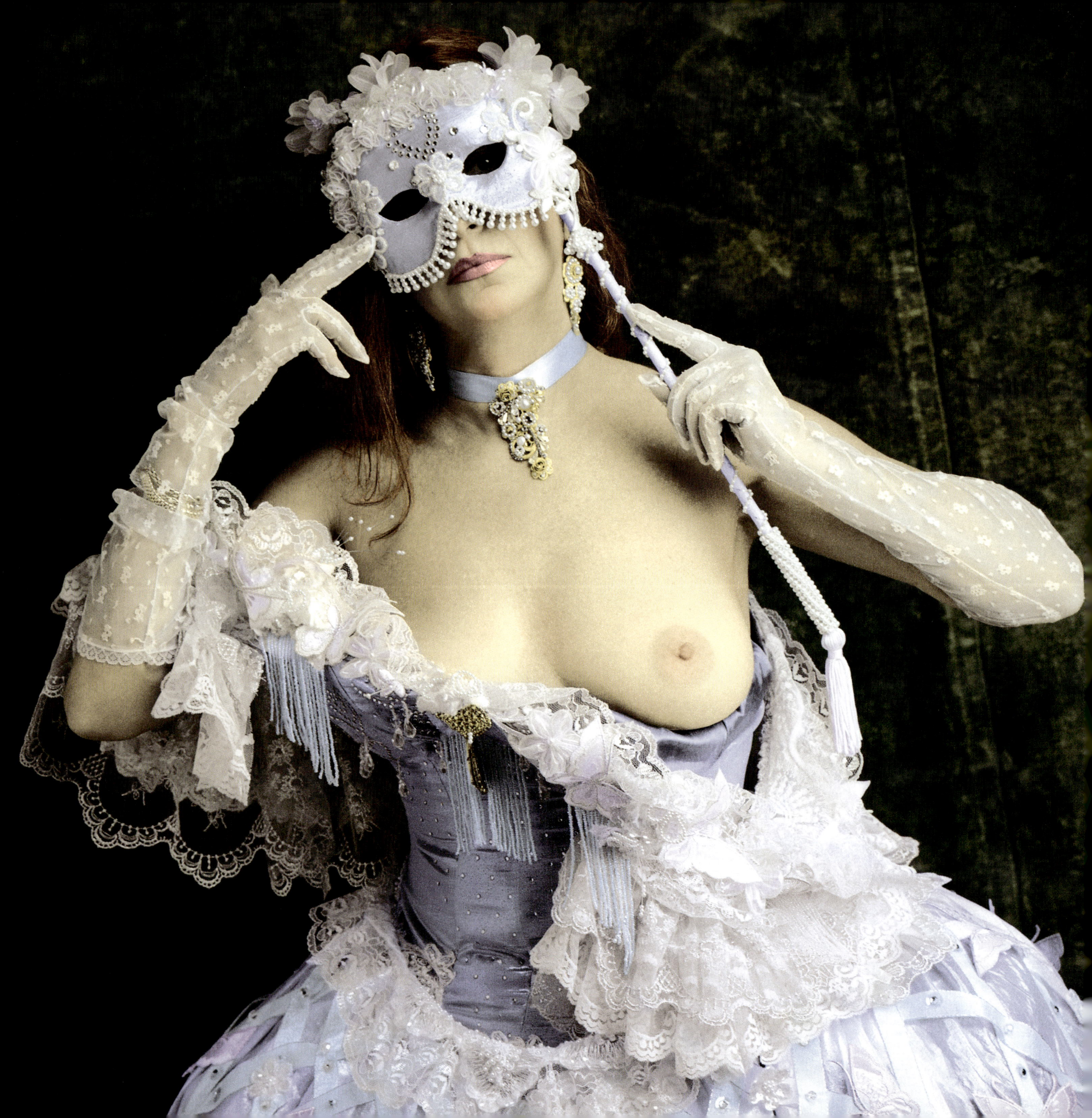

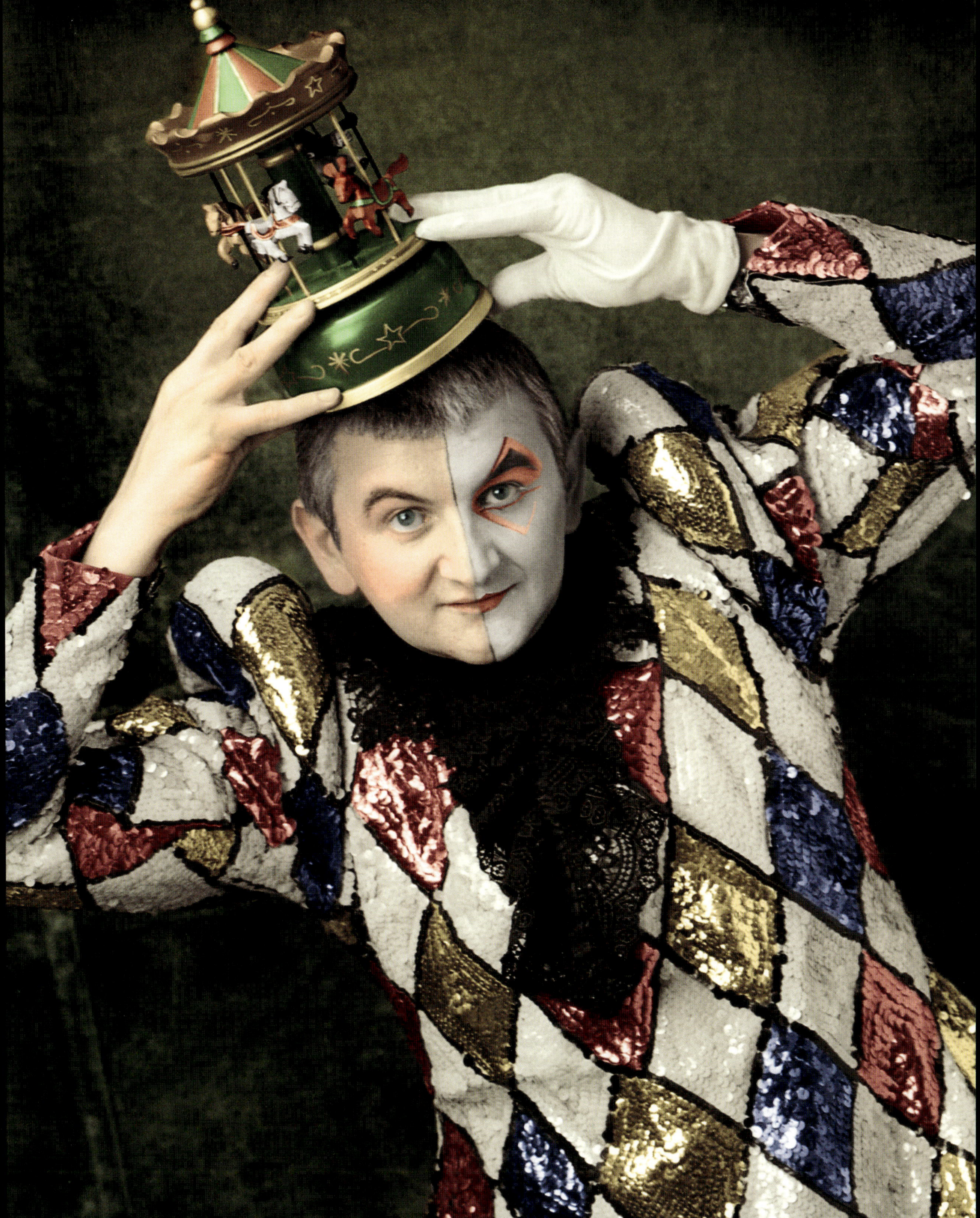

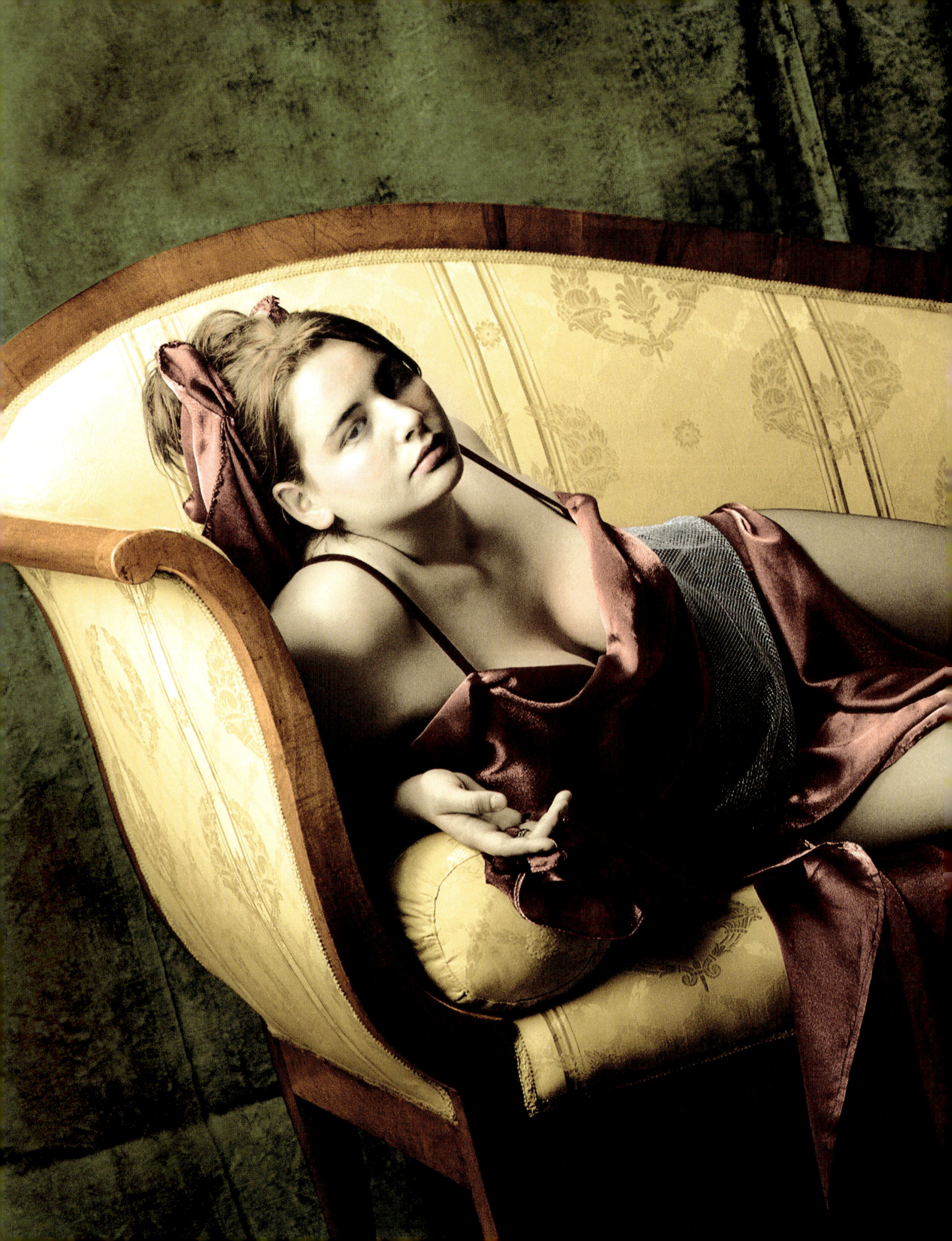

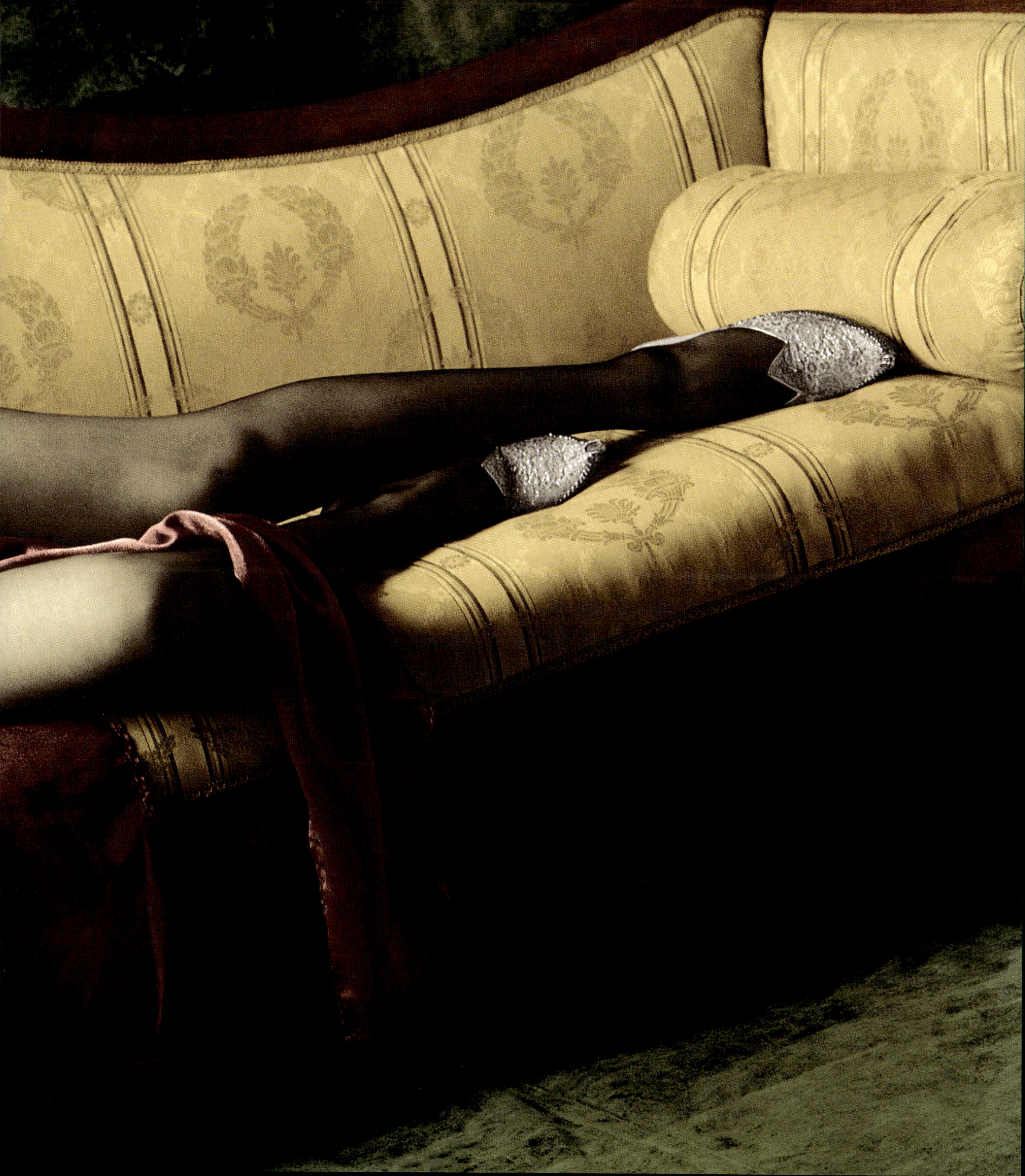

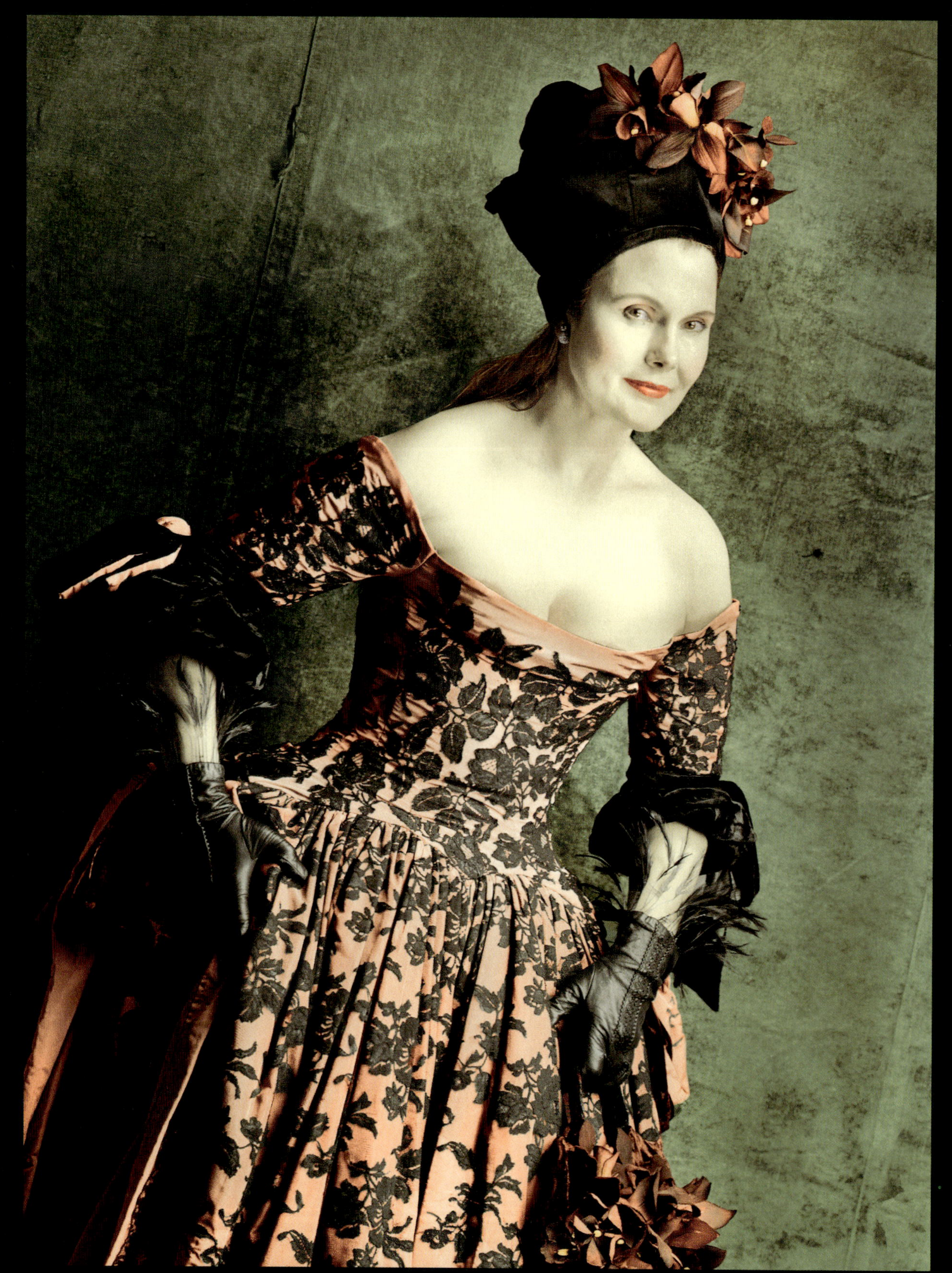

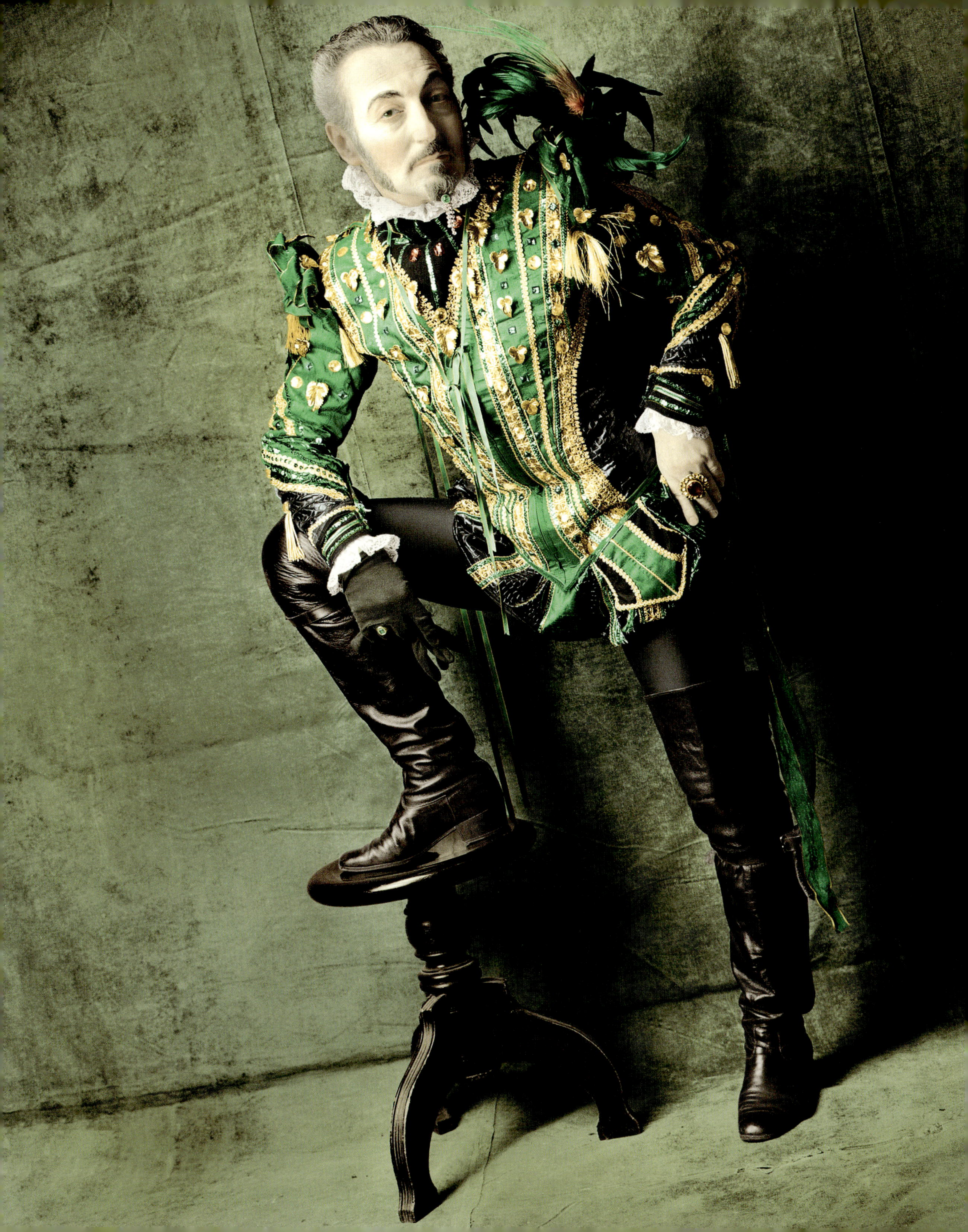

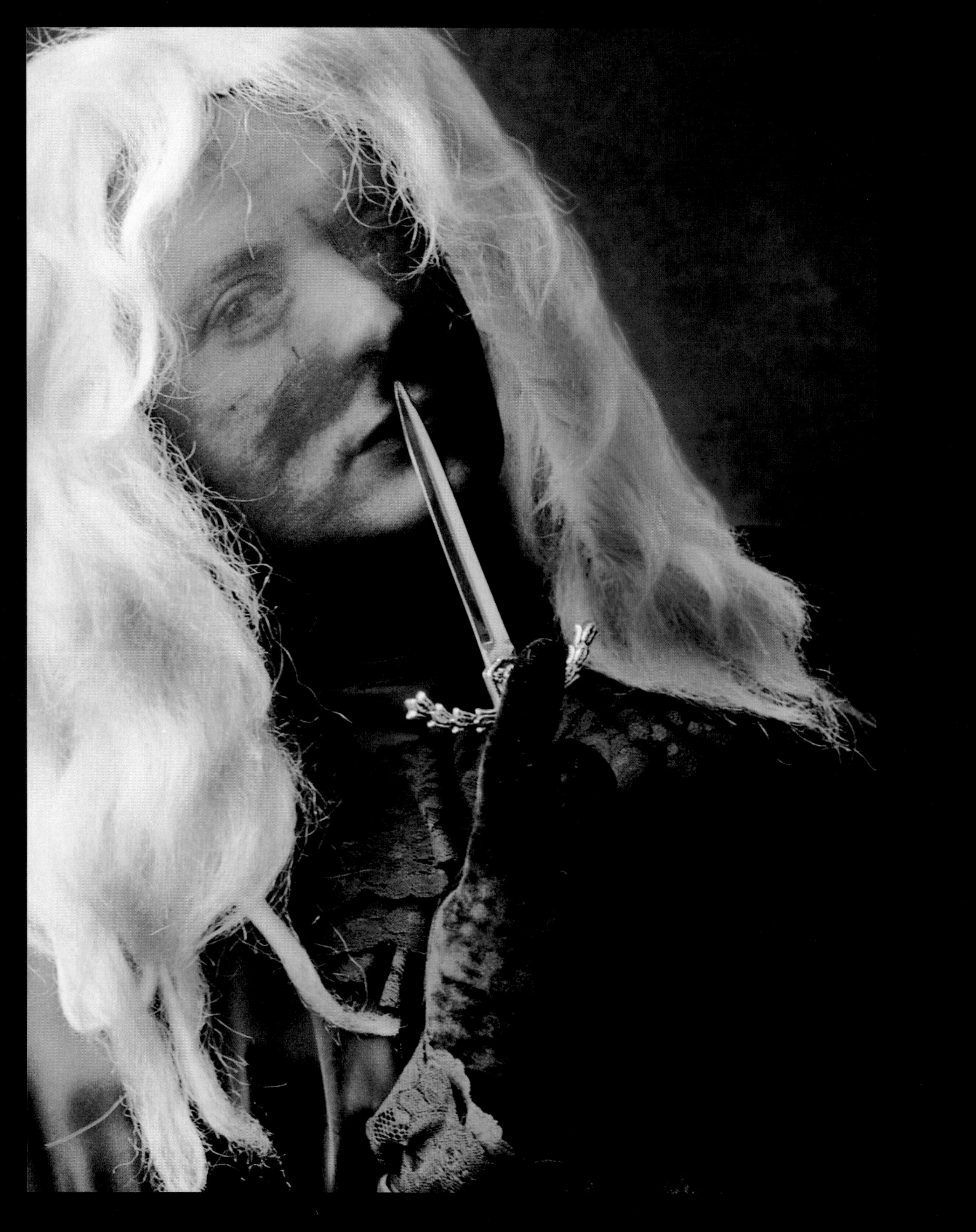

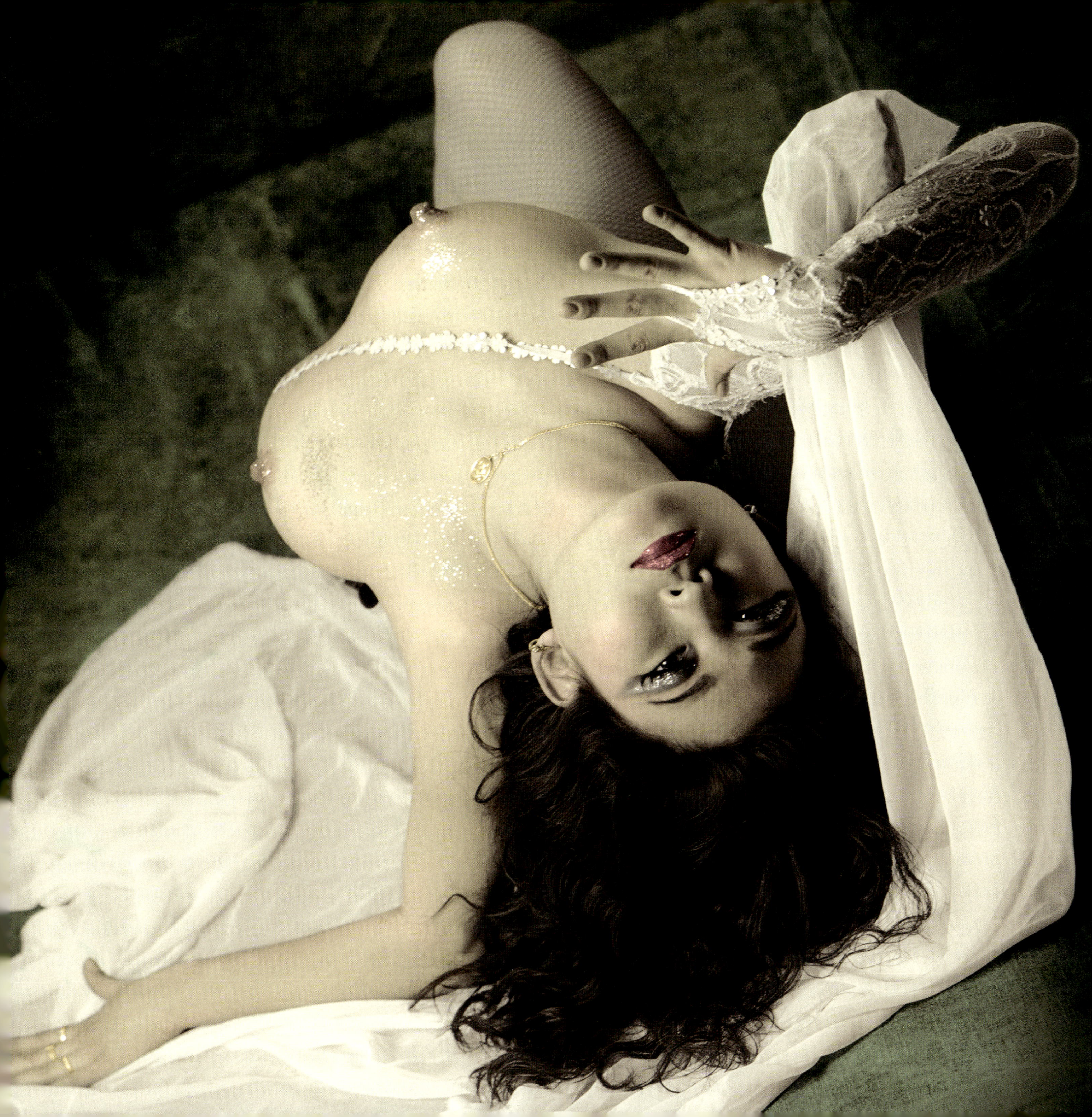

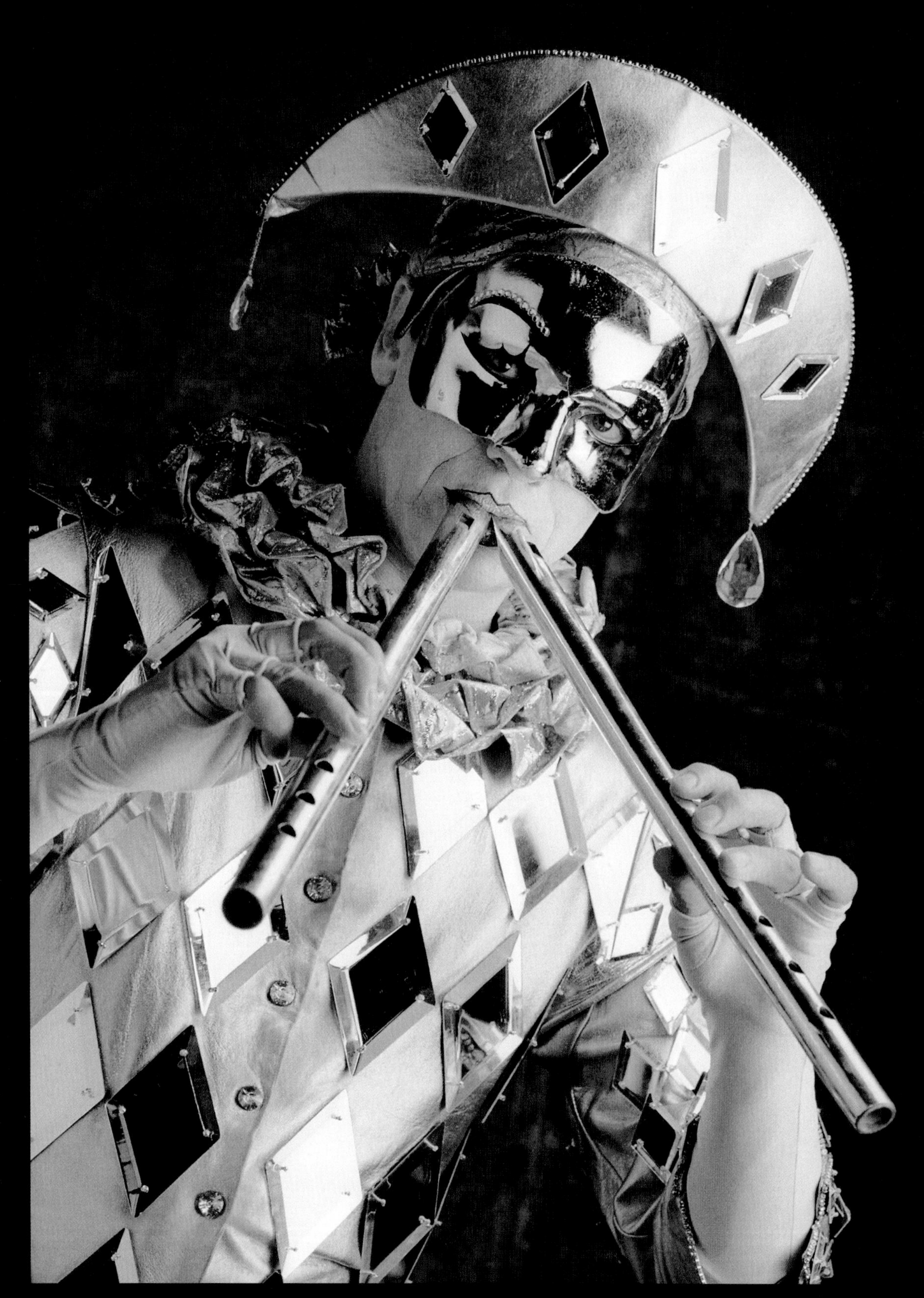

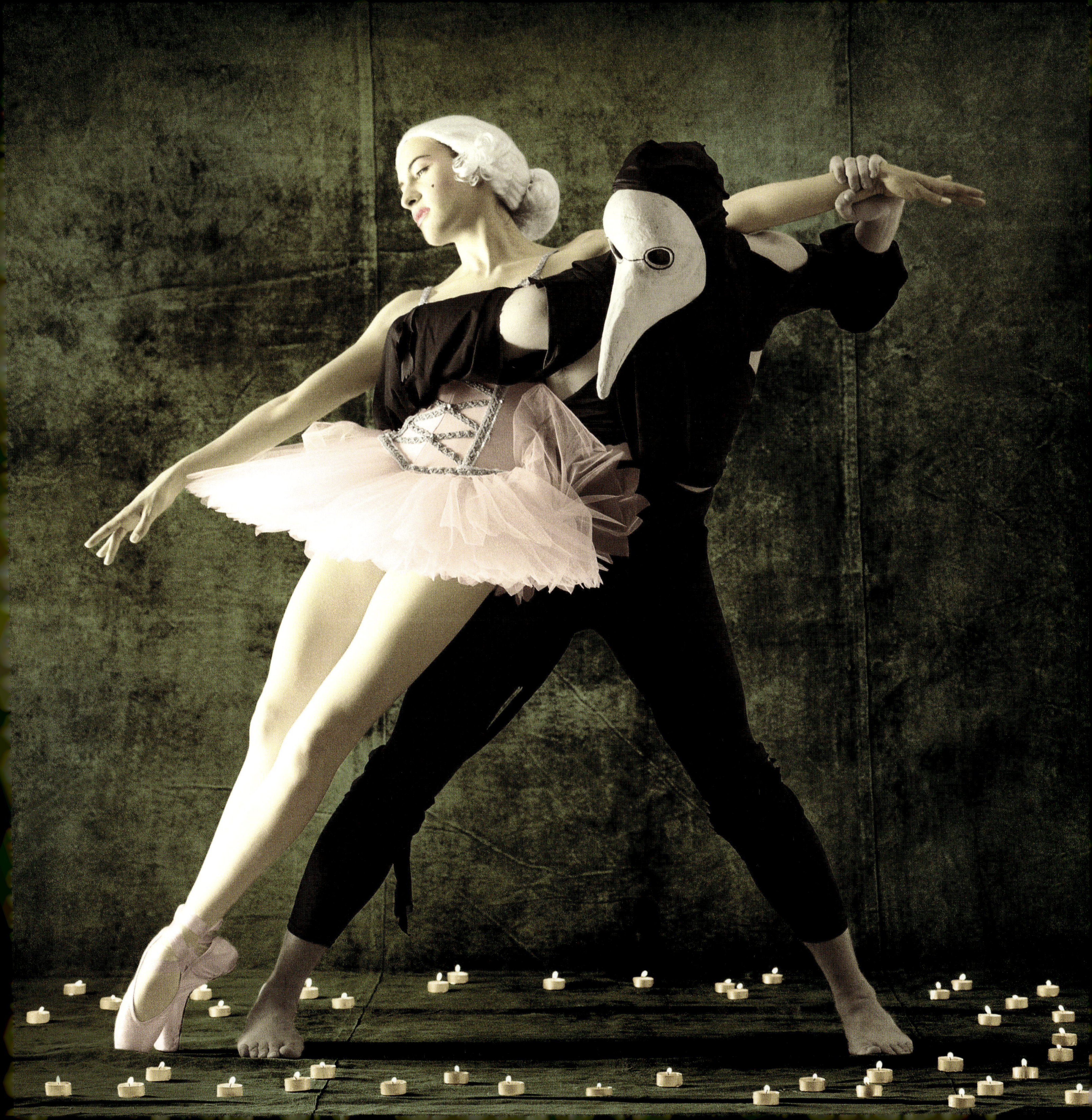

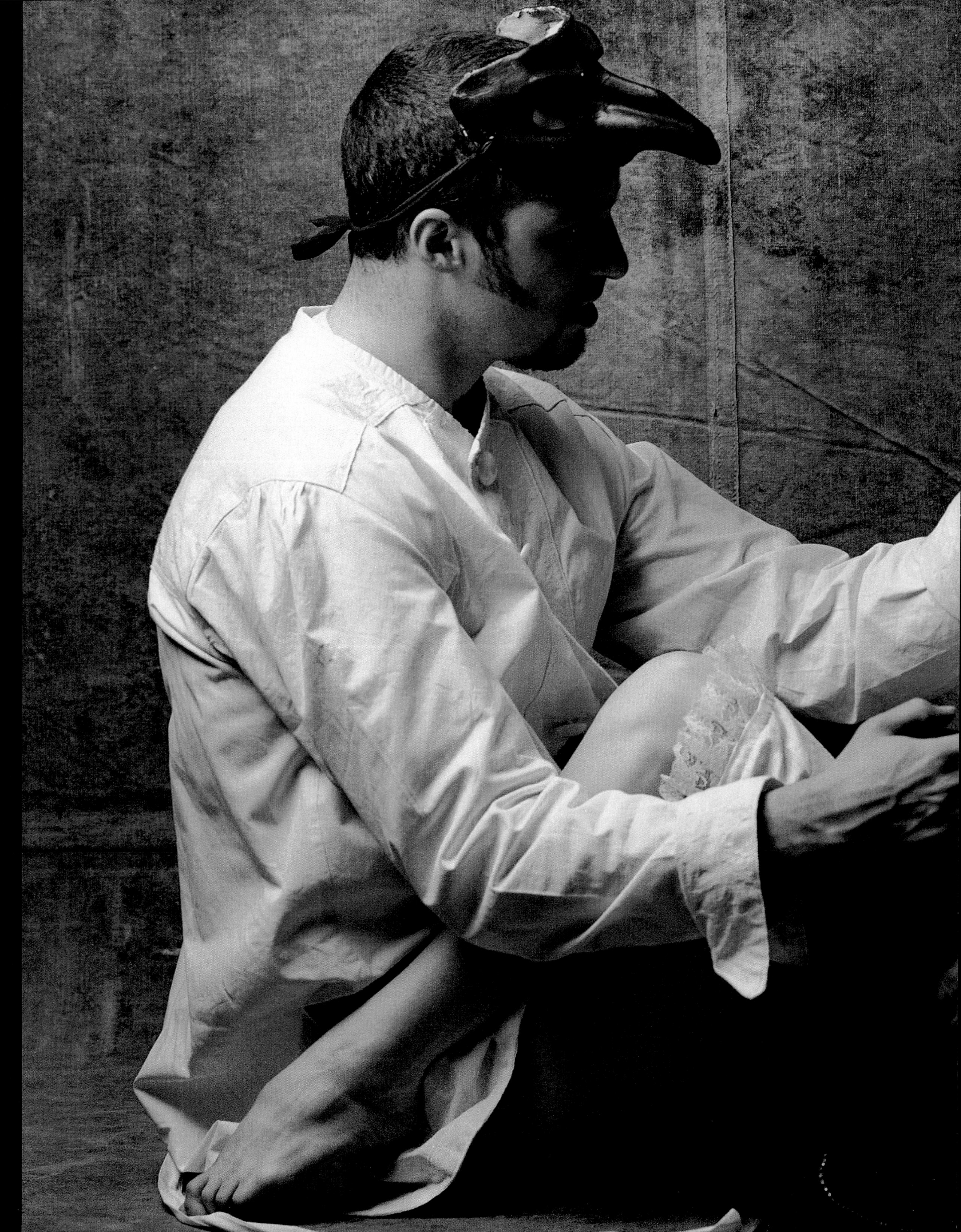

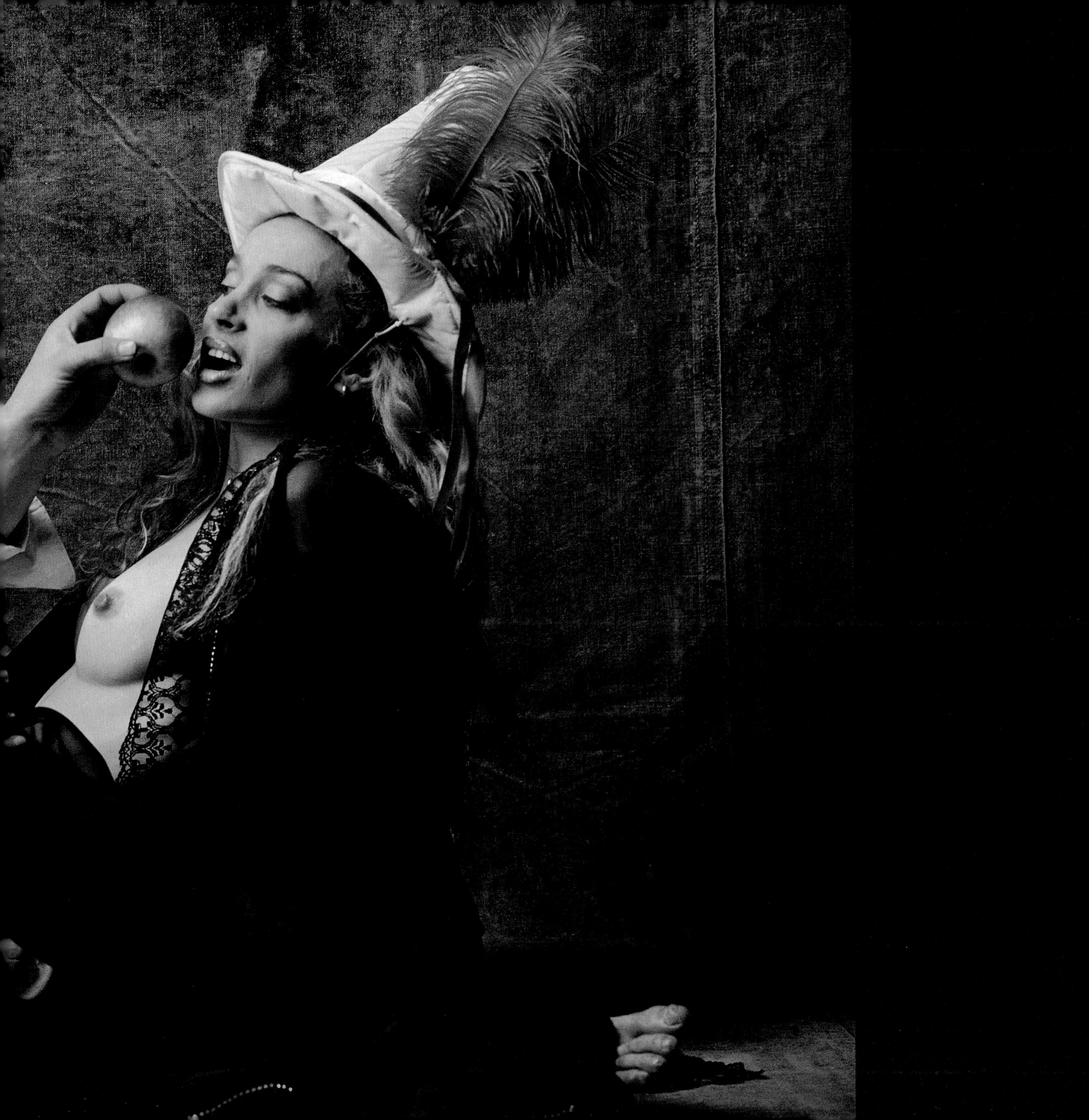

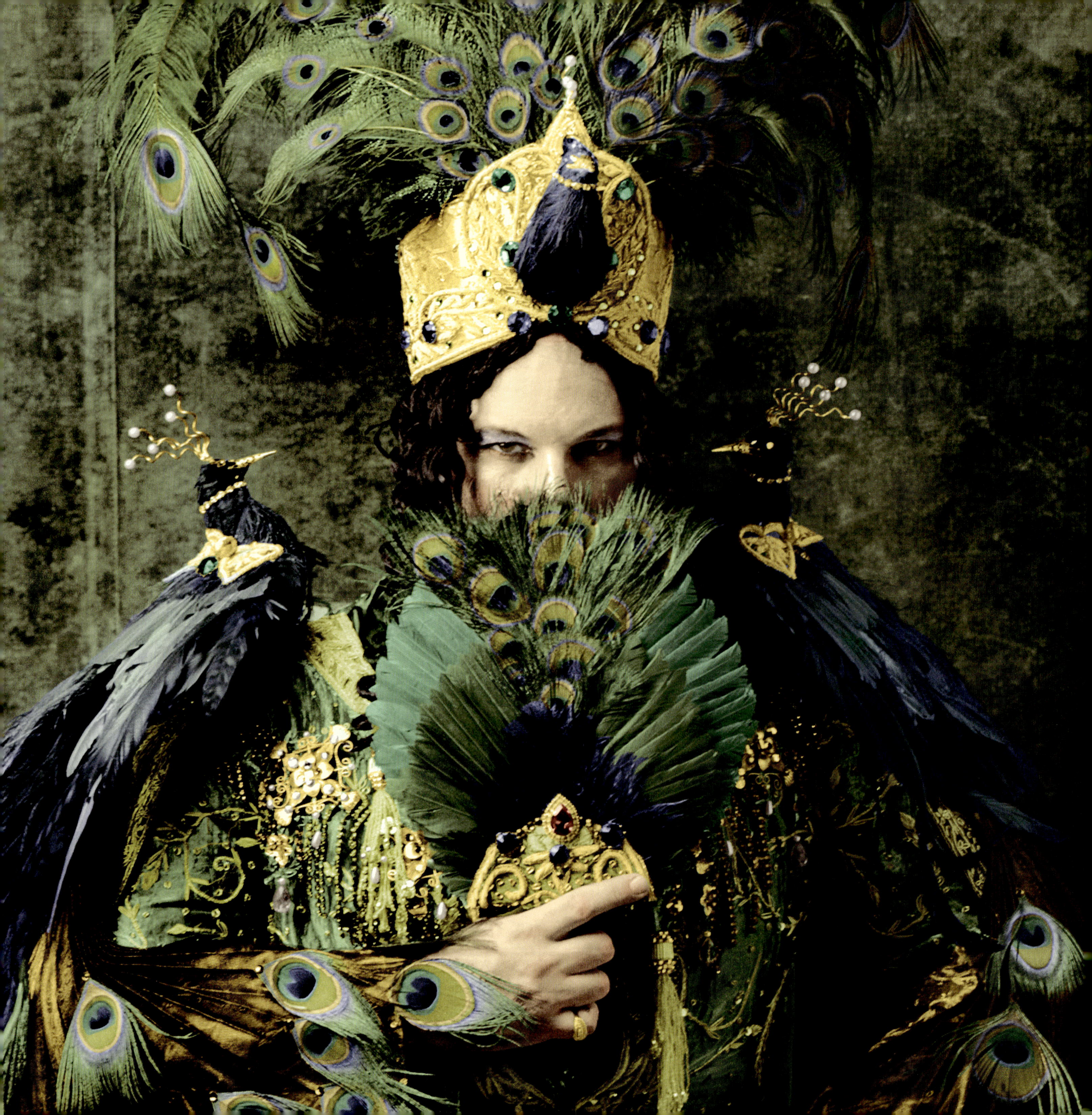

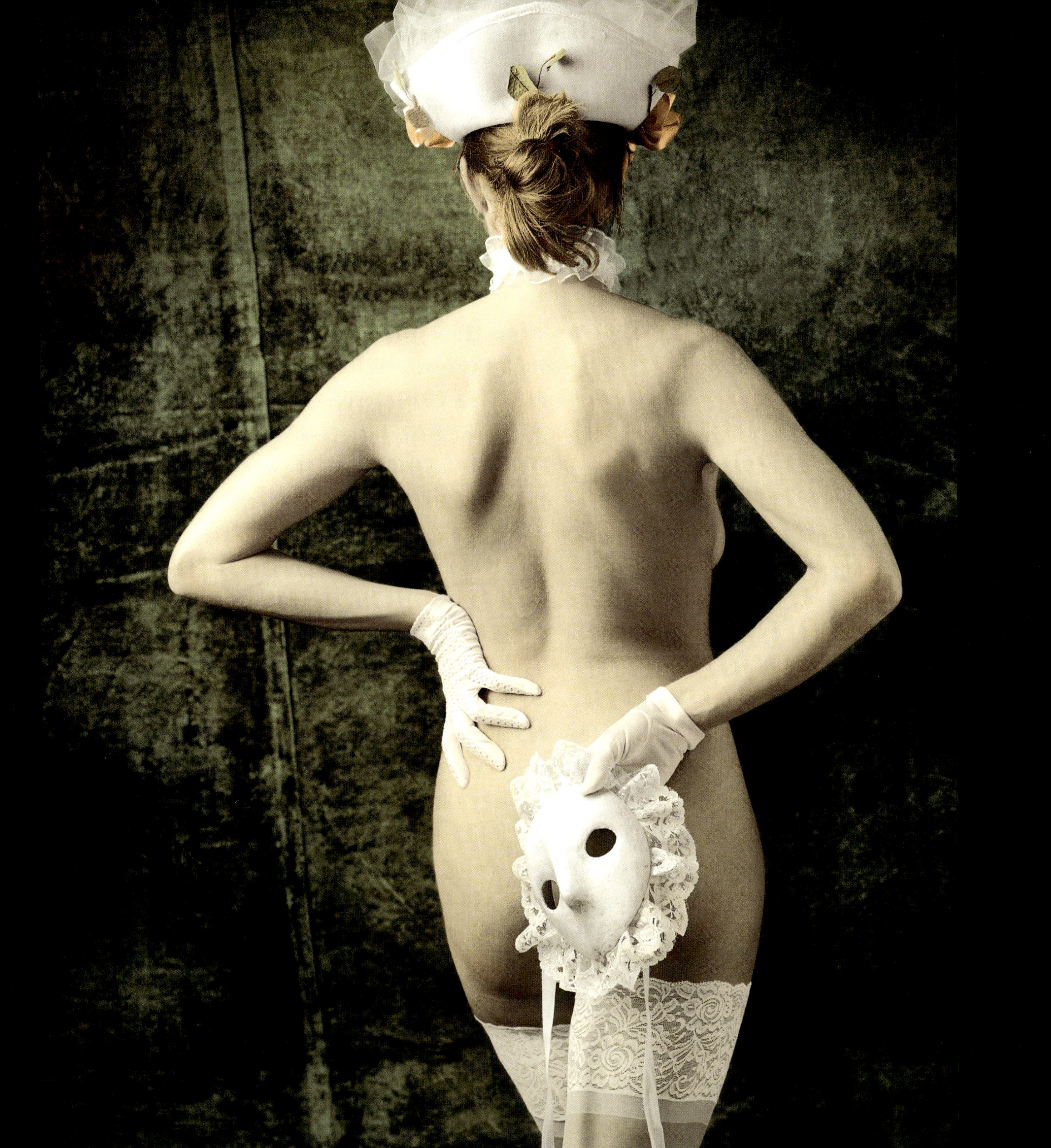

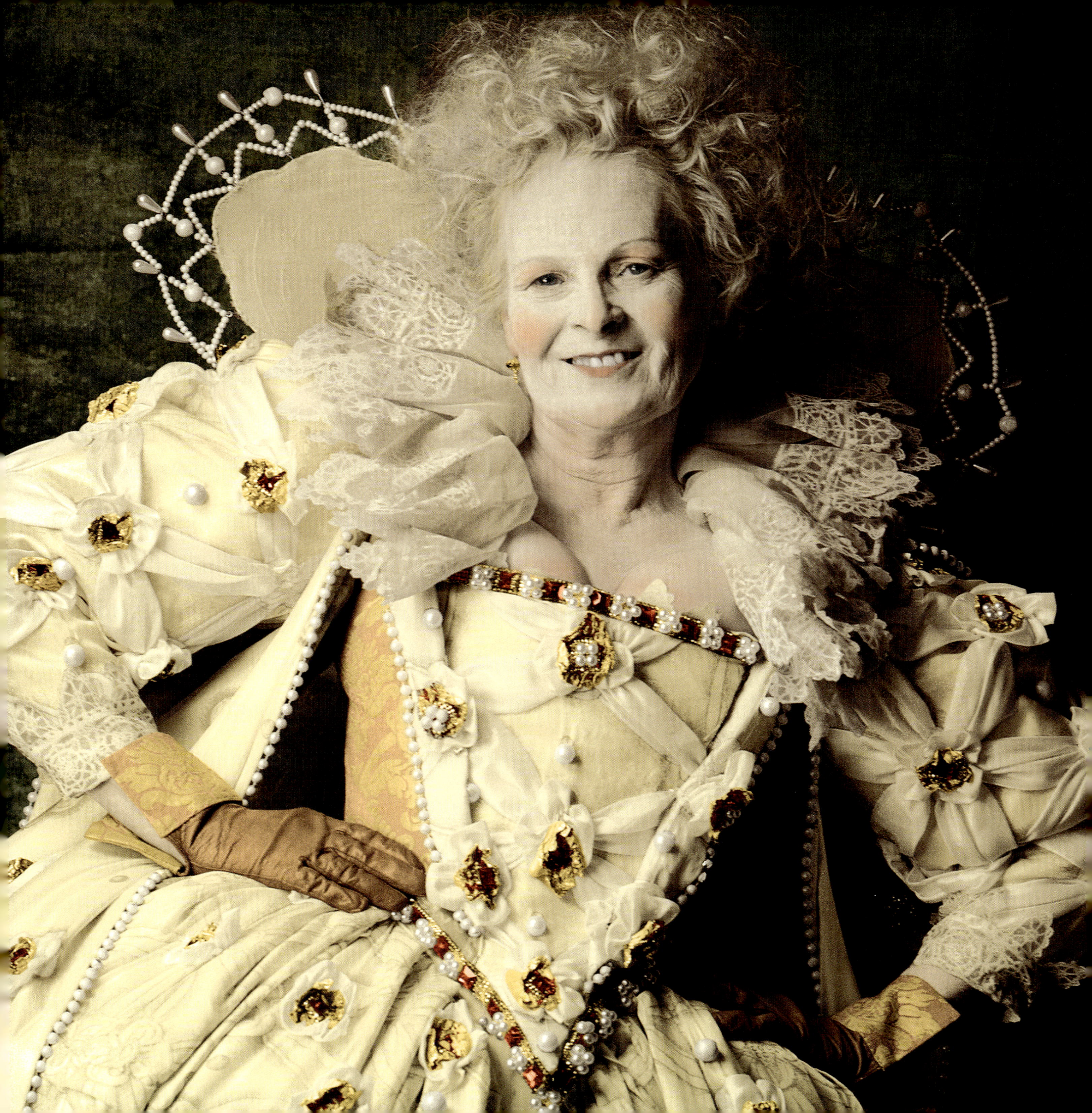

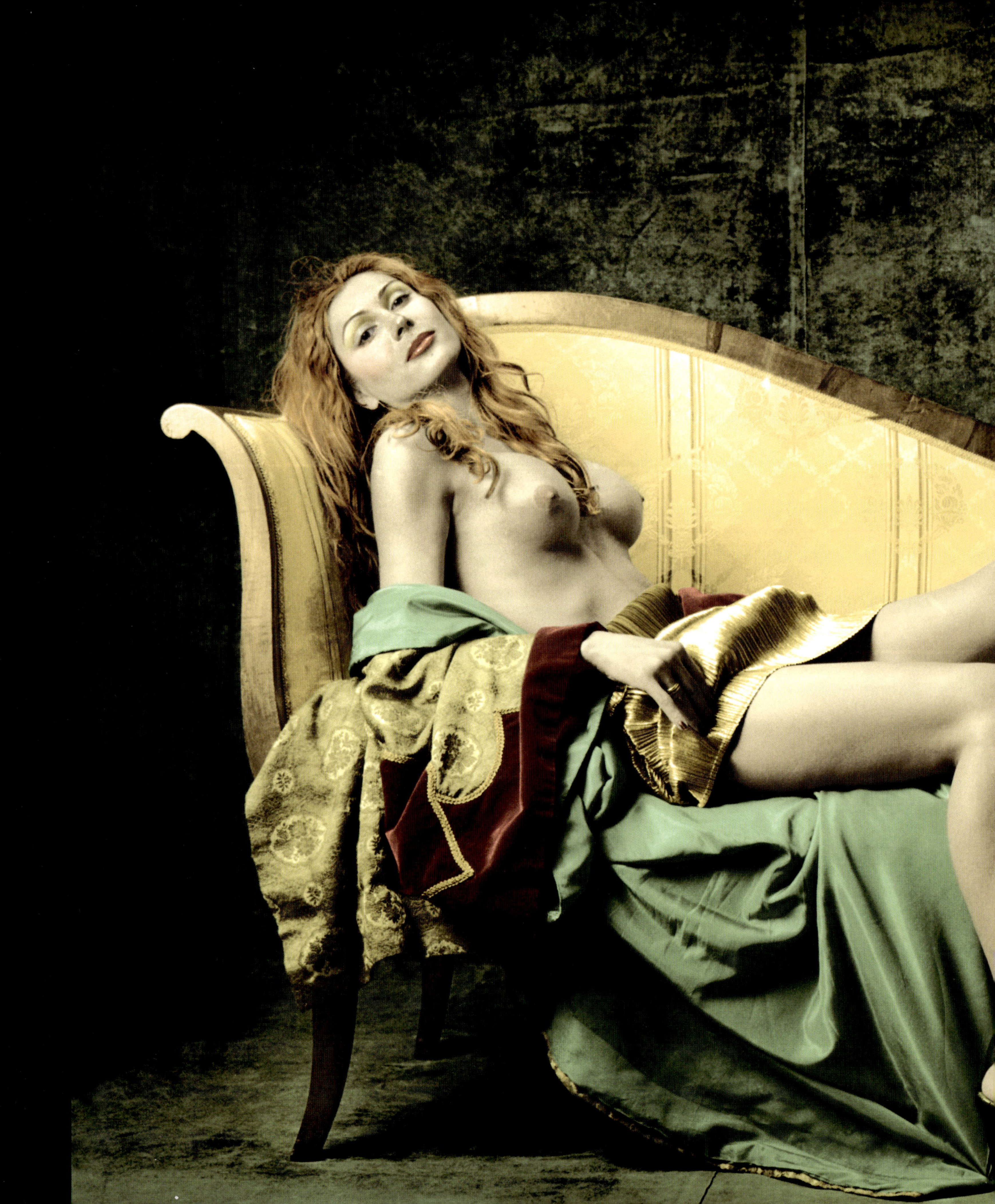

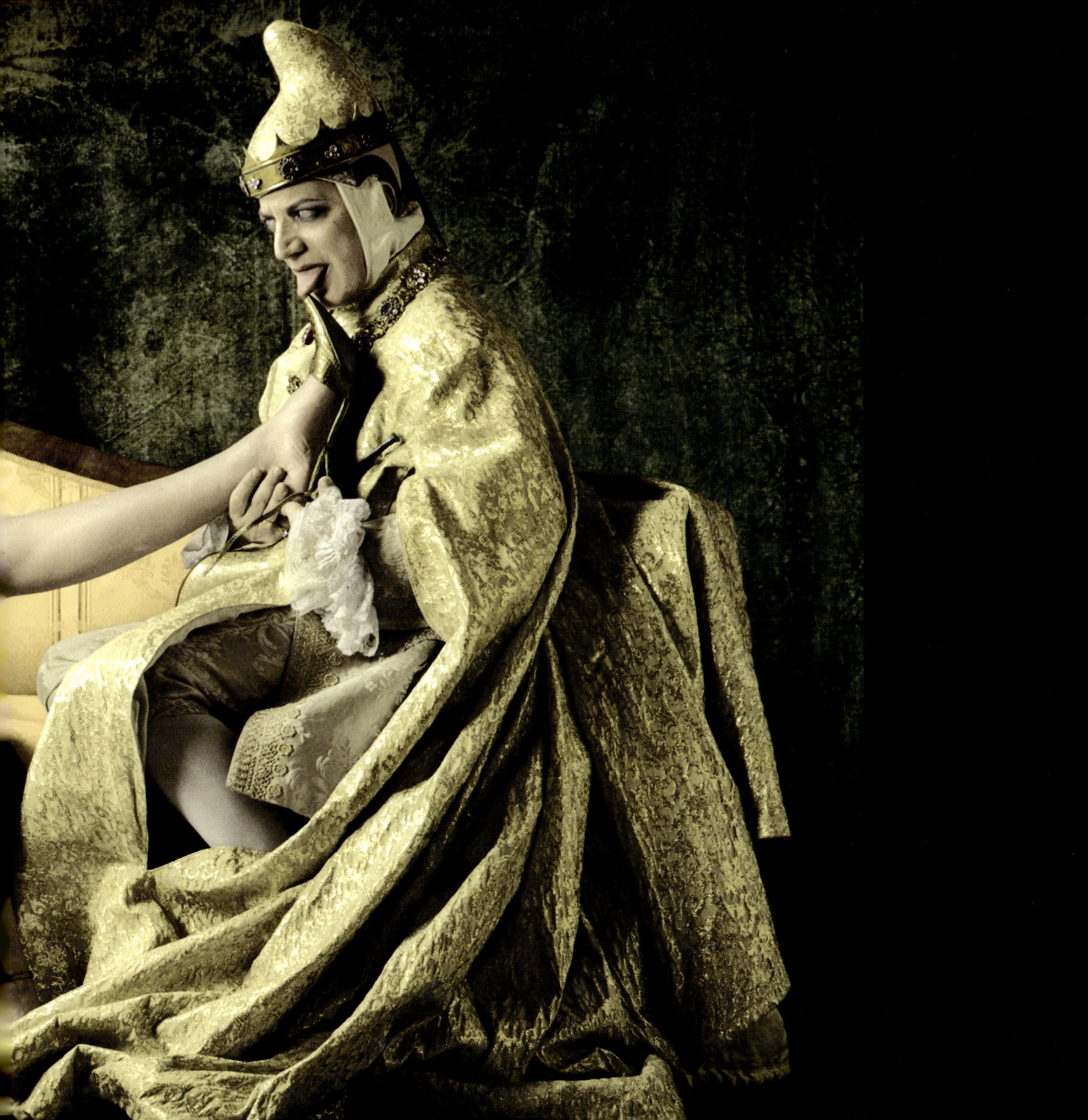

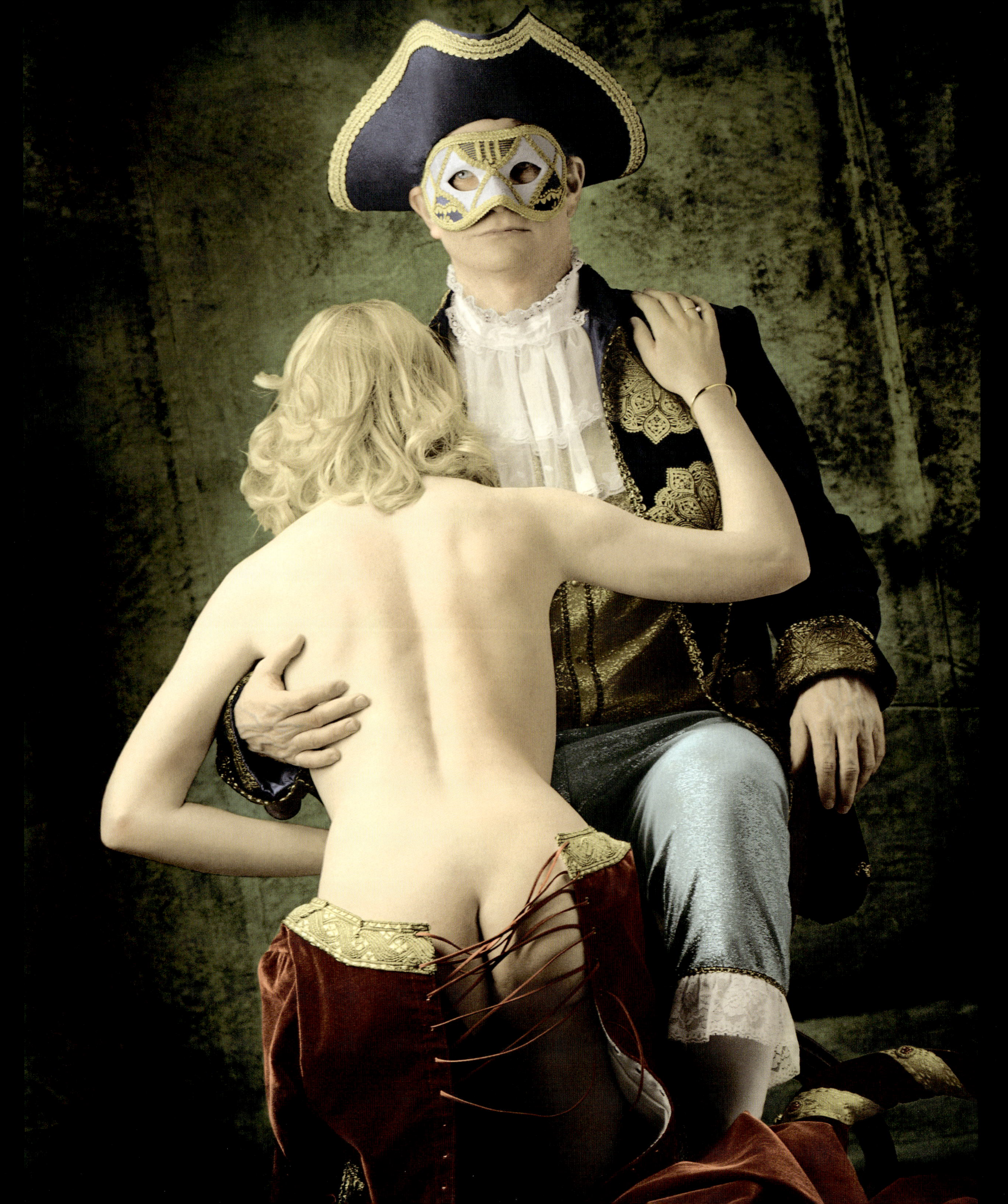

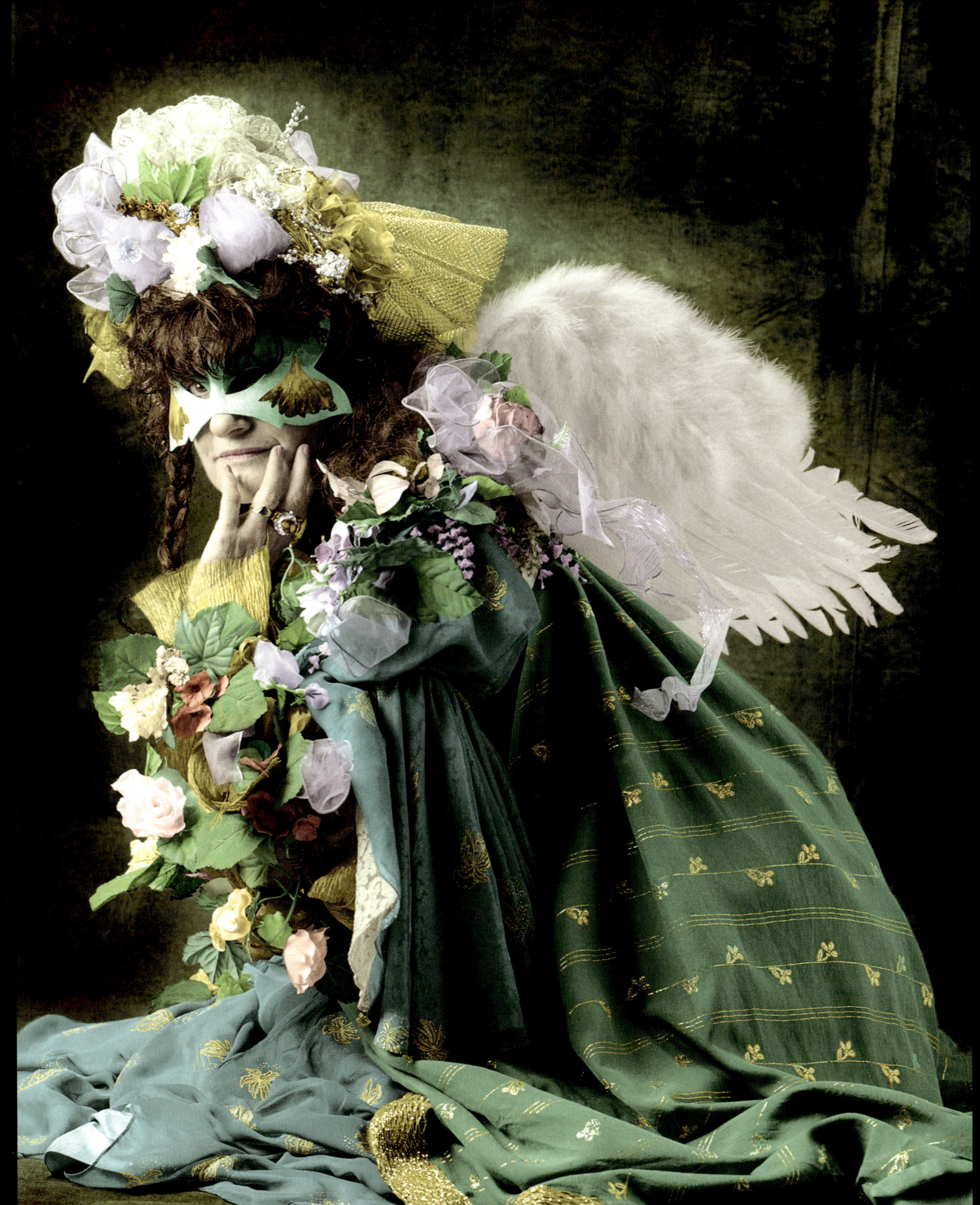

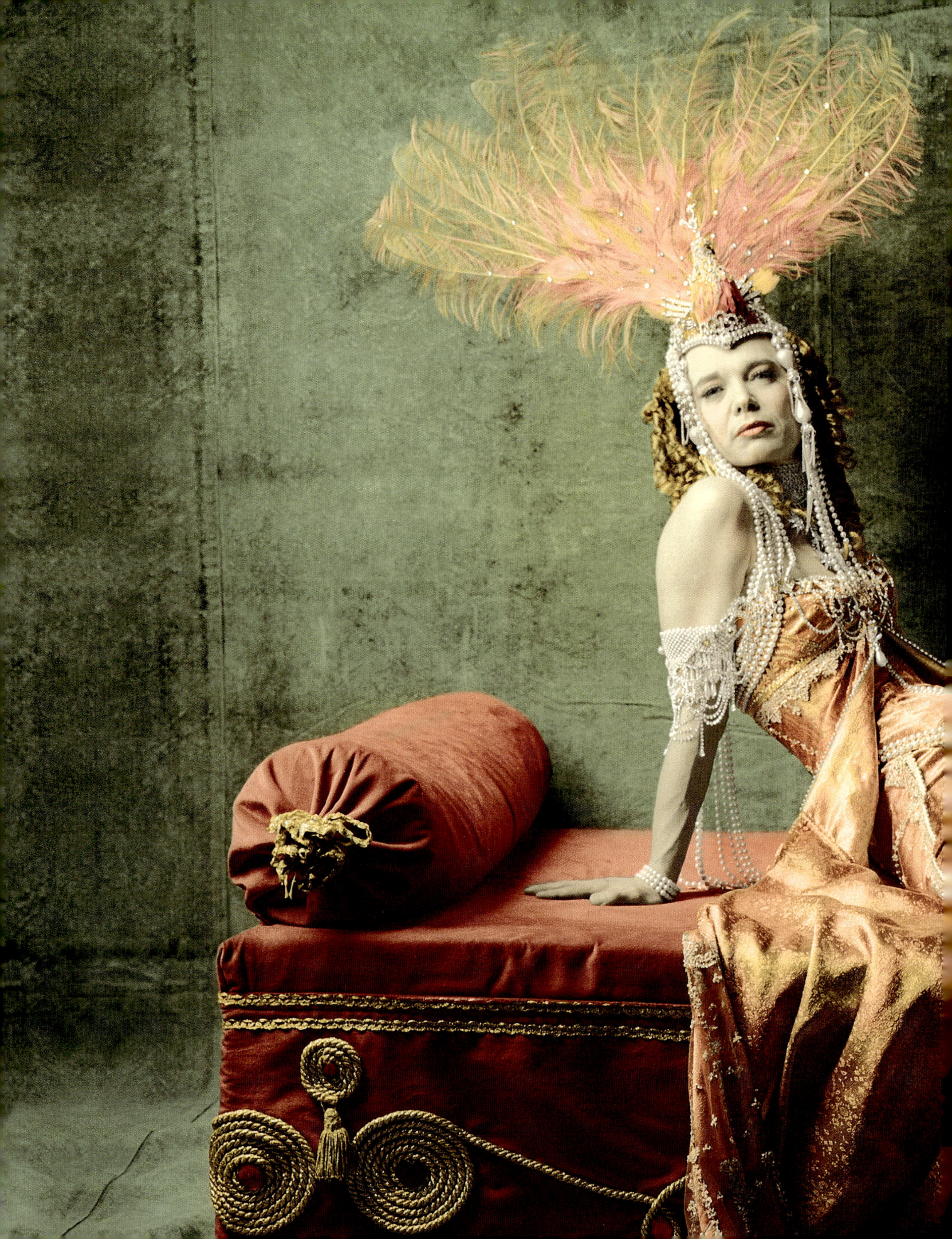

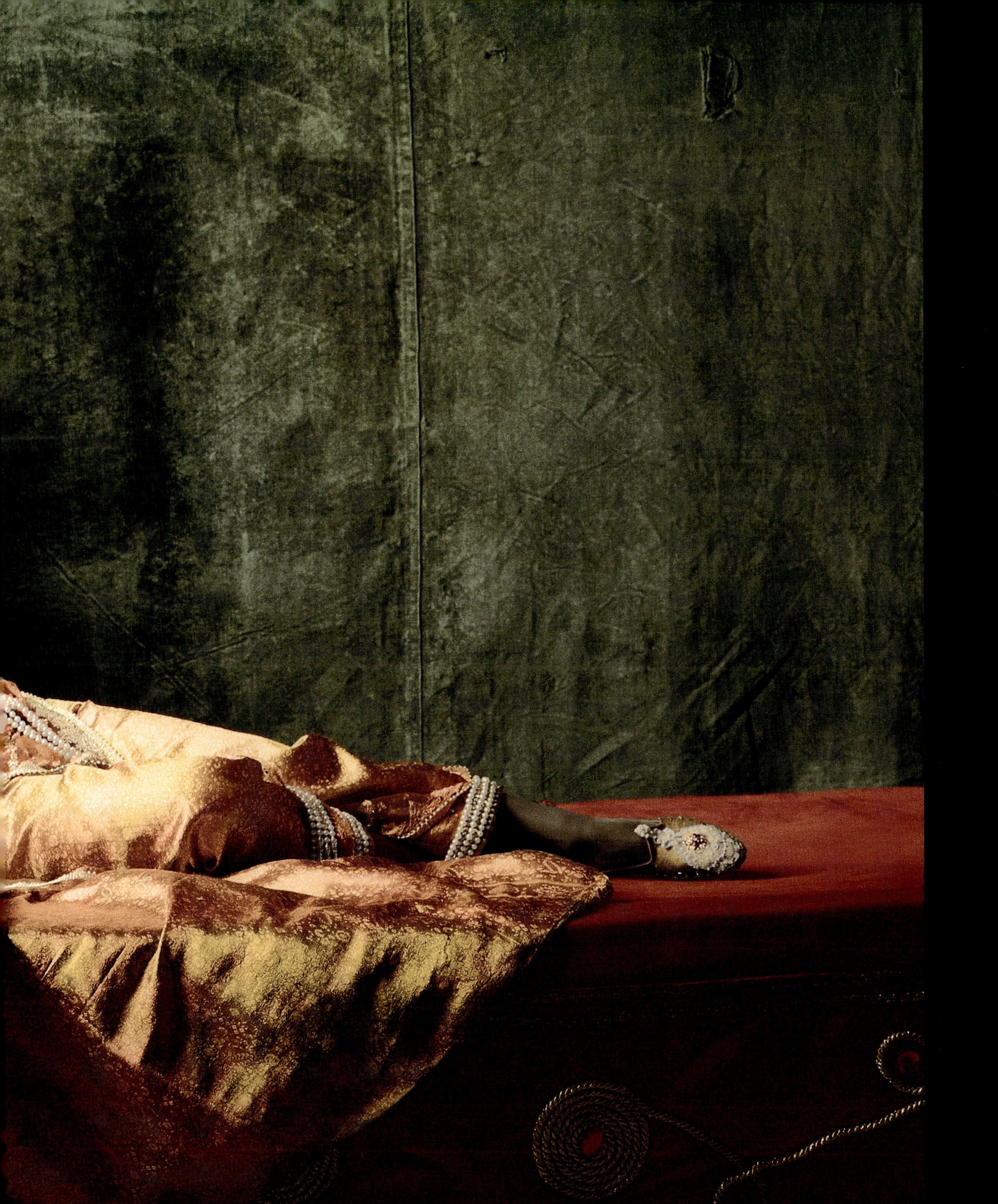

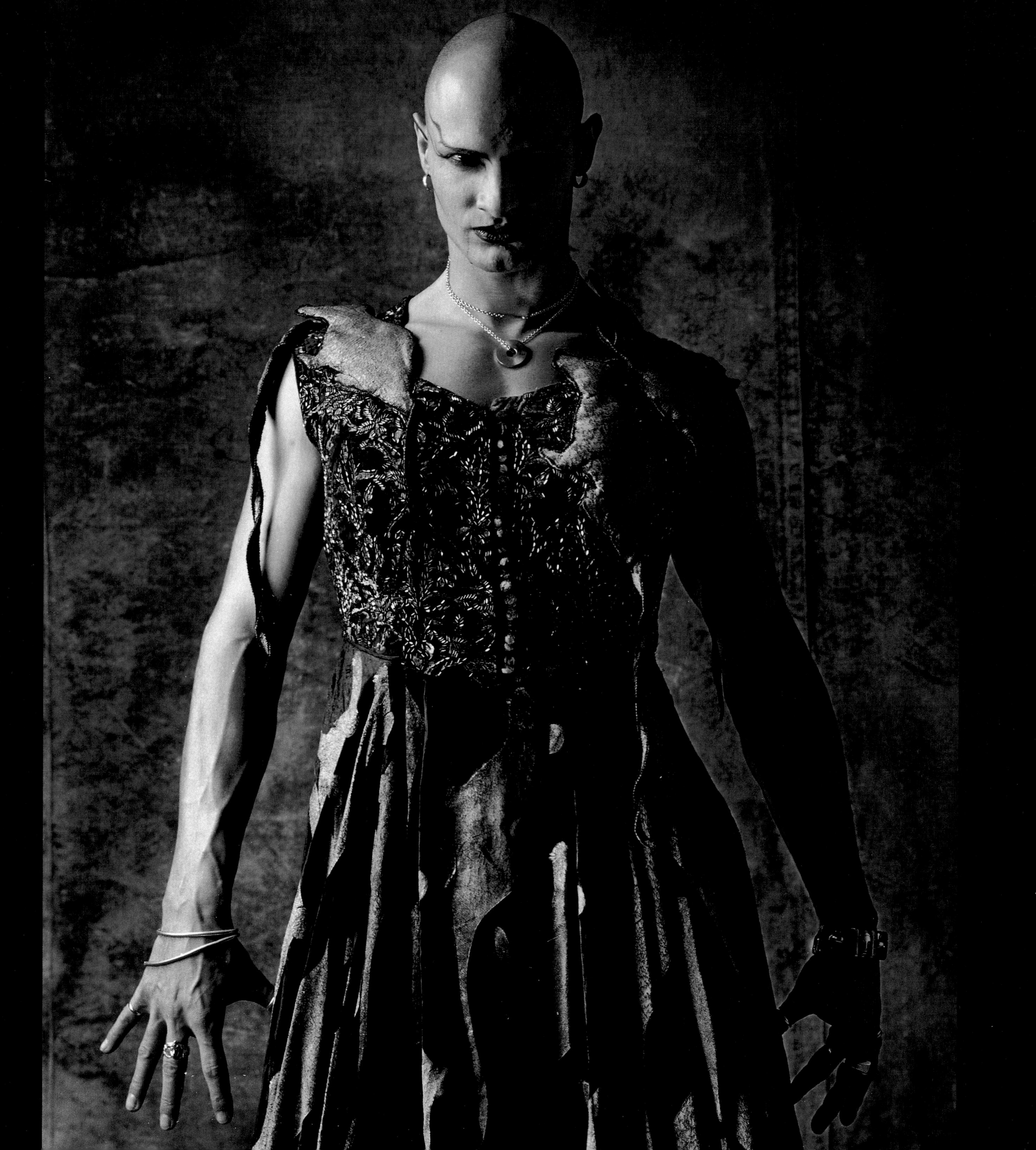

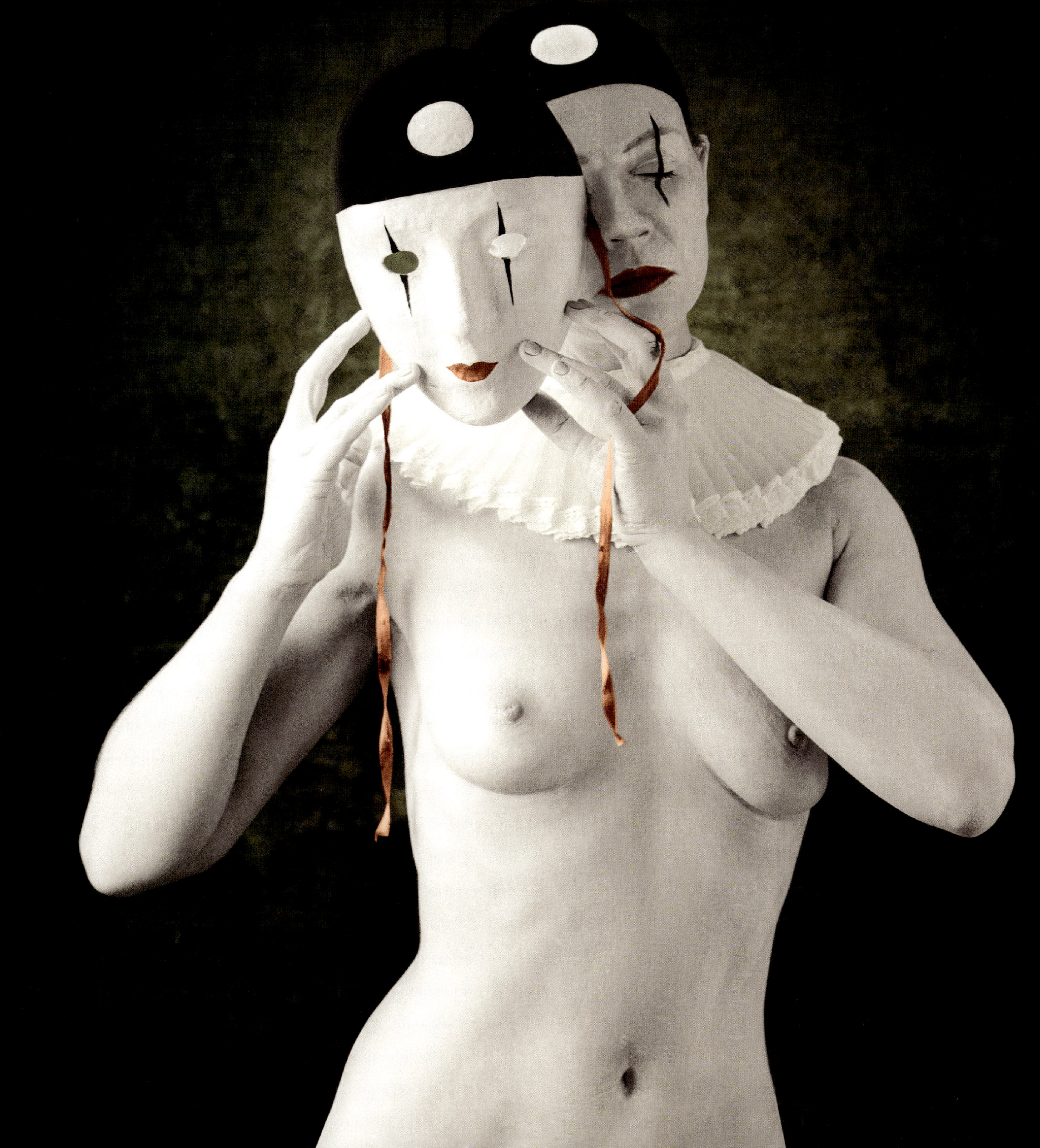

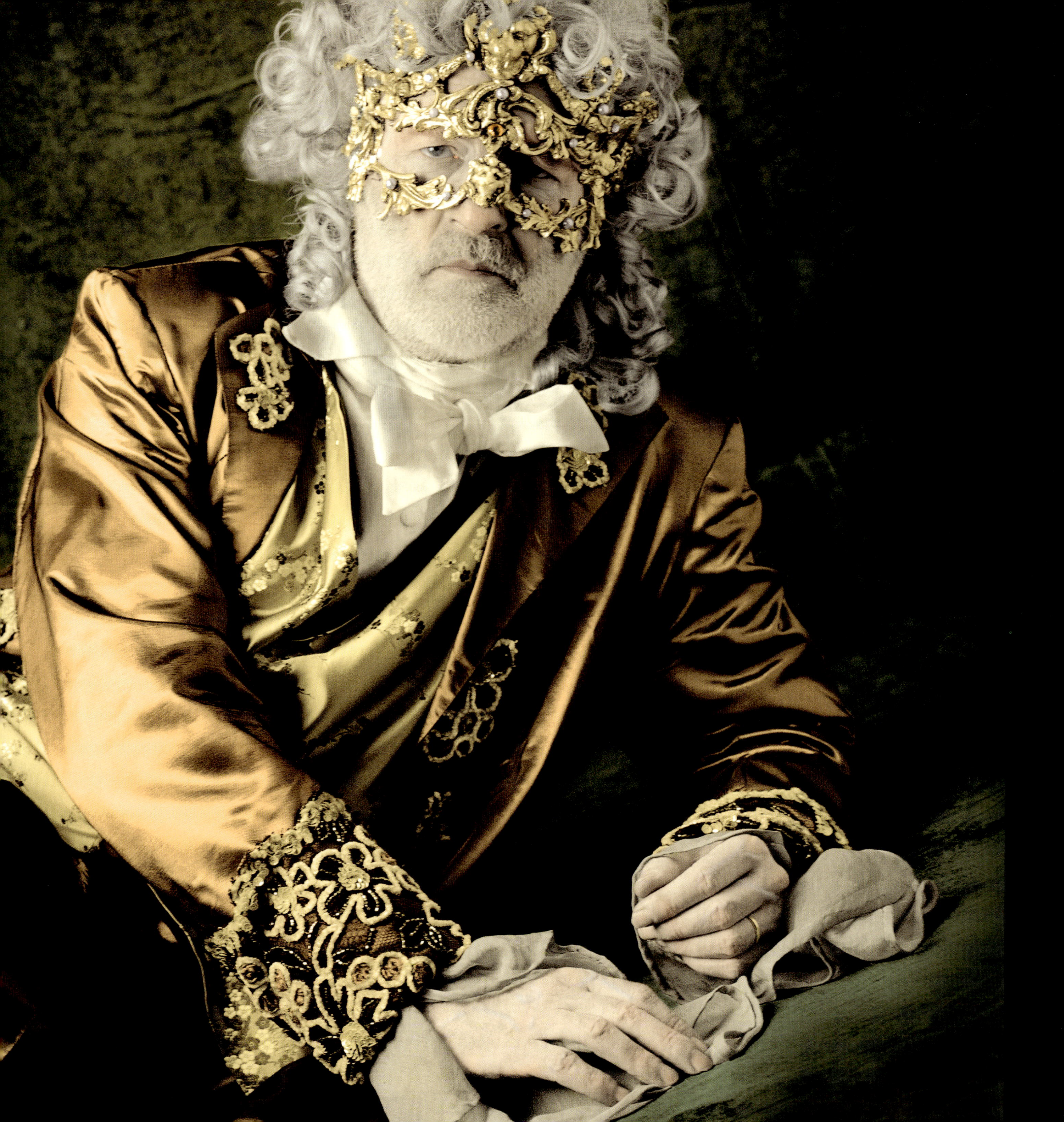

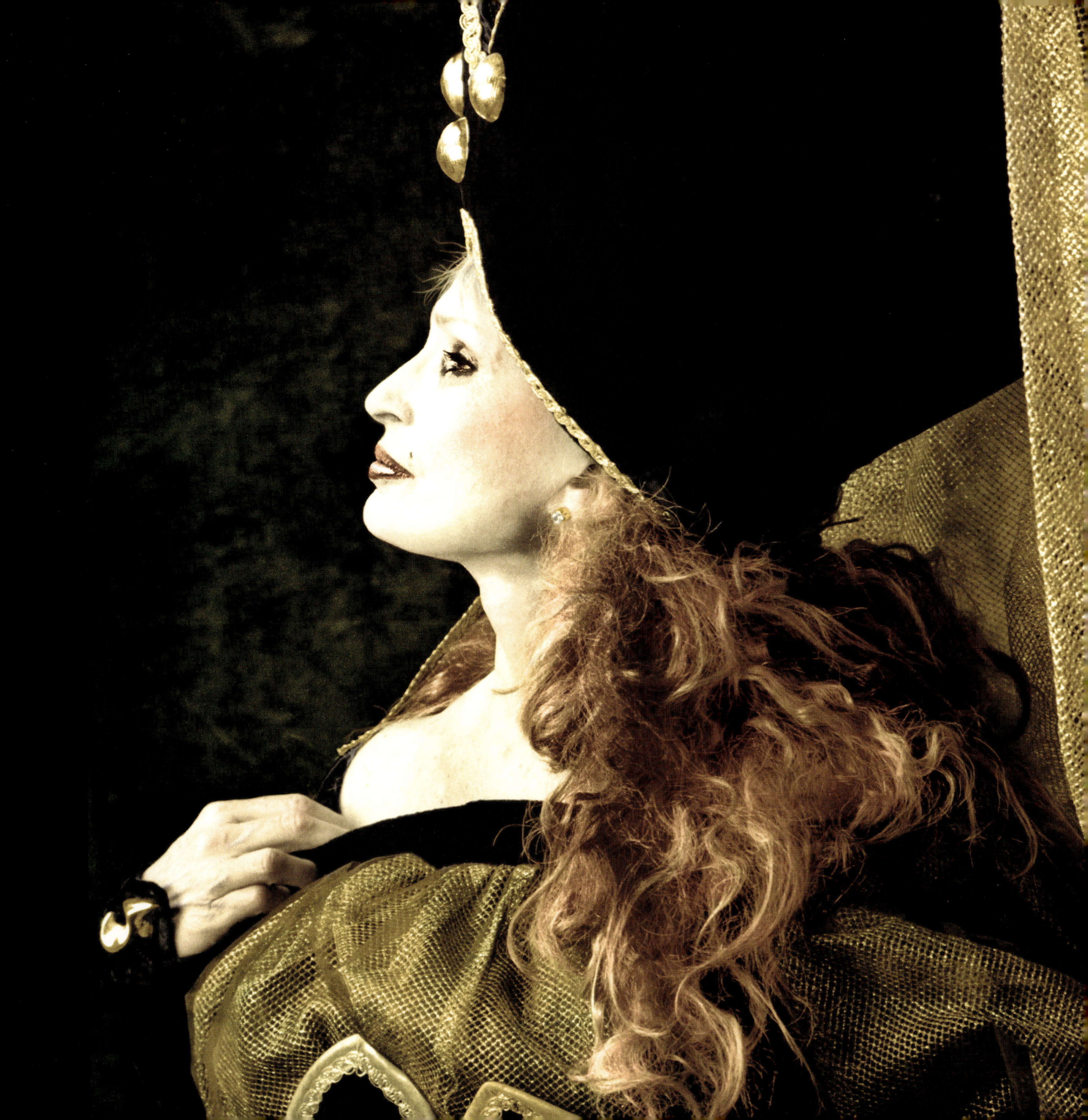

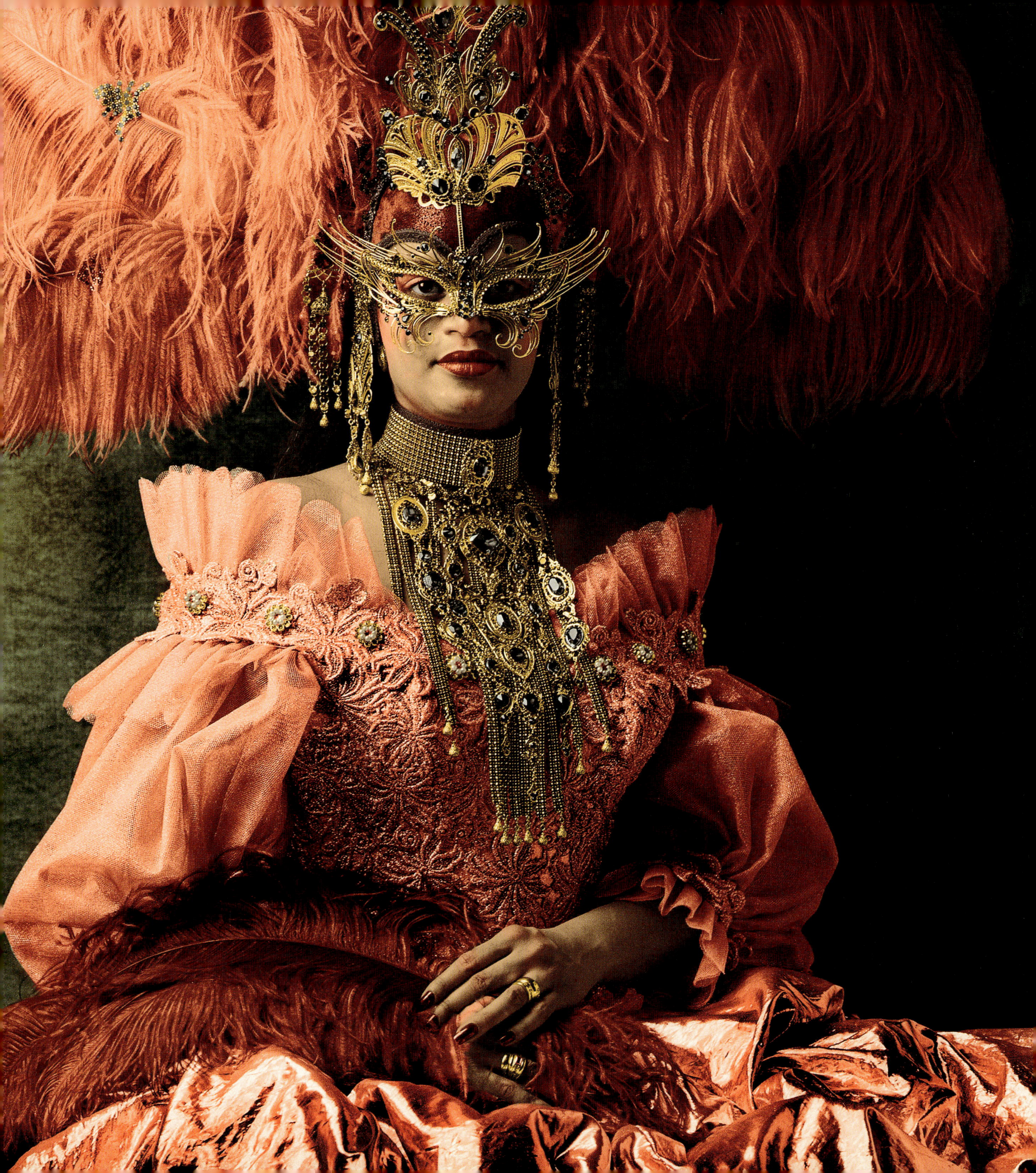

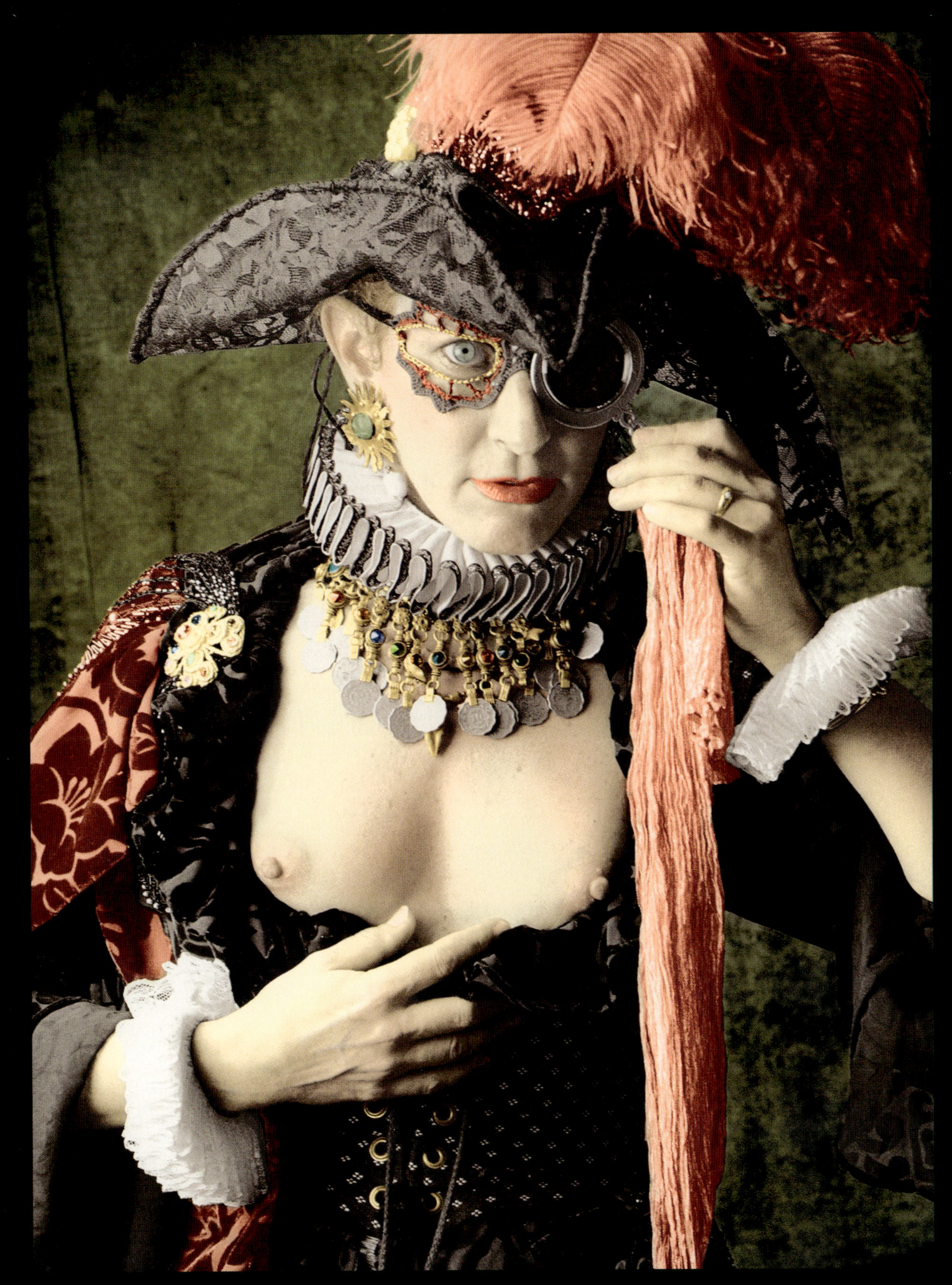

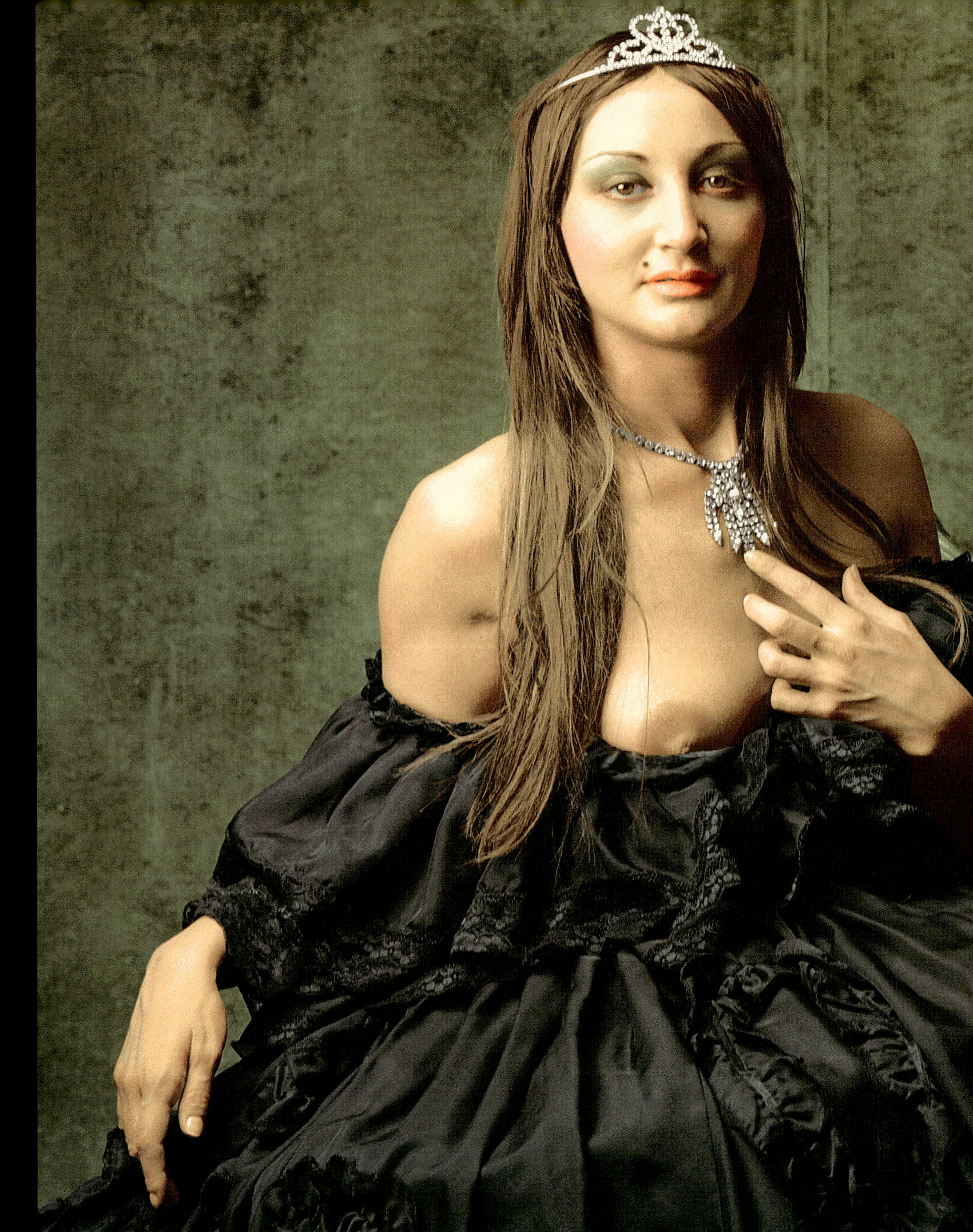

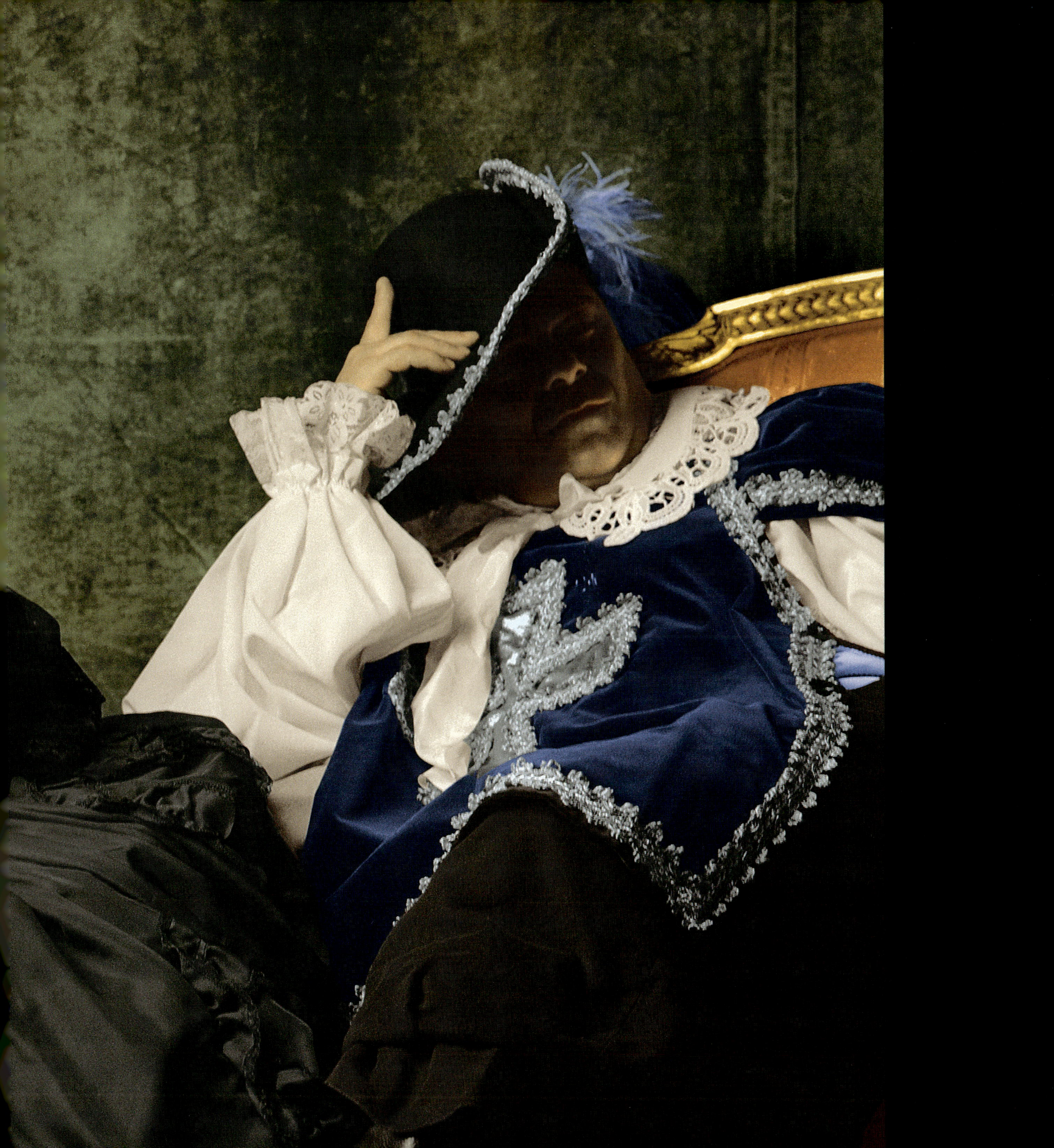

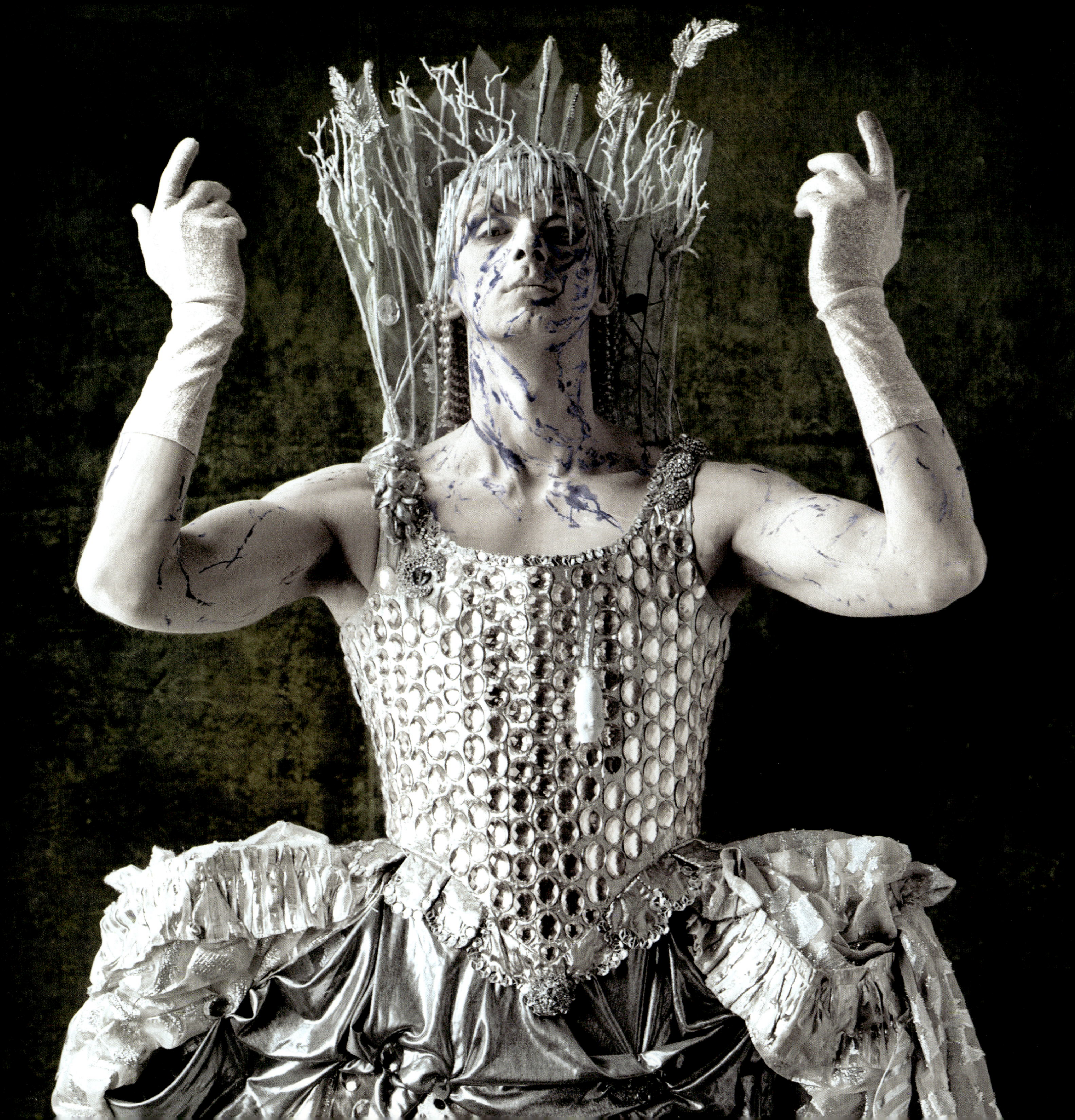

Contained and divided
The gesture restrained
In confused remains

Prehensile caress
Embroiders the silence
With wordy decorum

Boldly I touch
The joined silk
Balanced in wonder

Trembling and transitory
Diligent time
Glides fragile

Mute and irremovable
Suppressed premonition
Of fleeting tenderness

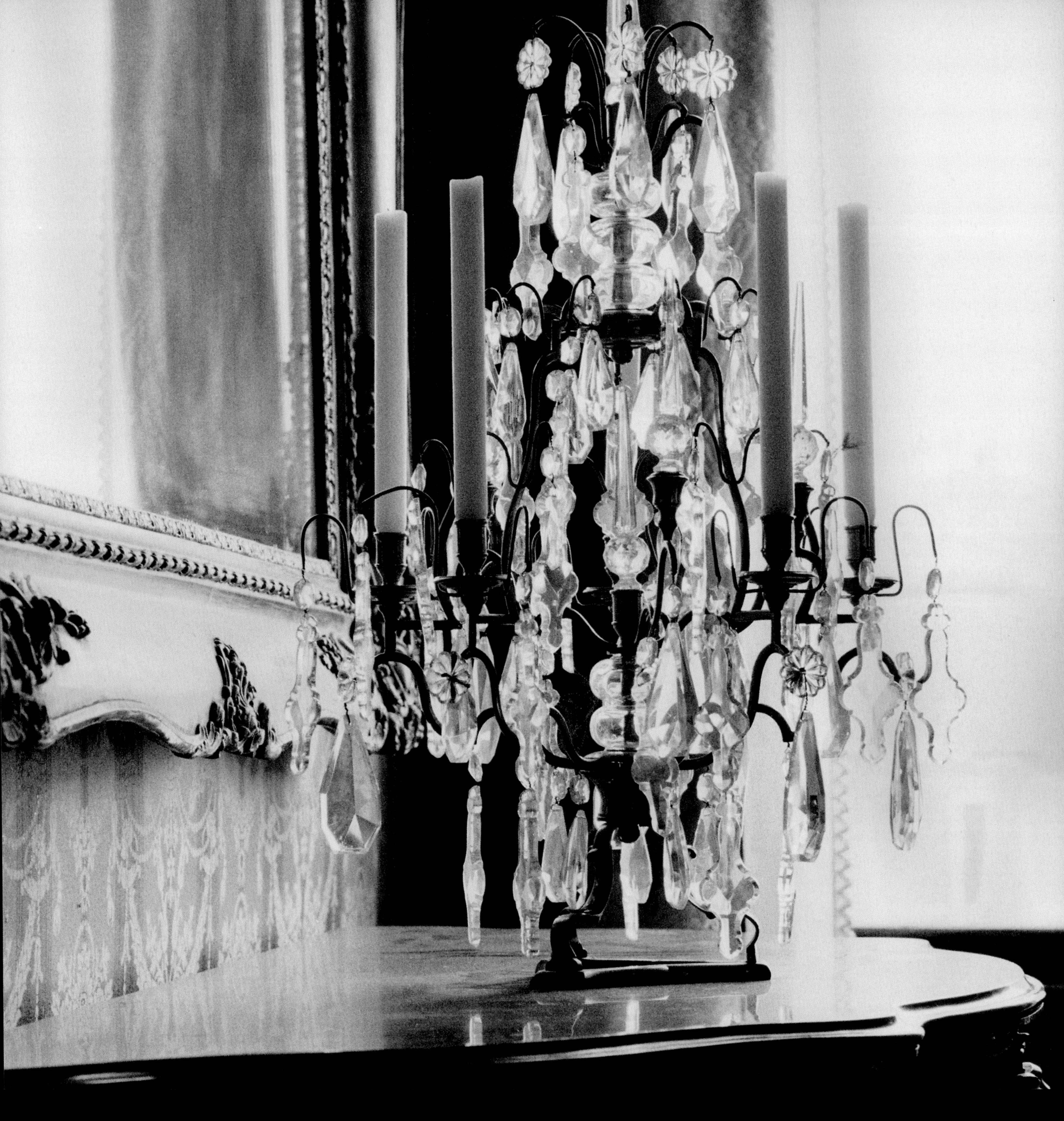

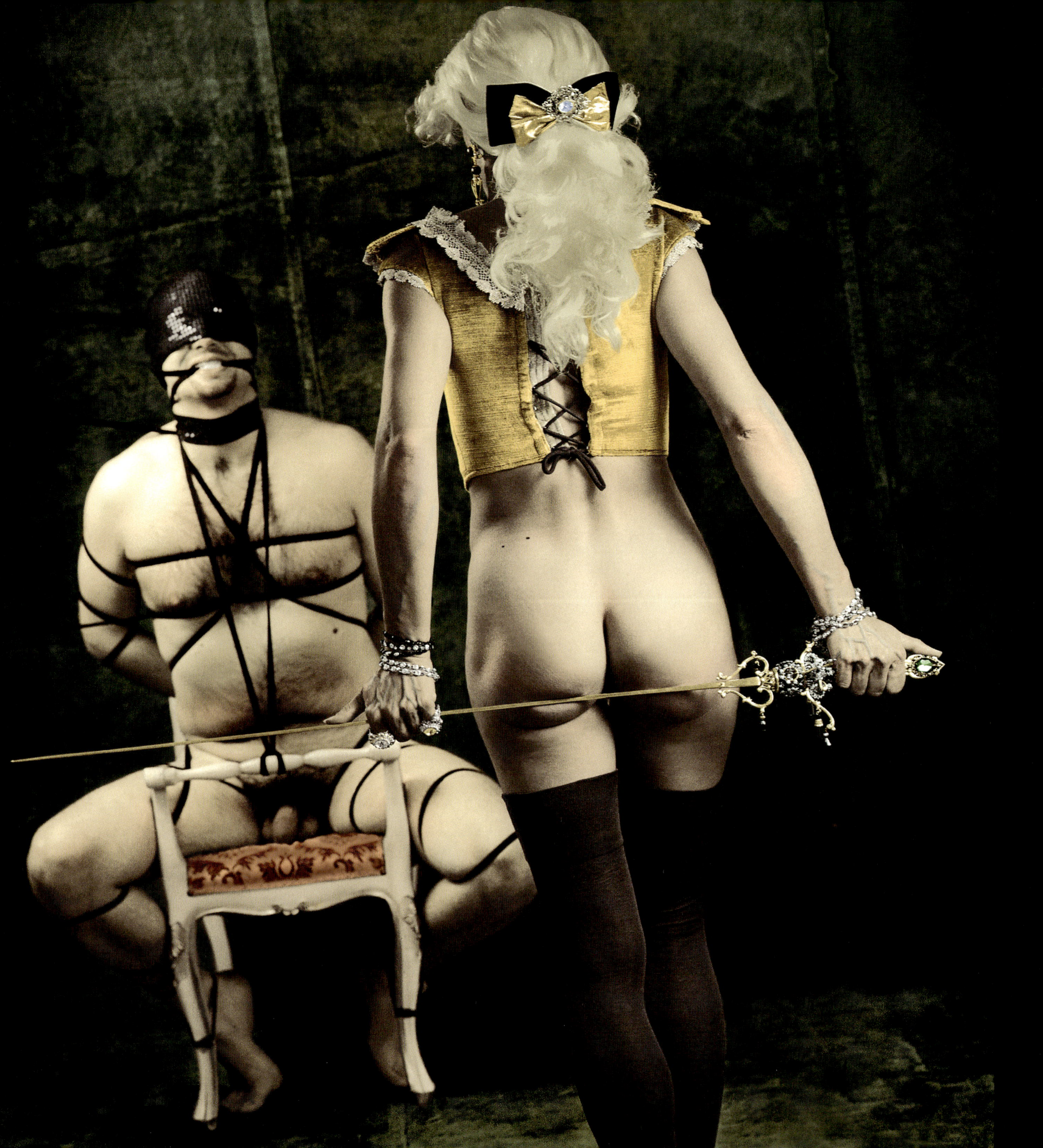

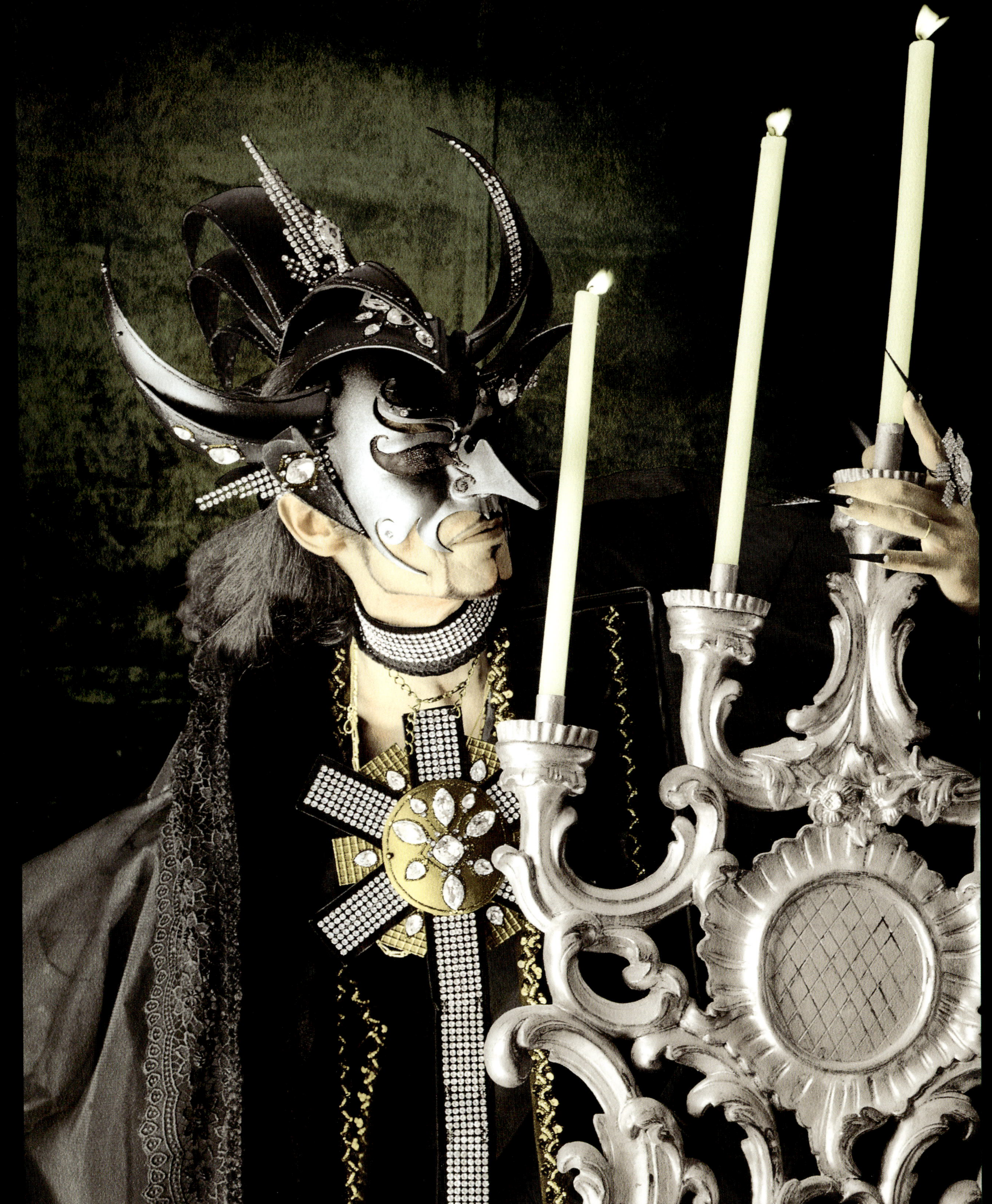

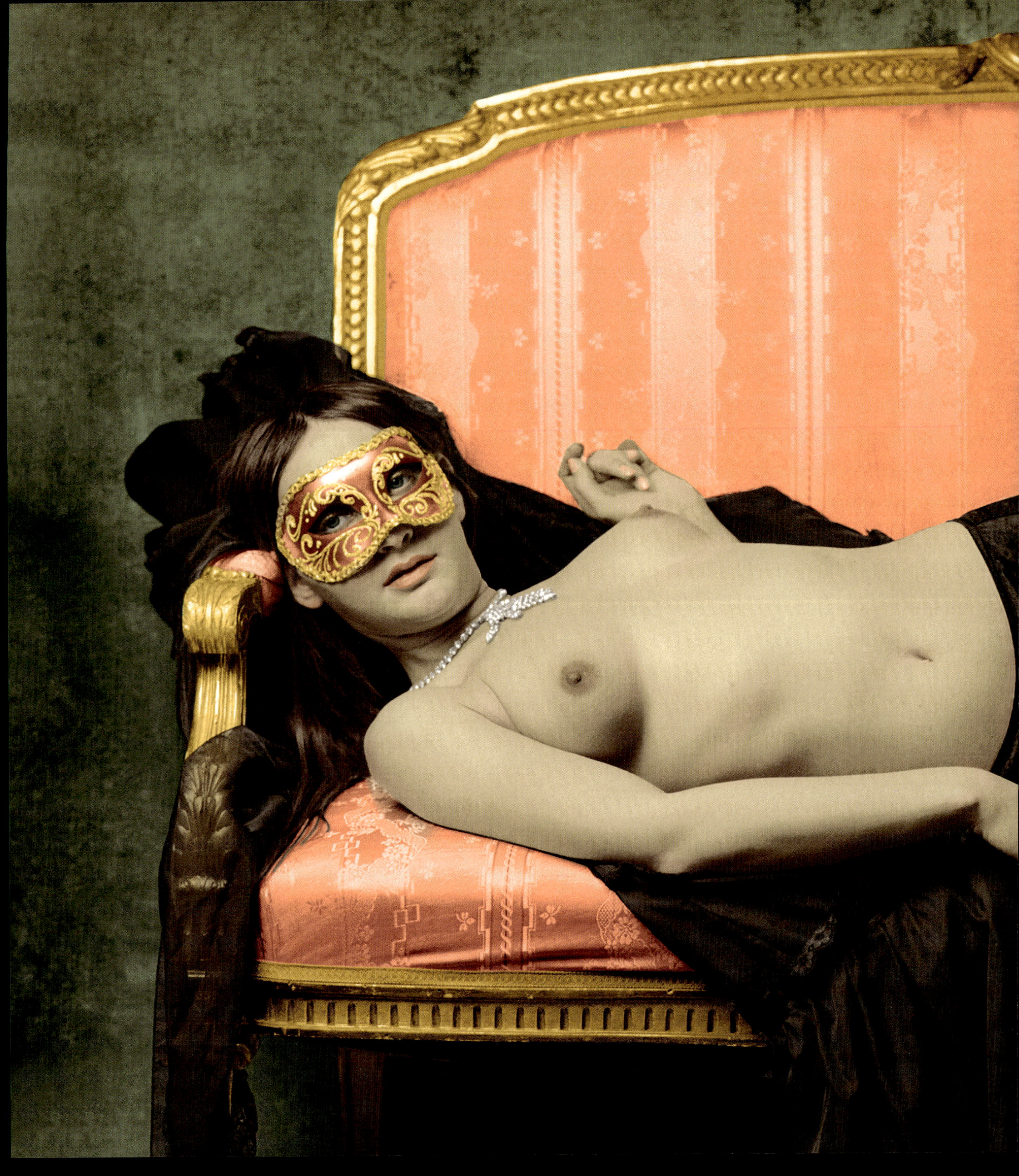

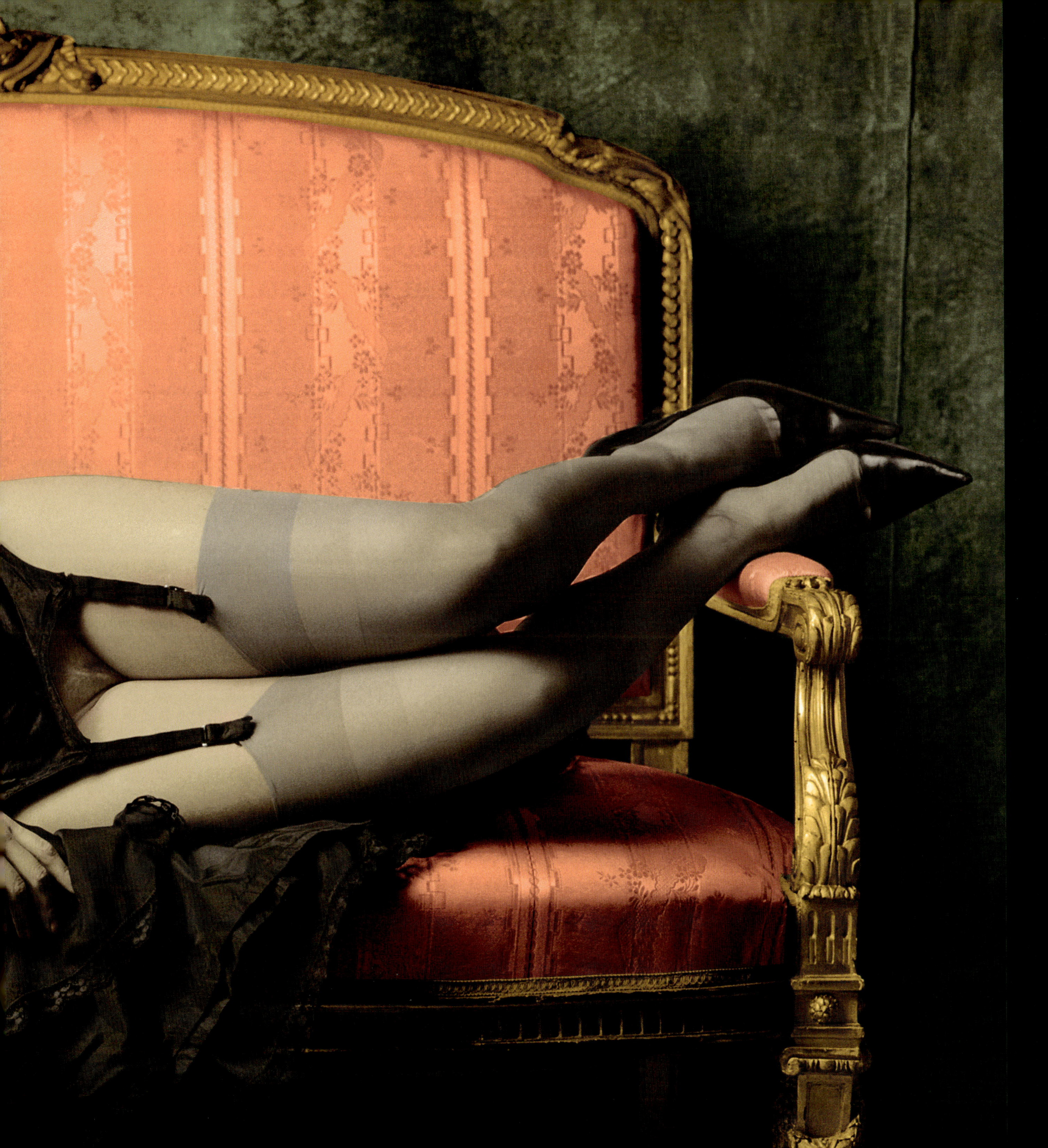

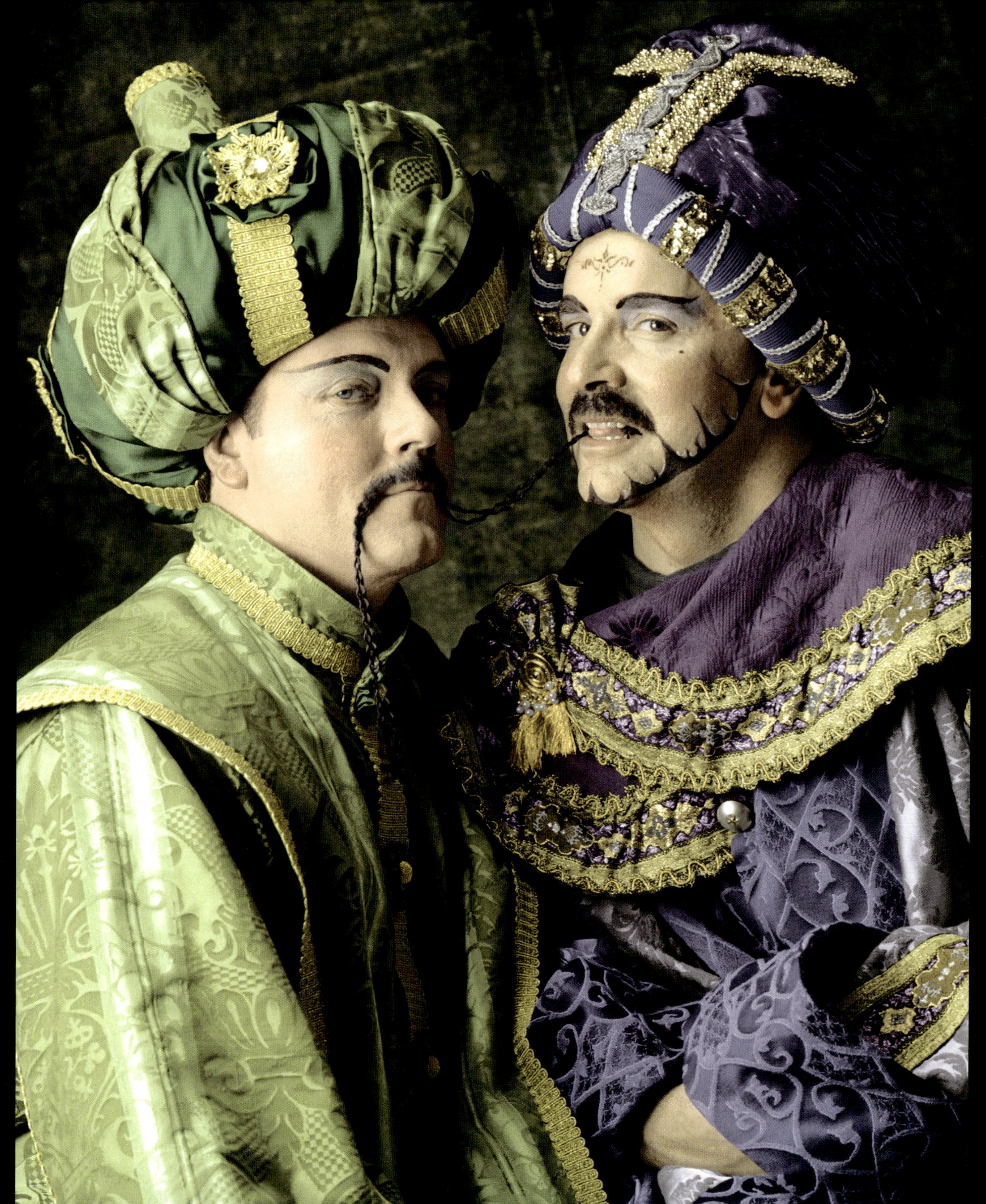

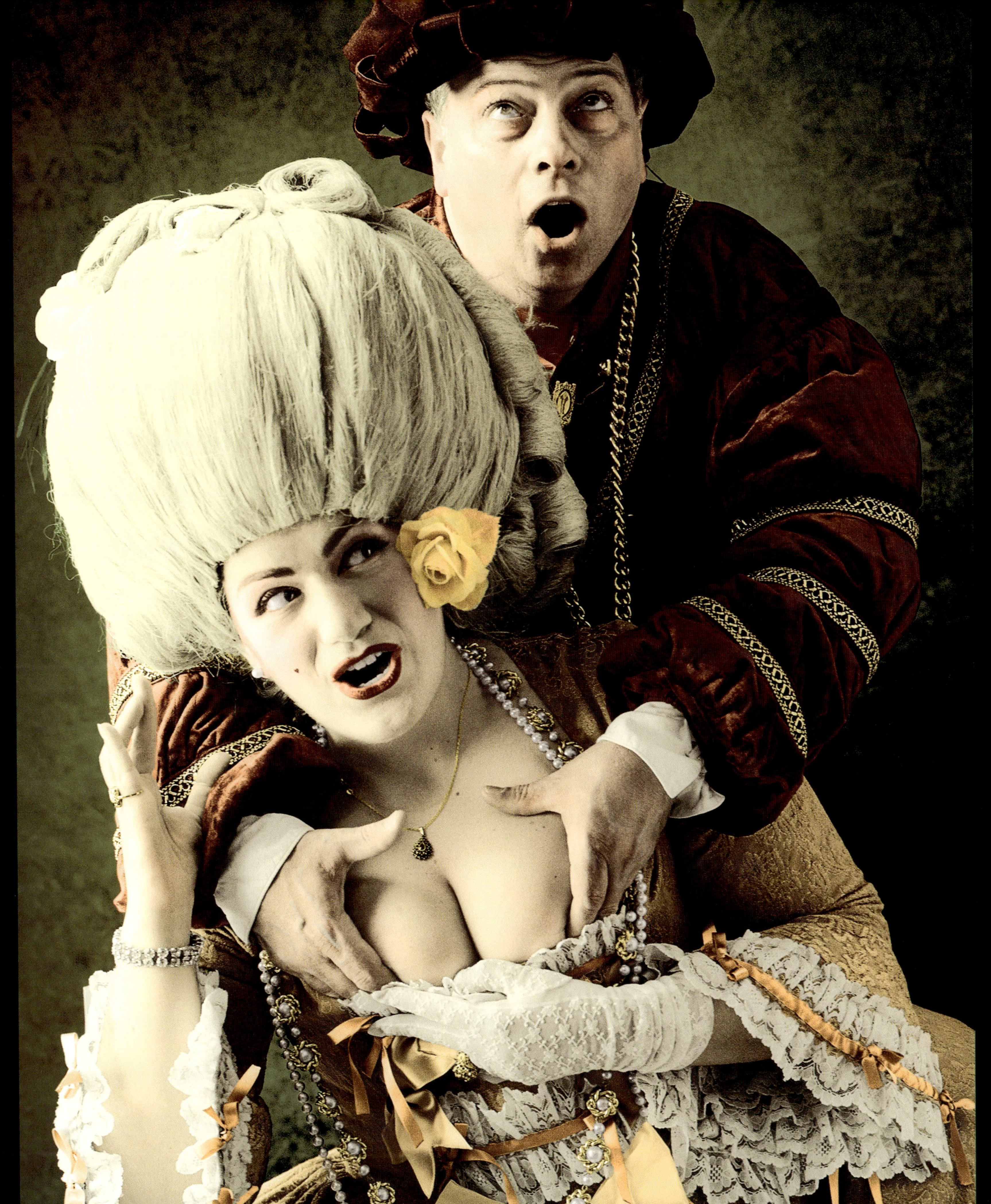

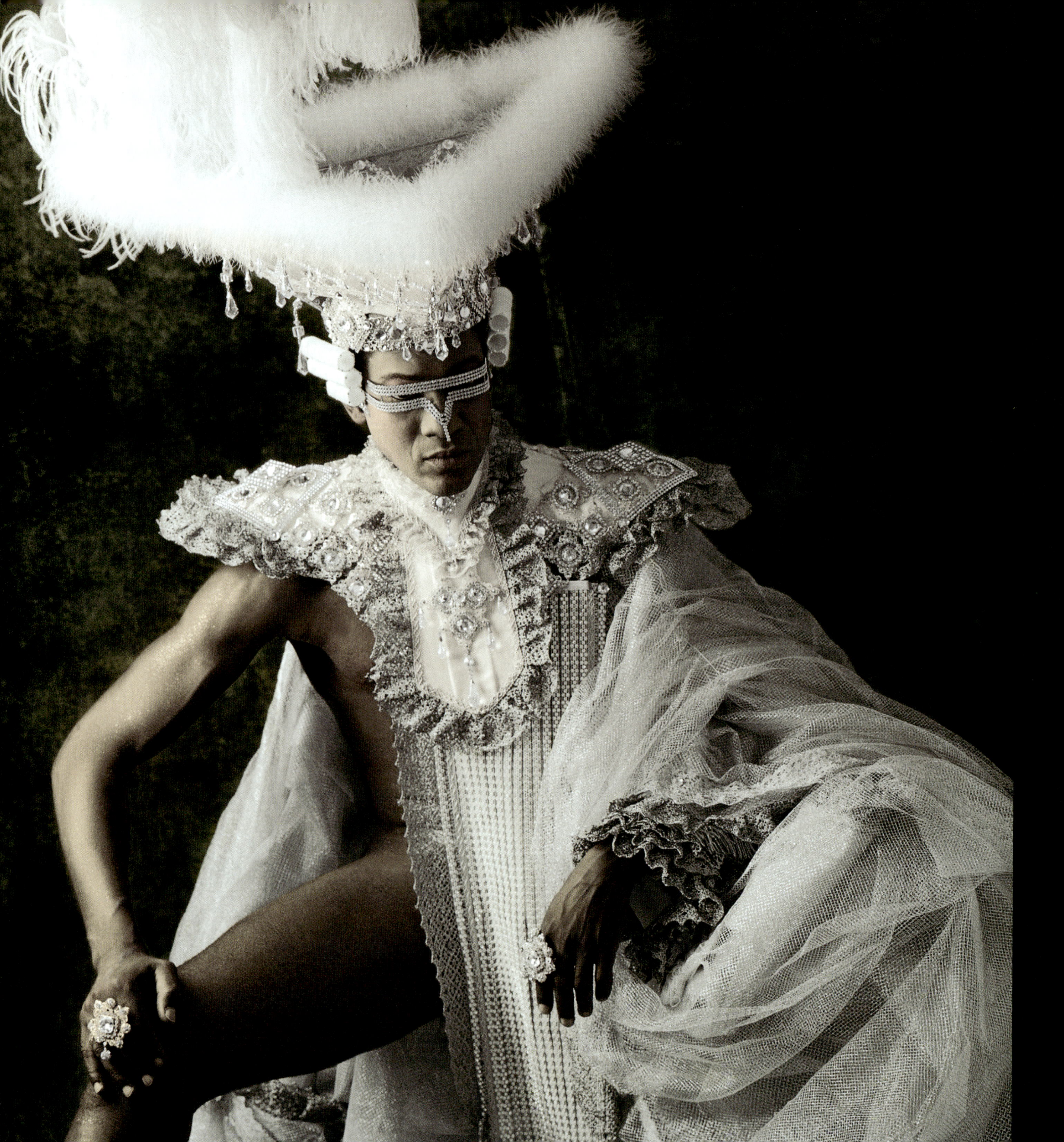

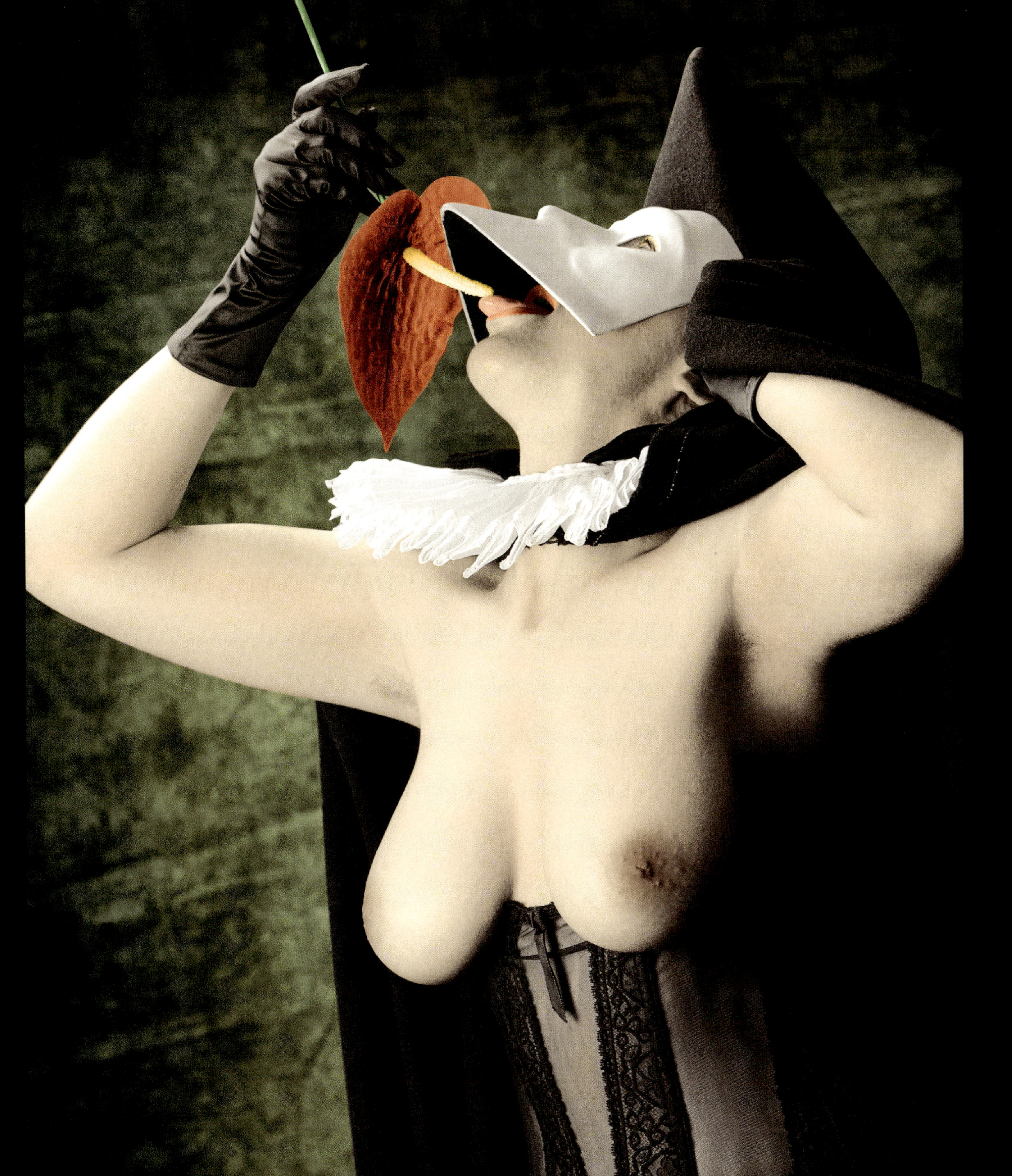

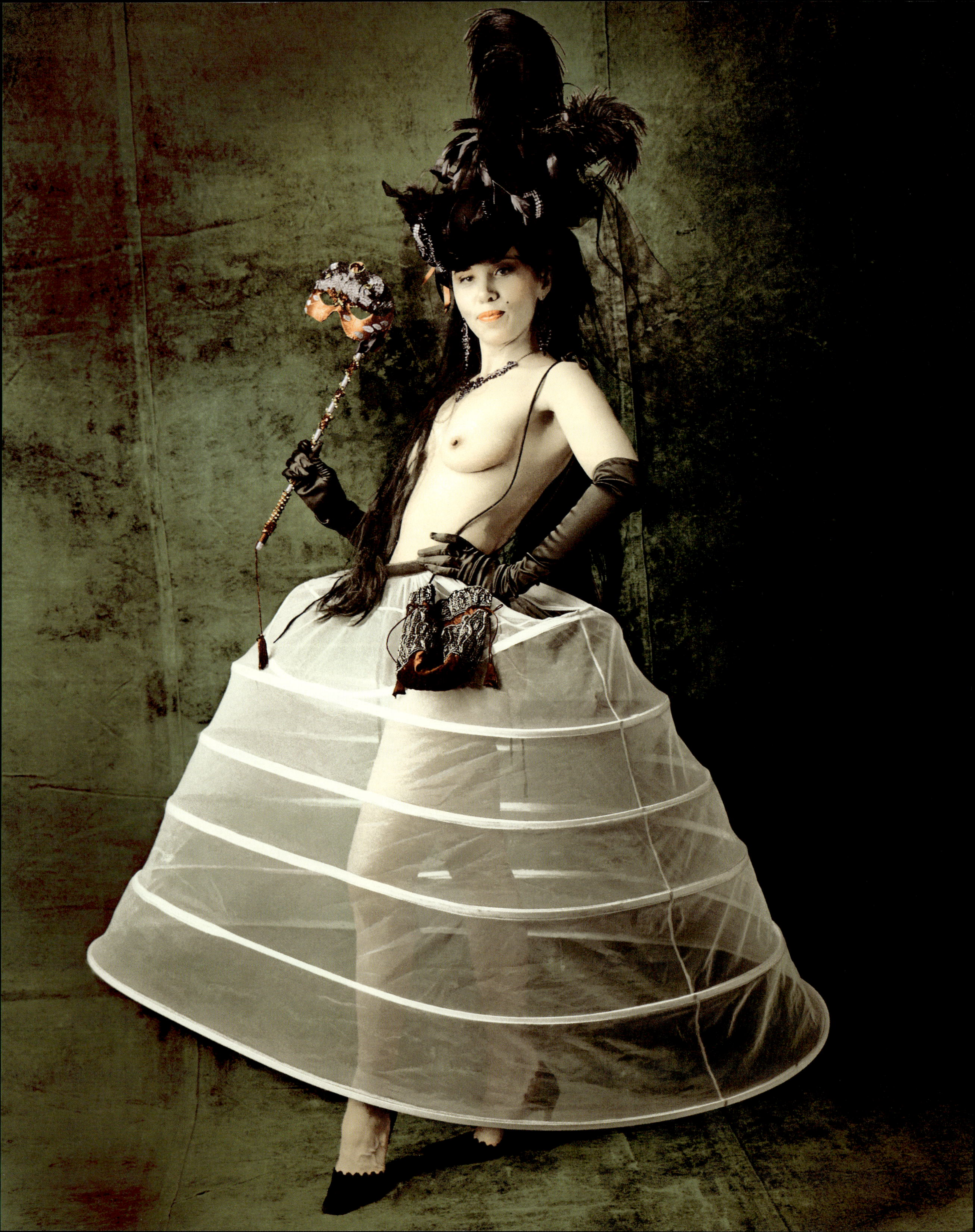

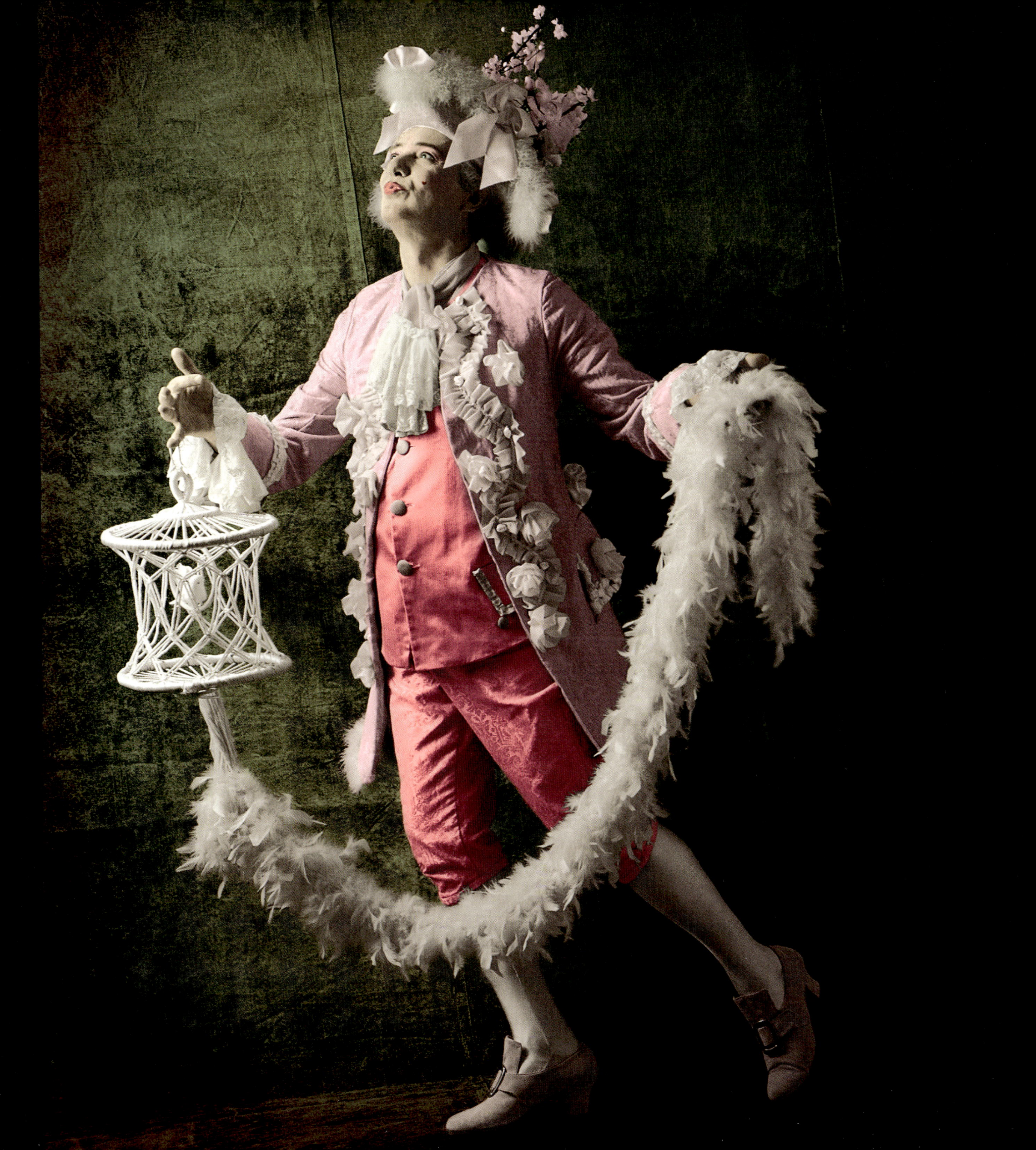

Ancient grazing touch
Heedless refuge
Of merry delicacy

Joy in disguise
The happening pastime
Dissolves and evaporates

Reflexes and deception
Instants extinguished
Of silky white.

Dazzling uproar
In lyric confusion
Exhausted and lost

Conscious certainty
The bonfire dying
Silently we vanish

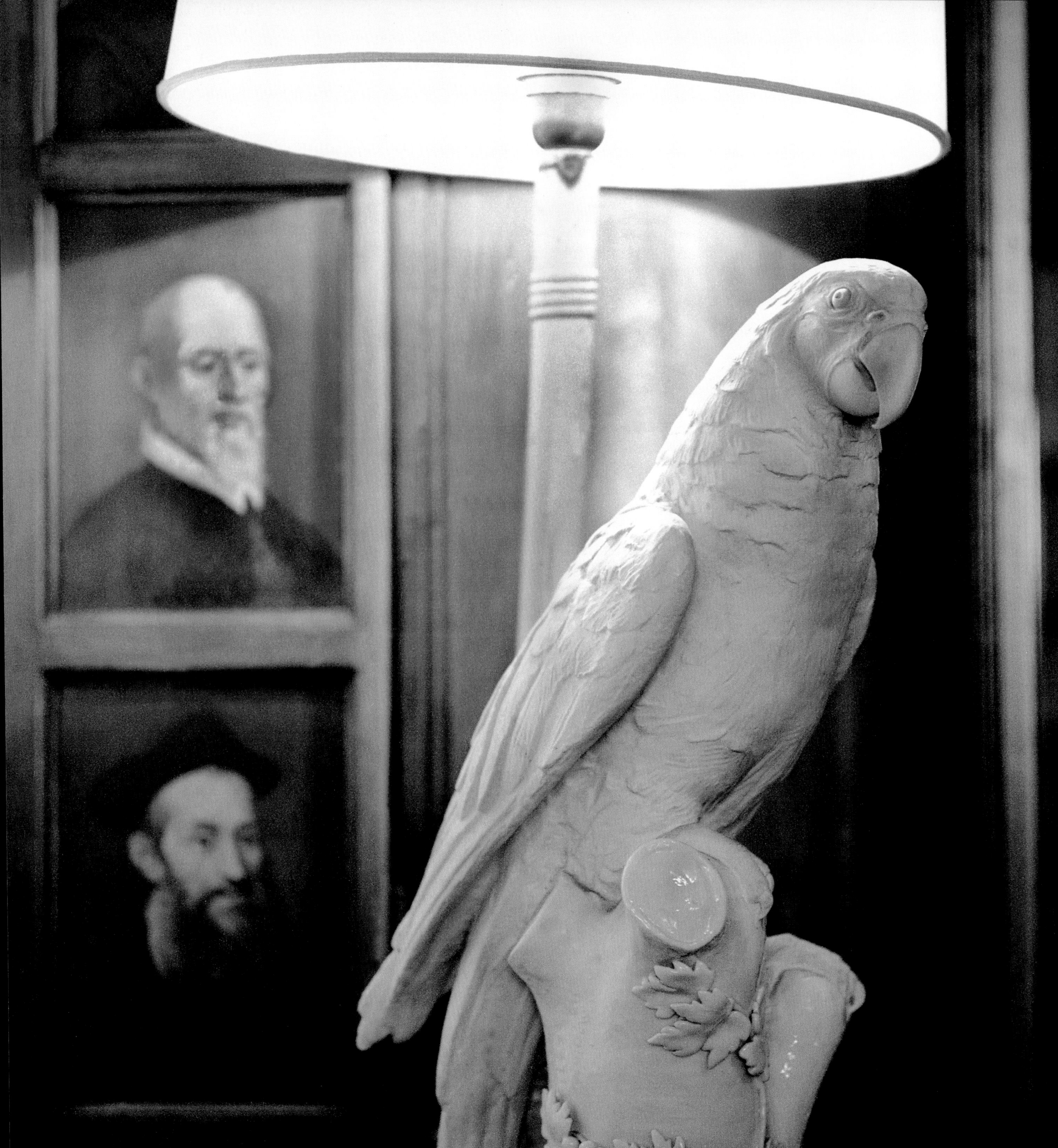

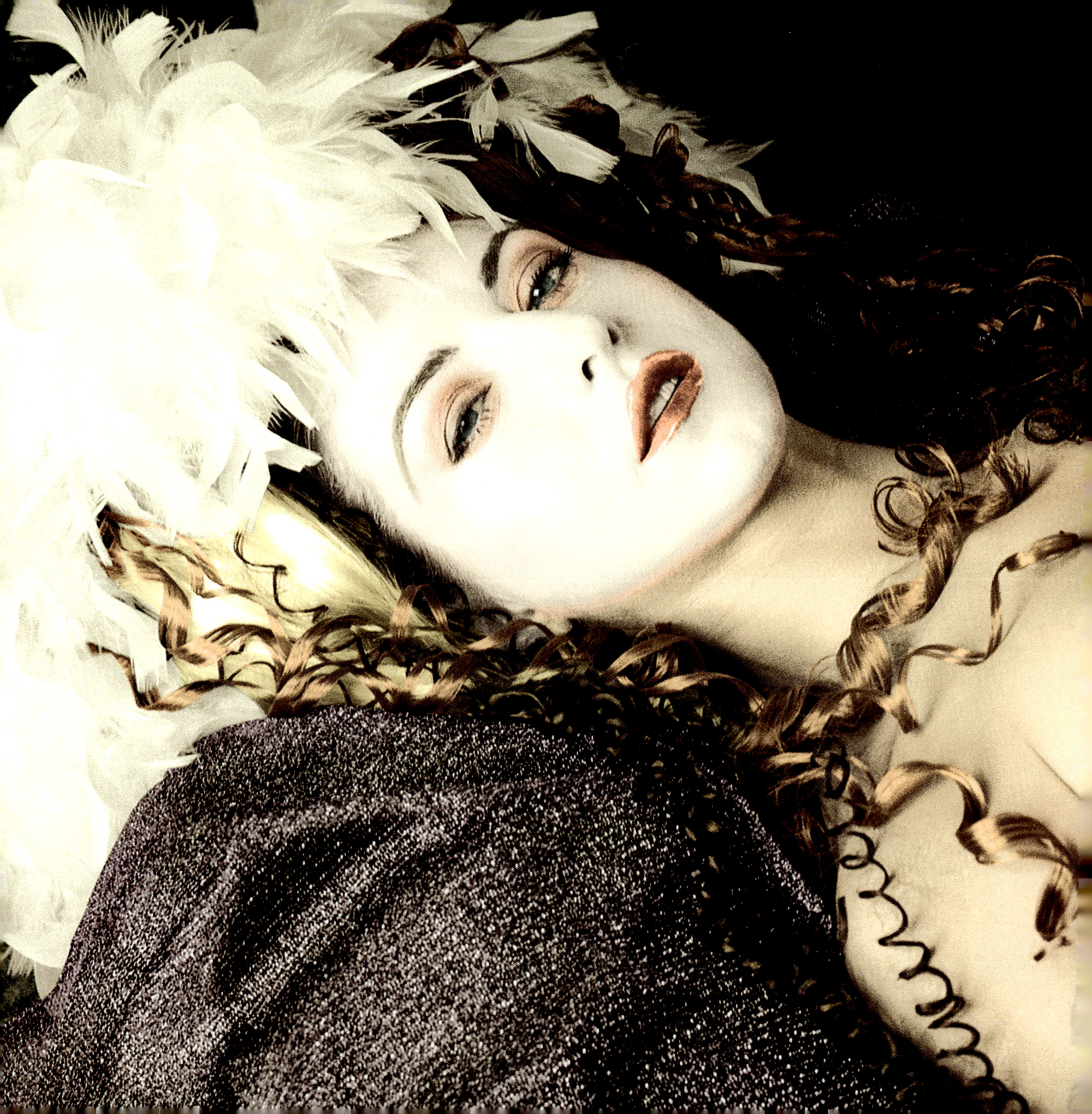

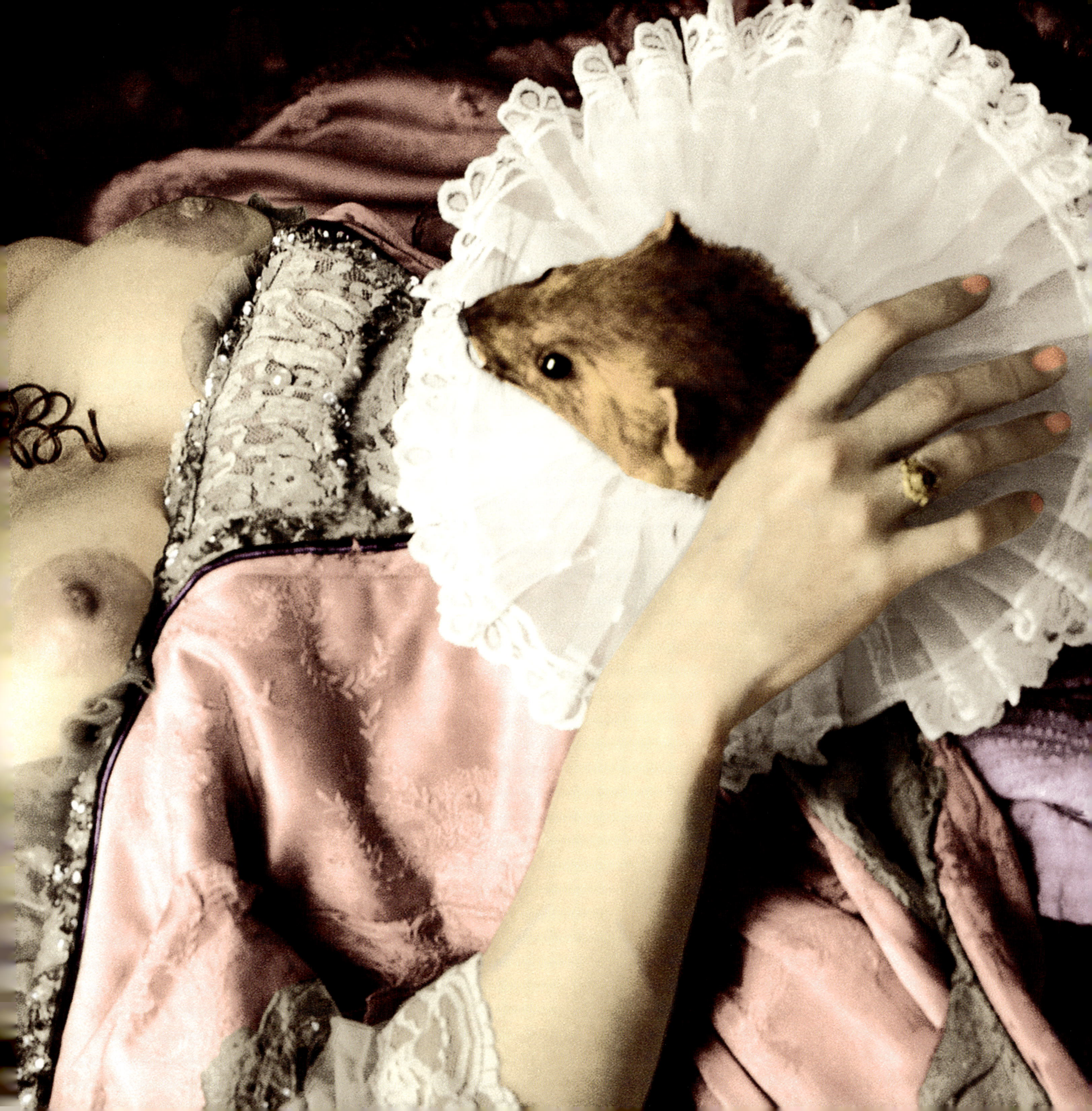

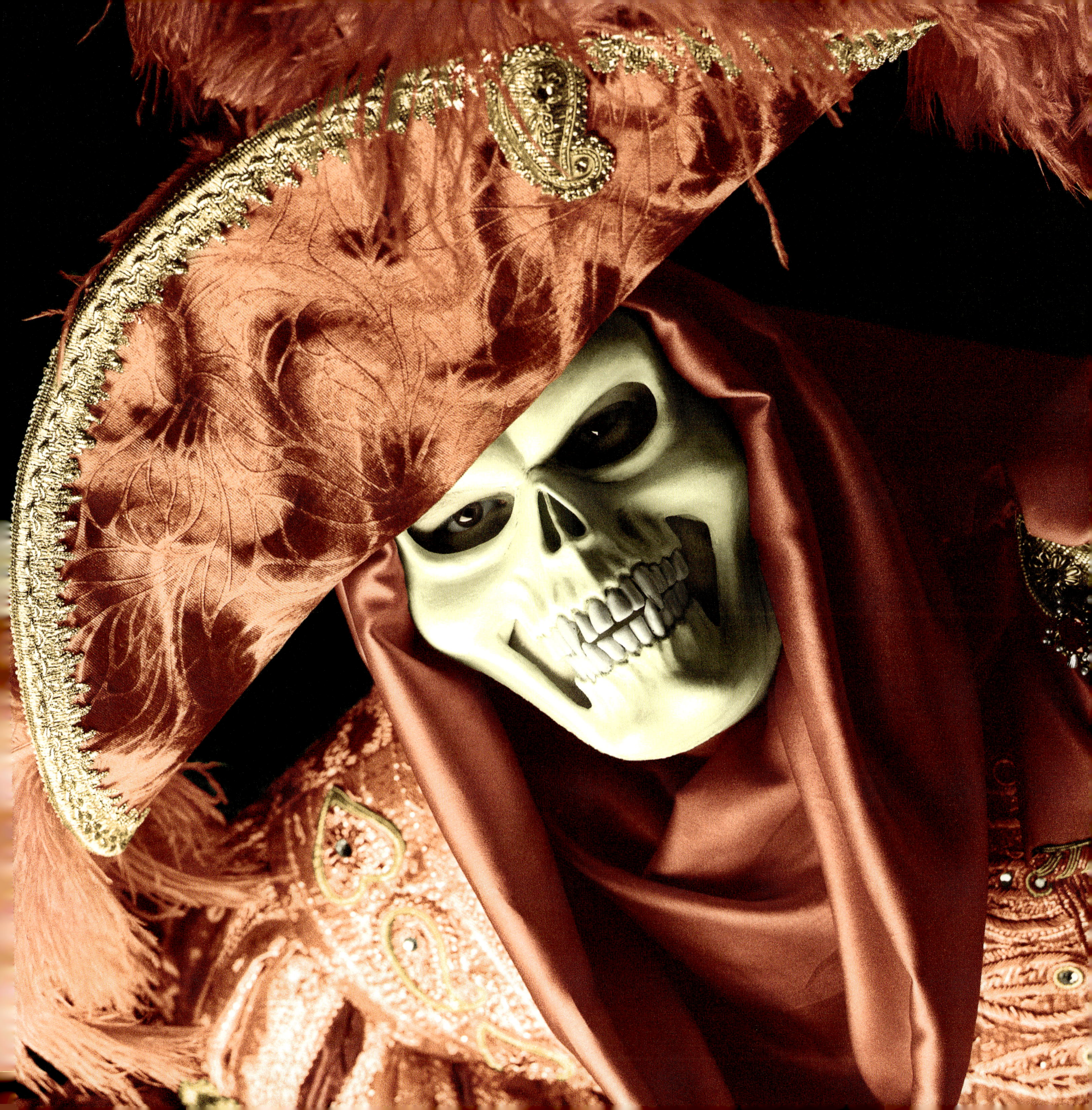

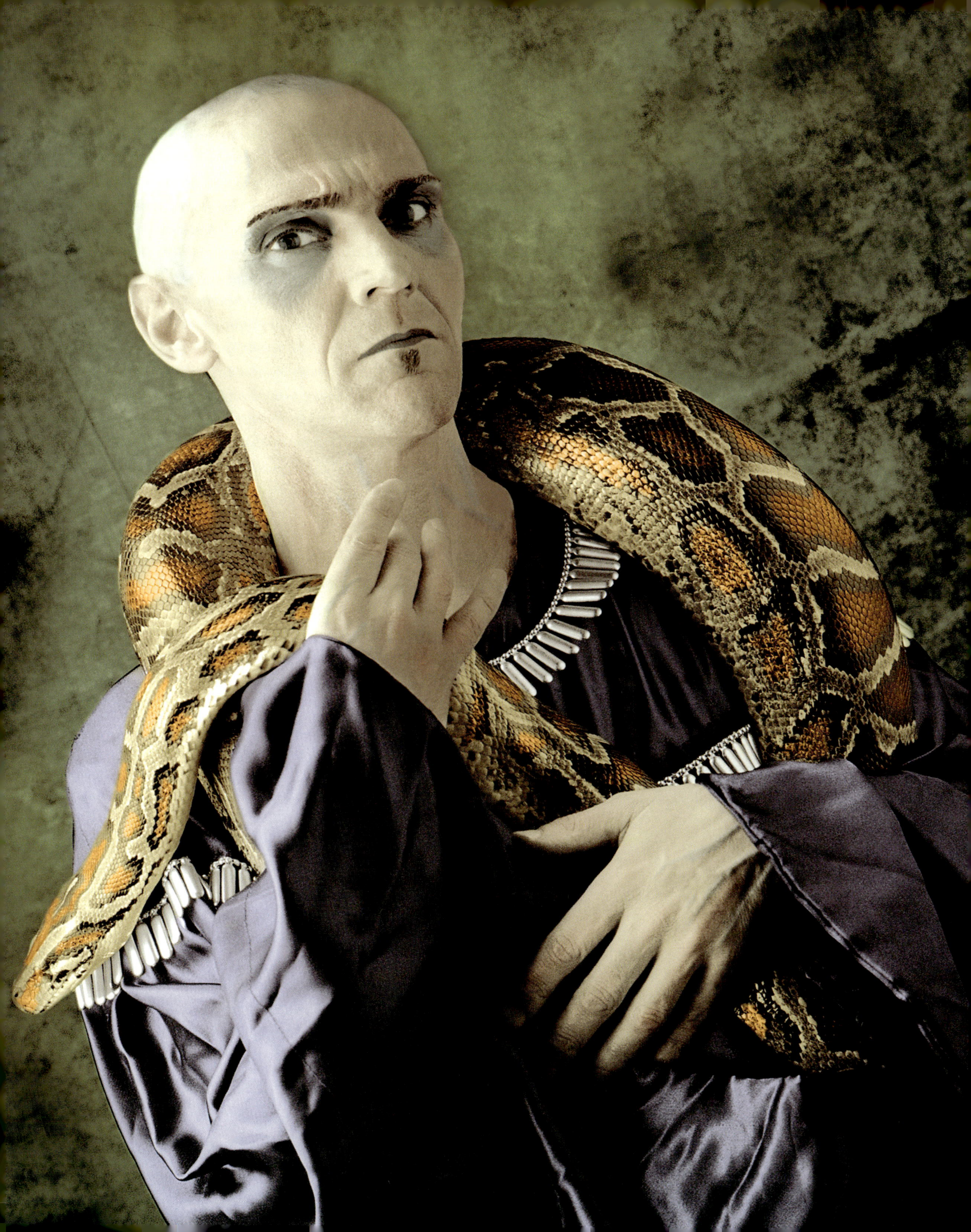

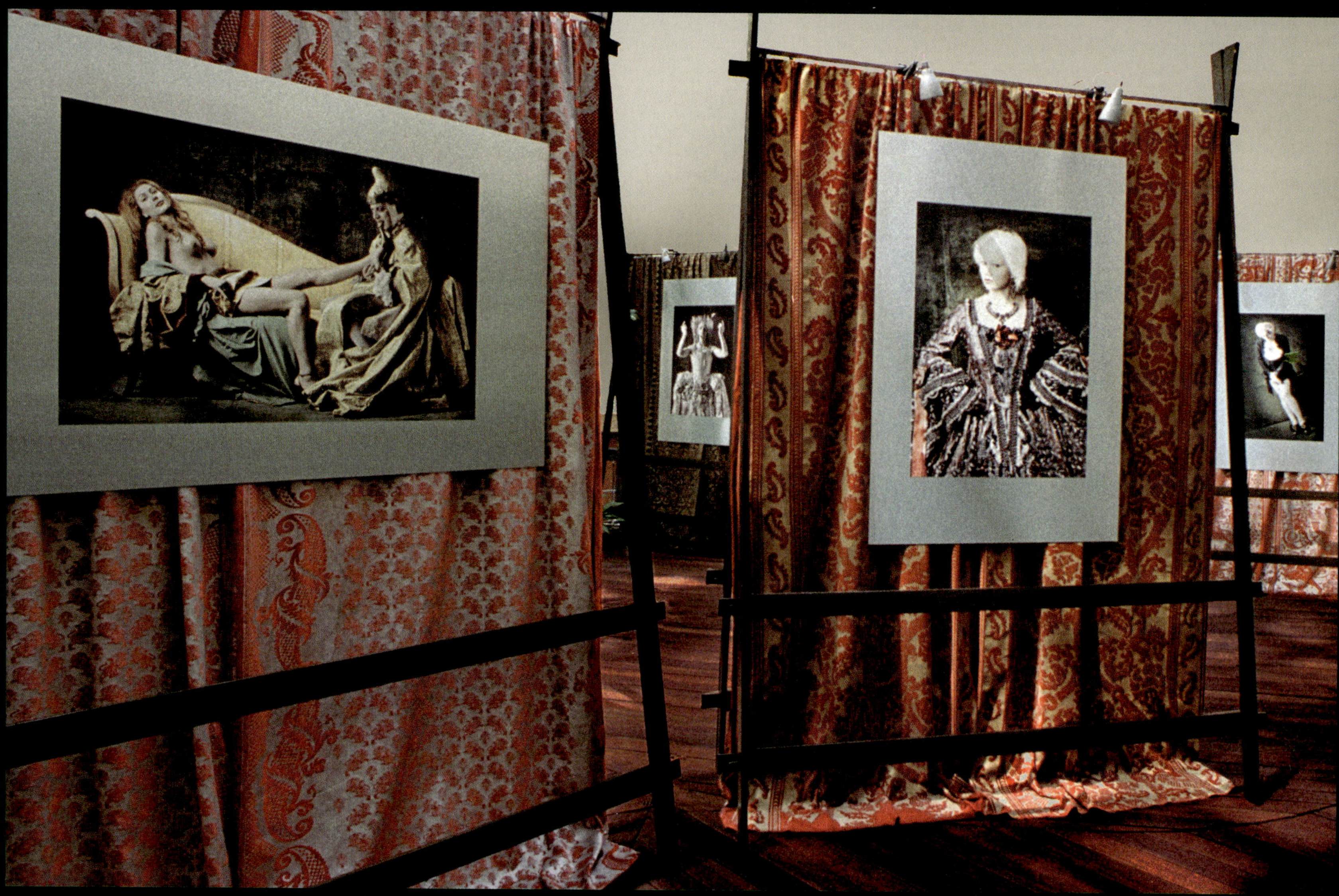

All of the photographs were taken with black and white film and later coloured by the author.

Masquerade is also an itinerant display.
All of the works, of large dimensions,
are exhibited on elegant fabrics
enveloped in precious hand-worked damasks
of Venetian inspiration by Andrè du Dauphinè.

Information:
Simoni Communication,
e-mail: simoni.art@gmx.de

CD 1

UNA FESTA VENEZIANA

Antonio Vivaldi (1678-1741)
Concerto in C major for two trumpets, strings and b.c., RV537
[1] 1. Allegro 2:37 - [2] 2. Largo 1:03 - [3] 3. (Allegro) 2:53
Ludwig Güttler, trumpet I & direction - **Mathias Schmutzler**, trumpet II - **Joachim Bischof**, violoncello - **Werner Zeibig**, double-bass - **Friedrich Kircheis**, harpsichord
Virtuosi Saxoniae
P 1992**

Tomaso Albinoni (1671-1750)
Concerto in C major for two oboes, strings and b.c., op. 7,11
[4] 1. Allegro 2:59 - [5] 2. Adagio 2:29 - [6] 3. Allegro 2:54
Hans-Werner Wätzig, oboe I - **Jürgen Apel**, oboe II - **Jeffrey Tate**, harpsichord
Kammerorchester Berlin - **Vittorio Negri**
P 1974*

Antonio Vivaldi (1678-1741)
Concerto in F major, op. 10,1 RV 433
"La Tempesta di Mare" (Storm at Sea), for transverse flute, strings and b.c.
[7] 1. Allegro 2:48 - [8] 2. Largo 1:44 - [9] 3. Presto 1:58
Eckart Haupt, flute - **Dresdner Barocksolisten** - **Peter Schreier**
P 1991**

Alessandro Marcello (1669-1747)
Concerto in D minor for oboe, strings and b.c.
[10] 1. Andante e spiccato 4:07 - [11] 2. Adagio 3:51 - [12] 3. Presto 3:56
Burkhard Glaetzner, oboe & direction - **Armin Thalheim**, harpsichord
Neues Bachisches Collegium Musicum
P 1992**

Antonio Vivaldi (1678-1741)
Concerto in G minor, RV 104
"La notte" (The Night), for transverse flute, two violins, bassoon and b.c.
[13] 1. Largo, Presto "Fantasmi", Largo, Andante, Presto 4:39
[14] 2. Largo "Il Sonno" 1:40 - [15] 3. Allegro 2:37
Eckart Haupt, flute - **Dresdner Barocksolisten** - **Peter Schreier**
P 1991**

Tomaso Albinoni (1671-1750)
Concerto in D major for two oboes, strings and b.c., op. 7,8
[16] 1. Allegro 2:13 - [17] 2. Largo 2:49 - [18] 3. Allegro 2:22
Hans-Werner Wätzig, oboe I - **Jürgen Apel**, oboe II - **Jeffrey Tate**, harpsichord
Kammerorchester Berlin - **Vittorio Negri**
P 1974*

Petronio Franceschini (ca. 1650-1680)
Sonata in D major for two trumpets, strings and b.c.
[19] Grave 6:04 - [20] Allegro 0:52 - [21] Adagio 1:24 - [22] Allegro 1:48
Ludwig Güttler, trumpet I & direction - **Mathias Schmutzler**, trumpet II - **Joachim Bischof**, violoncello - **Werner Zeibig**, double-bass - **Friedrich Kircheis**, organ -
Virtuosi Saxoniae
P 1992**

CD 2

DOLCE MIO BEN

Francesco Gasparini (1661-1727)
[1] "Dolce mio ben" (Aria) 5:07 - [2] "Cor nemico amante" (Aria) 3:36
[3] "Sparger no vò più lagrime" (Aria) 5:40

Francesco Bartolomeo Conti (1681-1732)
"Clori, sei tutta bella" (Cantata)
[4] "Clori, sei tutta bella" (Recitativo) 0:40 - [5] "Quando muove il tuo bel piede" (Aria) 3:35 - [6] "Sì, sì, Clori vezzosa" (Recitativo) 0:45 - [7] "Il mio cor" (Aria) 5:29

Nicola Matteis the Younger (ca. 1670-1749)
[8] Aria 1:47 - [9] La dia Spagnola 2:27 - [10] Chaconne (in A major) 1:43

Signore Magini
"Da che vidde il duo sembiante" (Cantata)
[11] "Dache vidde il duo sembiante" (Aria) 3:54 - [12] "E cagion ben lo vuole" (Recitativo) 1:28 - [13] "Io voglio sì sperar" (Aria) 2:41 - [14] "Ma se non vien' de' miei contenti il giorno" (Recitativo) 0:59 - [15] "Vanne à trovar ch'io t'ami" (Aria) 2:48

Luigi Mancia (ca. 1665-1708)
[16] Sinfonia 2:05 - [17] Solo 2:51 - [18] Allegro 1:48

Ruggiero Fedeli (1655-1722)
"Lasciatemi al mio duolo speranze adultrici" (Cantata)
[19] "Lasciatemi al mio duolo" (Recitativo) 0:41 - [20] "Se in aspetto men tiranno" (Aria) 2:21 - [21] "Ma più fiera" (Aria) 2:10

Nicola Matteis the Younger (ca. 1670-1749)
[22] Chaconne (in G minor) 2:09

Domenico Natale Sarri (1679-1744)
"Barbara Gelosia" (Cantata)
[23] Recitativo 0:23 - [24] "Son disprezzato da un core" (Aria) 4:03
[25] Recitativo 0:37 - [26] "Se d'Aquilon lo degno" (Aria) 5:04

Maite Beaumont, mezzo soprano

LAUTTEN COMPAGNEY
Birgit Schnurpfeil, violin
Anne von Hoff, violin
Ulrike Paetz, viola
Ulrike Becker, violoncello
Annette Rheinfurth, double bass
Mark Nordstrand, harpsichord
Hans-Werner Apel, baroque guitar · theorbo

Wolfgang Katschner, theorbo · musical direction

CD 3

MELODIE ITALIANE

Gioachino Rossini (1792-1862)
Il Barbiere di Siviglia (The Barber of Seville)
[1] Sinfonia 7:20
Staatskapelle Berlin - Otmar Suitner
P 1966*

Luigi Boccherini (1743-1805)
String quintet in E major, op. 13,5
[2] Menuett 3:58
Rundfunk-Sinfonie-Orchester Leipzig - Robert Hanell
P 1985*

Pietro Nardini (1722-1793) • **Emilio Pente** (1860-1929) (Arr.: C. Angellini)
Violin concerto in E minor
[3] 3. Allegro giocoso 2:59
Manfred Scherzer, violin - **Kammerorchester Berlin - Helmut Koch**
P 1972*

Giovanni Battista Viotti (1755-1824)
Violin concerto no. 22 in A minor
[4] 3. Agitato assai 6:59
Manfred Scherzer, violin - **Kammerorchester Berlin - Helmut Koch**
P 1972*

Niccolò Paganini (1782-1840)
Violin concerto no. 1 in D major, op. 6
[5] 3. Rondo. Allegro spirituoso 8:40
Egon Morbitzer, violin - **Großes Orchester des Deutschlandsenders - Robert Hanell**
P 1969*

Domenico Cimarosa (1749-1801)
Concerto for two flutes and orchestra in G major
[6] 1. Allegro 9:08
Werner Tast, flute I - **Eckhart Haupt**, flute II
Rundfunk-Kammerorchester Leipzig - Wolf-Dieter Hauschild
P 1981*

Pietro Locatelli (1695-1764)
Concerto grosso in E flat major op. 7,6
[7] 1. Andante-Allegro-Adagio-Andante-Allegro-Largo 7:48
Thorsten Rosenbusch, solo violin
Chamber Orchestra "Carl Philipp Emanuel Bach" - Hartmut Haenchen
P 1995***

Ottorino Respighi (1879-1936)
Antiche arie e danze
[8] 1. Italiana: Andantino 3:03 - [9] 3. Siciliana: Andantino 3:30
Rundfunk-Musikschul-Orchester Berlin - Jörg-Peter Weigle
P 1990**

Gioachino Rossini (1792-1862)
La scala di seta (The Silk Ladder)
[10] Overture 6:03
Rundfunk-Sinfonie-Orchester Berlin - Heinz Rögner
P 1972*

CD 4

SERENATA D'AMORE

Gustav Mahler (1860-1911)
Symphony no 5 in C sharp minor
[1] 4. Adagietto 10:00
Berliner Sinfonie-Orchester - Günter Herbig
P 1983*

Johann Strauß (1825-1899)
[2] Roses from the South, waltz, op. 388 8:29
Staatskapelle Dresden - Carl von Garaguly
P 1972*

Hector Berlioz (1803-1869)
Symphonie fantastique
[3] 2. Un Bal (A Ball)
Valse. Allegro non troppo 6:33
Dresdner Philharmonie - Herbert Kegel
P 1986*

Hector Berlioz (1803-1869)
[4] Le carnaval romain (Roman Carnival),
overture, op. 9 8:65
Gewandhausorchester Leipzig - Gerhart Wiesenhütter
P 1963*

Max Reger (1873-1916)
Boecklin suite, op. 128
[5] 2. At Play in the Waves 4:30
Dresdner Philharmonie - Heinz Bongartz
P 1970*

Max Reger (1873-1916)
A Ballet Suite, op. 130
[6] 3. Harlequin. Vivace 2:12
Staatskapelle Berlin - Otmar Suitner
P 1973*

Josef Strauß (1827-1870)
[7] My Life is Love and Joy, waltz, op. 263 7:30
Staatskapelle Dresden - Otmar Suitner
P 1981*

Piotr Ilyich Tchaikovsky (1840-1893)
Serenade for strings in C major, op. 48
[8] Waltz 4:07
Staatskapelle Dresden - Otmar Suitner
P 1969*

Giuseppe Verdi (1813-1901)
La Traviata
[9] Prelude to Act III 4:07
Staatskapelle Dresden - Giuseppe Patané
P 1973*

Maurice Ravel (1875-1937)
[10] Bolero 15:17
Berliner Sinfonie-Orchester - Günther Herbig
P 1979*

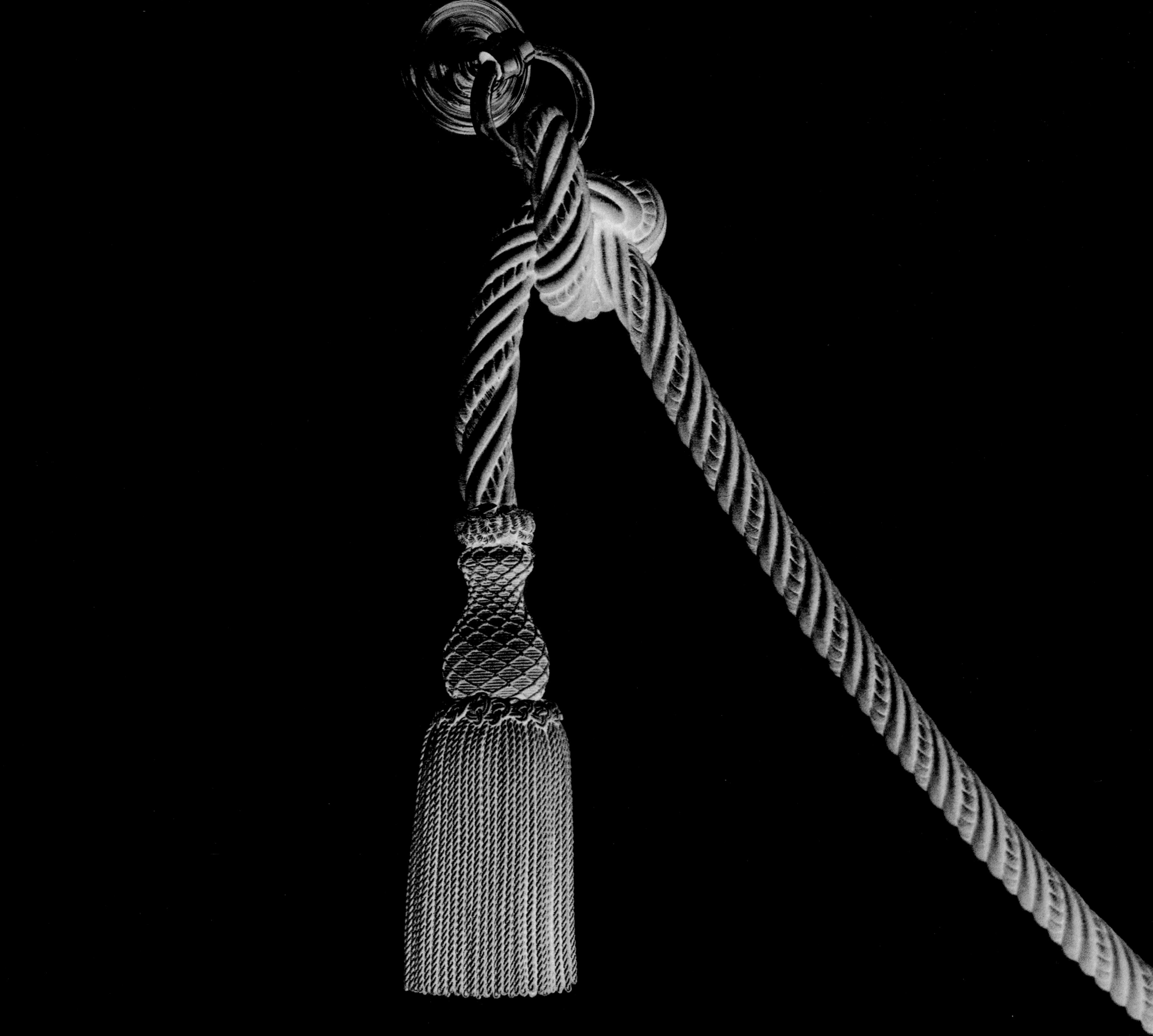